GLASS SLIPPERS, EVER AFTER, AND ME

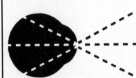
This Large Print Book carries the
Seal of Approval of N.A.V.H.

PROPER ROMANCE

GLASS SLIPPERS, EVER AFTER, AND ME

JULIE WRIGHT

THORNDIKE PRESS
A part of Gale, a Cengage Company

LIBRARY OF CONGRESS CIP DATA ON FILE.
CATALOGUING IN PUBLICATION FOR THIS BOOK
IS AVAILABLE FROM THE LIBRARY OF CONGRESS

ISBN-13: 978-1-4328-7712-5 (hardcover alk. paper)

Published in 2020 by arrangement with Deseret Book Company/Shadow Mountain

Printed in Mexico
Print Number: 03   Print Year: 2020

To Chandler
The sort of young man who treats
every young woman like a princess
regardless of her footwear.
I love you, buddy.

CHAPTER ONE

"If fairy godmothers existed, there would
never be an empty space in the freezer
where the ice cream goes. Any
responsible fairy godmother would keep
that space magically stocked at all times."
— Charlotte Kingsley,
The Cinderella Fiction
(The "Make Your Own Magic" Chapter)

My fairy godmother was all talk and no action. Like the tooth fairy, she was definitely
not someone I could depend on. I had a
sneaking suspicion the two had run off
together a long time ago and were now
downing drinks with umbrellas while they
lounged on a beach somewhere exotic and
peaceful. Somewhere I wasn't, as I hadn't
heard from either one ever in my life. That's
why my hand clutched my phone, which
contained the email that had popped up in
my alerts while I paced among the trees still

gripped by winter. Joggers along the trail narrowed their eyes at me and worked to avoid full-on collisions as I walked past without seeing them. *Do I open the email, or do I ignore it for a while longer?* I couldn't decide. I had worked myself up enough to not feel the cold of February in Boston. Every ragged breath of air I sucked in felt barbed and insufficient to fill my lungs without doing damage. *Please don't let this be what I think it is,* I prayed to the fairy godmothers of ink and paper. *Let the words contain magic instead of more poison.*

My father always told me that with a name like Charlotte Kingsley, I must be royalty. He would tug on the ends of my red braids and call me his princess. He insisted my freckles were a constellation map to treasure. Even after he and my mom divorced and he moved to California — since it was as far away as he could get from my mother without actually leaving the country — I still felt the pull of the fairy tales he'd spun for me as a child. It was his fault I believed in magic.

Magic.

What did I know about magic?

Nothing.

Ironic, since I wrote fairy tales for a living. Well . . . not for a living. I had yet to make any actual money off of my writing career. But I dreamed of earning a living off my art at some point. That's almost the same thing, right? With a grunt of disgust at myself, I walked home, still clutching the phone as if it were an explosive that would go off if I relaxed my grip even a little. My earlier plan to meet a neighbor for an evening jog because of the unusually warmer weather was entirely abandoned. Far better to do this within the privacy of my own walls than out in public view where there would likely be a scene.

No matter what the email contained, a scene not fit for public consumption would definitely follow. I would either be elated with an acceptance and then dance around screaming like a crazy, happy person, or, if faced with another rejection, I'd spend the better part of the evening screeching out the wails of a paid mourner.

Well, maybe not paid. Sadly, that's not how rejection letters work. If it were, I'd be a billionaire.

Inside my apartment, I paced for another forty-two minutes. My 480-square-foot apartment, filled with mismatched furniture and cluttered with puddles of various note-pads and book piles I always meant to put away but had yet to actually pick up off the floor, hindered any therapeutic result that might have come from pacing. And circling around and around in the same direction made me dizzy, so I'd had to get clever and change directions every few minutes in the name of equilibrium preservation.

The email on my phone could say anything. It could be a yes. Jennifer Apsley, the agent of my dreams, could want my book and the next ten books I write. She might have publishers already lined up, movie deals already in mind. She might have a contract attached to the email that was still unopened on the phone in my hand. Maybe when I opened the email, a tiara would magically appear on my head and a ball gown would swirl its way around me in a storm of glitter and possibilities.

But it might be a rejection letter. Jennifer Apsley might tell me to just stop already. She might tell me to never submit to her again because she's sick and tired of seeing my name in her inbox. She might have put out a restraining order against me on all future communication. And this might not be a rejection from just her; she might have warned all other agents that I am needy and pathetic and that they should steer clear.

But maybe it was an acceptance.

Or maybe it was a full-on renunciation in

which an evil sorcerer in a black suit would appear as soon as the email opened. The sorcerer would delete all word-processing programs from my laptop and laugh in that deep, booming, maniacal laugh that only evil sorcerers know how to do. He would break all the pens, pencils, and crayons in my apartment building and forbid me from ever thinking about filling a blank page again. Though in reality, any crayon I might have owned was already broken. There is something untrustworthy about a person who manages to keep their crayons intact.

But maybe the email was validation — with party favors, balloons, a unicorn, and a disco ball.

Or maybe . . .

I swiped open the email on my phone at 5:13 p.m.

"Dear Charlotte Kingsley . . ."

At 5:16 p.m., I reached into my freezer to find the spot usually occupied by Breyers raspberry fudge ice cream entirely vacant. Sometime between 5:16 p.m. and 5:17 p.m., the first tears rained down on my cheeks. That empty spot in the freezer felt like the time I had woken up on Christmas morning when I was seven to find all the space under the tree empty because my mom had decided I was too old to believe in North Pole legends, and she felt it would be easiest to rip off the Band-Aid so that my belief could bleed out in minutes rather than years.

That empty spot in my freezer was almost worse than the rejection that had led me to the freezer in the first place. After a lifetime of constant reminders that magic does not exist in the world, should it have come as a surprise to discover that my fairy godmother was a flake and had forgotten the magic ice cream after she'd already flaked on sending the magic book deal that came with a matching tiara?

Rejected.

Again.

I blinked back my own personal eye monsoon and sucked in a shuddering sob, determined to pull myself together long enough to function as I swept open the home delivery app for Bob's Grocery.

Once the essentials were ordered, and the little timer began counting down the twenty-six minutes it would take for the delivery person to bring me what I needed, I murdered my phone.

I can only assume the delivery came twenty-six minutes later, since I never set the clock on my relic DVD player and I couldn't check the time on the phone that lay in pieces below the newly-formed dent in the wall.

I forgave the DVD player for being a useless timepiece, readied it with the first disc of *The 10th Kingdom,* and settled in to overdose on rocky road ice cream — the life metaphor I planned to eat — and the Hallmark Channel fairy tales I would never have in real life, when my front door opened again.

It wasn't the delivery driver to tell me I had gotten her tip wrong, which I might have, considering I no longer had a phone to calculate such things for me.

Anders Nilsson stood in my doorframe, looking every bit the stereotypical Swede. Anders had emigrated from Sweden when he was a kid. If someone had given him a horned hat and a fur toga instead of the knee-length blue jogging shorts and Boston Red Sox T-shirt he wore, he'd definitely look ready for raiding some defenseless Norse village. His arms, chiseled straight out of Asgard legend, were poised with a camera in hand. Anders was a hobbyist photographer who took freelance photography jobs on top of his day job as a paramedic.

I narrowed my eyes at him. "If you take a picture right now, no one will recognize your corpse; that's assuming they find it."

13

He set the camera on the table by my door — *Was that the click of a photo being created I just heard?* — and crossed his arms over his chest. His head was already shaking like a blond-haired clock pendulum of shame. Back and forth. Back and forth. Shame, shame, shame.

It wasn't fair for me to think of it that way. Anders would never want to shame me. He was my friend, the type who wants to help whenever possible.

He entered my apartment without being invited, in much the same way he'd opened the door without knocking.

"I'm sorry, Lettie."

"How did you know?" I asked as my voice cracked. His showing up to offer comfort and solidarity made me want to cry harder.

"New driver at Bob's. She got lost. She stopped me for directions when I was on my way back into the building from my run. I noticed the bag with three ice cream tubs in it and figured . . . well, I figured."

I lifted three fingers in the air. "They only had three. What kind of crap store fails to prepare better for emergencies by having only three tubs of rocky road in stock? And they didn't have any raspberry fudge at all."

"Yeah. They're real monsters. I'd offer to go out and get you more, but I really think this habit of yours is incredibly unhealthy. Three is plenty." Anders stepped over the pile of murdered electronics on the floor and raised his eyebrows. "Well, that explains why it went straight to voice mail when I called. And it explains why you didn't meet me to go running."

He picked up the remote, probably to turn off my movie. I fixed him with my "I will kill you if you even twitch in that direction" glare. Anders took the intelligent road, leaving the television and the movie that was playing alone so he could sit by me on the couch. I snapped the fingers of my free hand at him to prompt him to hand over the remote.

He did, but he wasn't happy about it. "At least turn it down so we can talk."

I knocked it down one click.

Anders sighed. "You need an intervention," he said before looking at me and scowling. "And a spoon. I can honestly say I've never seen anyone use the scoop as a spoon before. What would your mother say?"

"She'd applaud me for being efficient. This saves me from having more dishes later."

That wasn't true. My mother would definitely *not* approve of me using a scoop

15

instead of a spoon any more than she approved of me going outside without a hat — because, according to her, the sun will cause the freckles scattered across my cheeks and nose to get so huge that they will become lakes of cancer in my old age. "Redheads are prone to freckling," she'd said to me a hundred times with that scowl of disapproval because my red hair came straight from my father. But what my mother didn't know wouldn't hurt me. I was twenty-six years old, writing advertising copy for eyewear, and paying my own bills. Didn't that mean I could go outside without a hat? Or use a scoop to eat ice cream if I wanted to?

"Lettie . . ." Anders's blond eyebrows were raised so high on his forehead, it looked like they were trying to reach escape velocity. "Your mother would beat you with that scoop before letting you do what you're doing."

He'd met my mother the one time she'd come into town to stay with me for a weekend so we could have "bonding time" while my stepdad and sister went on a father-daughter trip. I'd spent most of her visit hiding in Anders's apartment, even though he lived in a rather cozy — which was a nice word for cramped — studio apartment. Anders knew what he was talking about. He'd heard her make the "lakes of cancer" comment as well.

I shrugged. "It's a good thing she's not here then, isn't it? I moved away from her precisely so she doesn't get to know the details of my life choices. If you're going to get judgy, I'll move away from you, too."

Anders shook his head some more and looked longingly at the remote, but he didn't reach for it again, though he was clearly tired of having to talk over the on-screen trolls and the werewolf I'd had a crush on since I was thirteen and discovering the magic inside stories. He picked up his phone instead of prying the remote from my hand. He ordered Thai takeout from our favorite restaurant, The Thai Guy, to be delivered to my apartment — as if coconut curry could fix what was wrong with me.

No one makes bandages for broken hearts.

"What are you doing?" I asked.

"I told you. An intervention. You at least need real food."

I scrubbed my wrist over my right eye to remove the last bit of crusted tears. I used my wrist, as I wasn't willing to relinquish the scoop or the remote. "I don't need an intervention. I need inspiration. I need to write a book that the publishers want."

Anders's arm went over my shoulder. "Forget what they want. Write what *you* want. Write your authentic self. That's the only way to make real art."

I leaned back into the pillow his arm made for me and stared at my ceiling. "I don't need to make art. I need to make my rent payment. Besides, publishers don't want art. They don't want authentic. They want the hot new thing. It's time to put up the white flag and admit that the only writing I will ever be good for is descriptions about fun and sassy eyewear that leads to a fun and sassy life, which is actually the most fictitious thing I've ever written. Eyewear can't give anyone a fun or sassy anything." I sighed. "I'm over it. I'm done. I'm not writing anymore."

With that declaration, I sat up and dug my scoop back into the carton only to hear the dull thud of metal on cardboard. The ice cream was gone.

I stood to retrieve a new carton, making the mistake of dropping the remote onto the couch. Anders took advantage of my tactical error and hit the power button. He let out a purposely loud sigh of relief at the silence that followed.

"If you don't like the entertainment, you

can go watch your own TV," I called out to him.

"I don't have time for TV. I'm going out tonight," he called back.

"Chloe?"

"Yep."

"You've been dating her for a while now. What . . . almost two months."

"So?" he said.

"That's a long time — like eternity in dating years. She must be the one?" It felt good to think about something else — something not me. And it was a conversation I'd been meaning to have with him anyway. He'd seemed entirely absorbed by his admiration of her after their first date. All conversations were Chloe-this and Chloe-that, but now he spent more time in my apartment helping himself to my fridge than he did wining and dining his girlfriend.

He'd followed me into the kitchen, startling me when his voice came from directly behind me rather than the other room. "I don't know. She's pretty great, but I don't know."

I shut the freezer and turned to face him. "What don't you know? She's gorgeous. The woman's got legs that just never seem to end. I'd kill for legs like that. And her hair? All dark sleek and style."

19

"You make her sound like a car."

"What? This is nothing like a car. Cars don't have legs. Or hair for that matter."

"Whatever. Anyway, I *do* date women for reasons other than how they look. I'm not one of those shallow guys." Anders pulled out a bowl and spoon and handed them to me as if I might actually use them. He was adorable that way.

I put them back in the cupboard. My living room might have been a mess, but I liked my kitchen to be tidy. "I didn't say you were shallow. And it's okay to like how somebody looks. It's not like enjoying the beauty of another person is a bad thing. But, since you're being all weird about it, fine. Tell me what you look for in women."

"A good conversation for starters."

"And is Chloe good for conversation?"

"Yeah, actually. She really is." He frowned at my cupboard, though I couldn't be sure if it was because he didn't like that I put away the bowl and spoon or if he didn't like dissecting his feelings.

"Okay, she's pretty *and* a good conversationalist. We're back to why you're not sure about her. She sounds like she's worth taking home to meet Grandpa to me." The grandfather lived in Sweden. Anders said he'd know if a woman was right for him if

20

he actually wanted to take her home to meet his Swedish grandfather. Heckling Anders about his dating might be the only joy I received from the day.

"Let's not jump to conclusions, here. I mean, sure, she's great and everything, but taking her home for a visit with my grand-father? I don't think we're there. I just don't feel that yet. I don't know if that's something wrong with me or something wrong with her. Regardless, something's wrong."

The door buzzer rang, signaling that someone downstairs wanted into the building. Likely the Thai delivery guy. I tucked the ice cream back into the freezer with a grunt and hurried to buzz the delivery person up. I talked to Anders over my shoulder once we were separated by the kitchen walls again. "Dude, it's been like half a year. If you're not serious about her, you should probably cut her loose. It's not nice to hang on to something that you don't see going anywhere. She'll get the wrong idea."

He followed me as far as the kitchen entryway and leaned against it. "You are such a fiction writer. It has *not* been half a year. It's barely been two months. You just said so."

"I also said two months was eternity in

21

dating years."

"And like you're one to talk. How are things going with, what's his name? Aaron? Edward?"

"His name was Ian. And I cut that one loose already. See? That's what I mean about nice. If you don't see it going anywhere, cut them loose." I shrugged at him before reaching for the doorknob.

"I bet if you ask Ian, he won't see you dumping him as a kindness. Why are you always so dead set against long-term relationships?"

I shuddered. "Because long-term relationships lead to things like commitment, marriage, mortgage, kids. Ask my parents how that all went down for them."

He opened his mouth to likely remind me, again, that just because my parents had a crummy marriage didn't mean that all people had such bad luck, but I'd stopped listening, since the door was open and the Thai delivery guy was standing there with my coconut curry and, if Anders was the friend I knew him to be, mango sticky rice. I reached to my right, where my purse usually sat on the antique stand, the only bit of inheritance I'd received when my grandmother died, in spite of the fact that she had no other grandchildren, but the purse

22

wasn't there. I frowned and spun to survey the room to see where I might have left it.

Anders hurried across the room to hand the kid with the earbuds still in his ears some cash for the food.

"You need to let me pay for that," I said as I finally spied my purse sticking out from the side of the couch. I made more than Anders did. I always felt bad when he picked up the tab.

"I ordered it," he said, which meant he wouldn't be letting me pay him back. He tucked his wallet back into his front pocket. Anders was not a back-pocket guy. He deemed having a wallet in the back pocket unsafe for subway travel and declared it to be the ruination of proper spinal alignment. He had a phone in one front pocket and his wallet in the other. He called it balance. It made me glad I had a purse — a cross-body purse for proper spinal alignment or what-ever.

He continued, eyeing the remote on the coffee table, likely wishing he'd hidden it out of view, "I can't ask you to pay for something you didn't order or even ask for."

I looked in the bag and frowned. "There isn't much in here. Did you not get any for you?"

He lifted his shoulder in a half shrug.

"Date tonight, remember?"

"Oh. Right."

We sat together on the couch as I opened up my food on the coffee table.

"So what was wrong with him?" At my questioning look, he said, "Ian. The guy you were so nice to."

"Messy kisser." I shuddered to drive home the issue.

He nodded as he grimaced at the plastic fork and knife I'd set out on the coffee table. "I did tell them to not include environmental waste."

"I'll just take it back when I return the stash I've been collecting in my kitchen drawer." I got up again to fetch actual silverware and to dump the environmental waste in the collection drawer. I returned to the couch — the place where I'd determined to ride out the disgrace of another rejection.

Anders apparently decided that, since he'd preoccupied me with eating the food he'd bought me, he could act as my personal walking, talking, breathing motivational poster. "I hate it when you talk about putting out a white flag and walking away from writing." This began his illustrious pep talk. He followed up his beginning with a joke. "A writer died. Let's call her Charlotte."

24

"Is this you telling me I should kill myself? Because that's not very nice. It makes you a bad friend and a suspicious and creepy neighbor."

"Lighten up, Lettie! This is a joke."

"Killing me is not a joke."

"Sh! I'm telling you a joke."

I shushed and ate my coconut curry.

He continued. "Charlotte, the serious writer, was given the option of going to heaven or hell. Being a good writer, she decided to do her research and check out each place first. As Charlotte descended into the fiery pits, she saw row upon row of writers chained to their desks in a steaming sweatshop. As they worked, they were repeatedly whipped with thorny lashes. 'Oh my, this is awful,' said Charlotte. 'Let me see heaven, now.' "

I snorted at his interpretation of my voice.

He rolled his eyes but continued. "A few moments later, as she ascended into heaven, she saw rows of writers, chained to their desks in a steaming sweatshop. As they worked, they, too, were whipped with thorny lashes. 'Wait a minute,' she said. 'This is just as bad as hell!' But her tour guide replied, 'Oh no, it's not. Here, your work gets published!' "

He grinned wide at this and waited for

me to respond. I only blinked at him.

He grunted. "The point is that it's always work and effort, but the rewards *do* come."

"Unless, maybe I actually belong in hell and this is my punishment for not sharing my leftovers with the neighbor's cat or something." I looked in the bag, expecting the extra weight I'd felt there to be the mango sticky rice but instead found an intensely huge stack of napkins. It was like whoever packed my meal wanted to wipe out an entire tree in one go. "No mango sticky rice?" I asked.

"Steve doesn't have a cat, and you do not belong in hell. You're a nice, heaven-bound person, Lettie. And you have three tubs of ice cream. You clearly have dessert already covered."

I nudged the empty tub on the coffee table with my foot. "Wrong. I only have two tubs because I already ate one. So it *clearly* doesn't count." I stood and took the long walk back to my freezer.

"Is that all you have to say?" Anders, who had apparently gotten up to follow me some more, said.

"All what?"

"You've turned almost every conversation into a discussion about food. Why are you not willing to discuss your writing?"

I whirled around, the tears in my eyes sudden like a surprise rainstorm in the tropics. "Do you have any idea how many rejection letters I have?"

He fell back a step, clearly not expecting me to turn on him. "I don't see what the number has —"

"One hundred and eighty-seven," I interrupted him. "On *eight* different books. Do you know why?" I jabbed my finger into his chest. "I have eight books because I bought into that whole *work on another book while you have one on submission so the rejections won't feel so personal* crap. But you know what?" I jabbed him again. "That's the biggest lie ever. They *all* feel personal. They all cut a piece of creative soul out of me and burn it where I have to watch. Even the completely impersonal ones that don't have the decency to use my name, the ones that say 'Dear Author' are incredibly demoralizing, as they incinerate my hopes and dreams and belief in myself again and again and again."

I poked his chest at every *again.* Anders didn't give up any more ground though. He stood there and let me rant and vent and cry. "So if I want to call it quits, if I want to say I'm over being the abused spouse in this profession I've been chasing, I don't think anyone has the right to tell me I'm wrong. If I had a boyfriend who left me black and blue every time we went out, you would step in and drag me away and help me escape the cycle because you're a good friend. What I need right now is for you to be a good friend regarding my relationship with writing and support me when I say I want to break up with it because I. Am. Done. Being. Abused!"

Anders became a blurry kaleidoscope through my tears. I took a deep, shuddering breath and turned back to the comfort of my freezer. I pulled out the tub of ice cream, tugged off the lid, and tossed it in the garbage can.

"You might need that lid," Anders said quietly.

I swept past him to settle on the couch. I didn't even wait to sit before I tucked the scoop into the ice cream that was still soft because it hadn't had enough time in the freezer after being delivered. "I have no intention of needing that lid."

He rolled his eyes at me. "Look, I get that you're sad and frustrated. But you can't sad your way through three tubs of ice cream and still fit in any of the clothing in your closet later."

My head jerked up. "Is that a comment

on my weight? Are you trying to tell me that I'm fat?"

Flustered, Anders put his hands on his hips, which always made him look like a little schoolgirl. Teasing him about it usually entertained me, but not today. Nothing felt funny about today. "No!" he insisted, raising his voice. "Of course I'm not."

"Good!" I said, raising my voice to match his. "Because I might have to live with a lot of things in my life, Anders Nilsson. I might have to live as a failed writer and a quitter, but I will not live the life of a cover model, especially now that I'm certain no fairy godmother will be bringing me a ball gown to worry about fitting into anyway. I am not buying into the Cinderella fiction anymore!"

I pointed the scoop at him, flicking ice cream on my carpet and on my wall, only just missing him. And then I blinked and repeated my last sentence to myself. I repeated it softly but out loud, tasting the words on my tongue. "The Cinderella fiction . . ."

I stabbed the scoop in the ice cream and then dropped the tub to the coffee table before jumping to my feet and shoving Anders toward the door. "You have a date. You should get going. Thanks for dinner."

"Lettie? What's going on? What are you

doing? Why do you look like you're about to do something crazy?"

"Have fun on your date! I'll text you later!" I opened my door, handed him his camera, pushed him through the door, and shut it again, locking it so he couldn't come back in.

I spun to face my apartment. Anders was right. I was about to do something crazy. MIA fairy godmother or not . . . rejection or not . . . abusive relationship or not . . . I was about to write another book.

CHAPTER TWO

"On occasion, the princess deserves a broken heart. On occasion, the Evil Queen deserves love. Because all of us are both and experience both at some point in our lives."
— Charlotte Kingsley,
The Cinderella Fiction
(The "Know Yourself" Chapter)

I didn't leave my apartment for nearly three weeks. I took my paid time off at work and stayed home in my pajamas ordering Thai takeout and various grocery necessities from Bob's Grocery. I had to use the derelict phone in the basement office to get the Thai takeout, since the restaurant didn't have a reliable computer app, which meant I had to be sticky-sweet nice to Shannon the building manager, who probably lived in the woods in a cottage made out of candy and who probably spent her nights shoving kids into ovens. But until my new phone came — the one I bought used off eBay, since I didn't want to dip into my savings — kindness to my resident witch was the price I had to pay to stay fed.

The nice thing about having broken my phone was that no one could disturb me. I received no phone calls from my mother asking me if I was dating anyone; I wasn't. Or phone calls from my stepfather asking me to please return my mother's calls; I wouldn't. Or calls from Ian because he was under the impression that we should get back together; we shouldn't. After spending so long with the freedom of no phone, I wondered why society had ever become servants to that digital baggage.

Then I remembered how much I didn't love asking to use Shannon's office phone.

Anders popped in every now and again to take candid photos of me, which I'm sure he thought was hilarious, and to check on me to verify that I had eaten. Each time, I assured him that of course I had and could show him the takeout boxes in a garbage bag off to the side of the couch to prove it. He complained that he wished there was a garbage bag full of empty soap dispensers and shampoo bottles as well to prove that I'd been showering, but there was no such evidence because I *hadn't* been showering.

Though Anders was pretty much my best friend, his interruptions were entirely unwelcome. Especially when he started complaining about my hygiene. After his fifth intrusion of my intense creative burst, I decided it was time to lock the door.

On his sixth visit, he stood in the open doorway and held up the key. "I know where you keep this," he said. "And don't pretend you're locking the door for your own personal safety. We both know you never lock up properly because you think the lock on the outside door leading to the street is safe enough in spite of the fact that I tell you that Steve down the hall is kind of creepy, and you should be looking out for yourself."

He was proud of himself for knowing about my key.

To be honest, I was proud of him, too. I'd forgotten having put the key behind the framed print of the fish in the birdcage that Shannon had convinced the building owner to buy because she said it made the building seem trendy and cool when really it felt like a freaky metaphor of how we were trapped in our lives. I'd have moved a long time ago to a cheaper apartment if it weren't for my dear friend who couldn't seem to comprehend my locked door. "Anders, you

33

know I love you, but I really need to be working. I'm onto something here. This has never happened before. I've never had words just fly out of my head and onto the screen, and I need to keep it while I've got it."

Anders shook his Asgardian blond head from side to side and gave me his I-am-definitely-not-listening-to-you look, and then he said, "That's ridiculous. Creative energy can't be sustained if it isn't fed. What you need is a break. What you need is sunshine. You're starting to look like a member of the undead. I'm about to call a doctor to check for fang growth."

With a frown, I ran my tongue over my definitely-not-fangy teeth. They were more troll-like in that they felt like they were covered in moss.

"Besides all that, you're a human hazmat crisis. I mean this as a friend when I say you smell awful and need a shower."

I pinned my arms to my sides, determined not to give in to the impulse to lift one and take a whiff to verify the truth of his declaration. I probably bore the sour stink of unwashed human, and why would I want to smell that? I glared at him. "You weren't actually invited in for sniff-testing, so feel free to leave." With the intent of physically throwing him out, I moved off the couch for the first time in days and actually did catch a whiff of myself. It wasn't pretty.

"I'm just asking for a short walk," he said, putting his hands up as if to defend himself from getting kicked out. Or maybe it was to defend himself against the smell. "Just a walk. I'm not even going to make you run this time. We're just going to move slowly along a premade path. When was the last time you moved farther than twenty steps to the fridge or thirty steps to the bathroom?"

He actually made a good point there. My muscles were starting to atrophy. And the truth was that I happened to be stuck at that exact moment on a particular chapter that had me in a bit of a . . . well, not really a writer's block . . . more like a writer's stumble. The current chapter needed some thinking and walking. But would that thinking be better off done alone?

"Please, Lettie? Please, please, please? I really need you."

I blinked. Anders *needed* me? Only a monster could say no to that. We were friends. That meant we dropped things — or did things we normally wouldn't — when one of us needed the other. Like the time Anders had needed a date to accompany him to his work Halloween party the year before but wasn't dating anyone. I hated wearing the kind of costume that made people stare as they figured out what, exactly, it was supposed to be, but I went to his party because it mattered to him. We went as lightning and thunder. He was dressed as a black rain cloud with tufts of cotton stuffed in his ears, and I was dressed as a lightning strike victim, complete with the charred remains of an umbrella in my hand.

Everyone looked at us because the costumes were, indeed, very funny. And it's true that if anyone else had been dressed up that way, I would have loved it. But this was me, and being the center of attention was at the bottom of my list of things to do. Still, when your true friends need you . . .

"Fine," I said. "But not for very long. I really do have work to do."

"Deal," he said. He was serious about not liking my smell because he insisted on waiting while I showered quickly and dressed in clothes that *hadn't* been on my body for the last week and a half straight.

While cleaning up, I realized how much of this book belonged to Anders. So many of the words I'd written were fragmented pieces of things he'd said to me over the time we'd lived as neighbors in the same apartment building. One could probably go as far as to call it the book of Anders.

The work in progress was my first nonfiction experience. Before that, my writing had consisted entirely of fairy tales, fractured fables that twisted into stories that would matter today if any publisher would ever just say yes to me. I was a great believer in fairy tales, in writing things the way *you* wanted them to be. Why would anyone want to write about real life? Wasn't living it enough? I had certainly never wanted to venture into things that actually *were.* Until now. And, certainly, an author could hardly write nonfiction without pulling from her very own reality. Anders was a huge part of my reality; so of course he'd ended up in this book. Thinking and talking things over with Anders would probably help me get over my stumble.

But our walk wasn't really about me. He had said he'd needed me. The walk was about him. Once I was finished getting dressed and we were off, I peppered him with questions to keep us on topic.

Anders displayed more than a willingness to talk. He had forced me out into the fresh air because he was having girl trouble.

"She wants to get married." He blurted

37

this out as if it had been building up inside of him like floodwaters slamming up against a dam before it breaks.

It took my mind several moments to process the words he'd used. *She.* I could only assume that *she* meant his girlfriend Chloe. *Wants to get married.* I could only assume that the person she wanted to marry was *him.* Once my brain had finally taken all of those words apart, sorted through them, and then put them back together, I stopped walking and looked Anders directly in the eye. "You're getting married?"

Why did it feel like he'd slapped me across the face? Why did it feel like he'd punched me in the gut? Why did it feel like he'd stomped on my foot and then asked me to dance only to laugh at me, stomp on my foot again, and walk away, leaving me broken on the dance floor? Why did it feel like I had just lost my best friend?

Anders swallowed hard. His rather sharp Adam's apple bobbed with emotion. I didn't think I had ever seen Anders swallow like that before. Anders was not one of those nervous types that swallowed the words he was going to say before replacing them with new, different, untrue words. Anders was the guy who said what he thought. He never had to take that extra moment to reassess, replan, swallow words back down.

And that was when I became afraid. If Anders had to rethink what he planned to say to me, then it must be serious. It must be true. He was going to get married. The news shouldn't have bothered me. It's not like I had any claim to Anders beyond that of downstairs neighbor and friend, but it *did* bother me. Hadn't he, just a few short weeks ago, told me that he wasn't sure how he felt about her? Wasn't he the one who'd said he didn't want to take her home to meet Grandpa yet? For Anders, taking a girl home to meet Grandpa meant buying her an airplane ticket. That was a serious step. Was he taking that step?

And suddenly, the idea of Anders taking Chloe to Sweden with him made me hope with all my heart that all of those Swedish legends and fairy tales were true. I hoped the trolls would kidnap her while she was there and take her away to the troll lands and no one would ever see her again. I gave myself a small shake, realizing that this kind of fantasy smacked dangerously of jealousy.

Was I jealous?

No.

It's not like *I* wanted to get married. Anders did. It was one of those "we-are-so-not-compatible; it's-a-good-thing-we're-not-a-thing" things we laughed about. How could I be jealous when I didn't want what was happening to him to happen to me?

"Tell me what you're thinking," Anders said, his voice a pleading keen.

He'd been talking. And I'd missed most of what he'd actually said because I had been so caught up in the racing thoughts in my head.

"Let's start at the beginning," I said. "How did all of this happen? Tell me exactly what was said, where you were, and what the end result was."

Anders smoothed his hands over his jeans and licked his lips. "I hardly know where it started. One day we were just dating and doing what we did: going out, having dinner, seeing plays or a movie every now and again, and then the next day we were talking about how many kids she wants and do I like dogs."

"Kids, huh? How many kids *do* you want?" I asked, genuinely curious, since this was something that had never come up in any of our conversations.

Anders shrugged. "I don't know. Three? Three always sounded good to me. You know I like the rule of thirds." As a photographer, it was one of his favorite things.

"How many does *she* want?" Why was I

40

asking these ridiculous questions? Why wasn't I grabbing him by the shoulders, shaking him hard, and telling him that he couldn't get married because he already had a job as my best friend and neighbor? The husband job would be way too time-consuming to possibly fit in with his already-stated duties.

"She wants one. One. It seems awfully singular doesn't it?" How he managed to frown while keeping his eyes open wide in confusion was a mystery to me.

"One *is* awfully singular," I repeated. And didn't I know? No matter how many fairy-tale characters I'd read about and had considered to be my friends, I had still grown up singular for the bulk of my life.

"Does she like dogs?" I already knew that he did. Anders loved dogs regardless of breed, color, or fur length. If it barked and had a wagging tail, he fell in love. But did she? Did Chloe love dogs like Anders loved them?

Anders was already shaking his head. "No. She actually hates them. She's more of a cat person."

"But you're allergic to cats." A frown formed on my own face as I trailed my fingers along the cold, black rails of a wrought iron fence next to the sidewalk we were on.

"I know," he said. "That's why she said she didn't mind if we didn't have any pets at all."

I imagined the offspring of Anders and his not-troll-kidnapped bride and decided such offspring would likely end up having to daydream of being kidnapped by trolls because that would be far superior and far more interesting than growing up as an only child with no pets.

"Poor kid." I hadn't meant to voice that out loud. Sure. Probably tons of kids grew up like that and were fine. But I hadn't been one of those kids. I grew up like that and *wasn't* fine.

It wasn't fair for me to think that way. Just because my childhood had been a harsh, glaring reality with no frills or perks didn't mean all sibling-less, pet-less kids were like that. And I *had* ended up with a sibling when my mom remarried. I actually even loved my stepsister — in spite of what the fairy tales said I should feel about her.

Besides, any kid of Anders would be insanely lucky because Anders was fun to spend time with. Who needed siblings or dogs when Anders was around? But the woman in question? She was *packaging,* not *person.* It had never occurred to me to not like her until I realized at that moment how much like my own mother she was. And, of course, that realization hadn't come until she threatened to steal my best friend. How shallow did that make me? I'd been fine with her before. I'd even goaded Anders about marrying her back when the possibility of such a thing seemed so incredibly unlikely.

"She did say that we could probably do goldfish or maybe a pet canary or something as long as it didn't smell bad." Anders gave me a smile that looked as thin as a prisoner in a king's dungeon.

"That's nice." I had to say that. What else could I say? I was his friend, wasn't I? Friends support each other even when bad decisions are in fashion.

But really? A goldfish? A goldfish isn't a pet; it's an emergency snack during the apocalypse.

"Yeah," he said. "Nice. Nice. Goldfish are nice." But he didn't sound convinced of that.

It was his lack of conviction that gave me the courage to ask the hard question, the one question I had to have an answer to. "Are you actually engaged, Anders?"

He didn't answer right away, which honestly freaked me out a lot. What was the

43

silent answer? I understood that a *yes* answer might mean that I had to readjust the way I thought about Anders. I wouldn't be able to look at him as my best friend anymore because being married to someone required you to be the best friend to whomever you married. I knew that a *no* answer also meant that I had to rethink the way I viewed Anders. The fact that I flared with jealousy at the idea of him being engaged to someone else made me realize that I was more emotionally involved in this friendship than I had previously thought.

But the answer of silence? What did that mean for me? What did that mean for him? What did that mean for us?

Since he chose not to speak, and the silence was becoming unbearable, I filled that silence with more questions. "So did you tell her that you're agreeable with the idea of marriage? Or did you tell her you're thinking about it? Or maybe did you tell her that you aren't ready yet?"

Door number three, Anders. Pick door number three.

He finally opened his mouth, but only a choking sound that could have been a cough, maybe a laugh, or maybe he was actually choking — it was hard to tell — came out.

"I . . . I'm not really sure."

I deserved an award for not rolling my eyes at such a statement. What was *I'm not really sure* supposed to mean? Was this the same thing as he wasn't really sure about her but he was going to keep dating her anyway instead of letting her off the hook the way I'd told him to? Which would kind of make him a punk because, honestly, any guy who's not sure about a relationship has no business talking about marriage in that relationship.

"What exactly aren't you sure about?" I asked, feeling my patience wear out. My tone must have been frosty because the people we happened to be walking past cast me a look that said they thought I was a monster and Anders a look that said they pitied him for being stuck with such a monster.

Anders wasn't paying attention to the people passing us, so he didn't realize that he was, in fact, dealing with a monster because the look he gave me was filled with something else entirely. Fear, uncertainty, and something I didn't recognize. "I like Chloe. I even can honestly say I love Chloe. But I just don't know about Chloe with me on a permanent type of basis. And honestly, Lettie, I don't know if she's in love with me so much or if she's in love with the idea of playing house. I get the feeling that marriage is kind of one of those bucket list items for her, and she's just standing over her list and impatiently tapping her permanent-ink Sharpie ready to check it off."

He'd hesitated, but he'd said the word. Even with his doubt, he'd said the word. There was so much strength to be found in the word *love.* To have used that word to describe his feelings for her meant he had to mean it. Which meant this was not a good time for me to say, *hey, I think I might be interested in you because I'm feeling jealousy, and that's a new feeling for me.* Because that would make me a jerk friend. And the last thing I wanted to be was a jerk friend, not when he walked next to me with his face so open and vulnerable and in need of confirmation and confidence all at the same time.

I hunched deeper into my coat. "You did say you loved her. And you have been together for an awfully long time. And you refused to break up with her even when I told you to a few weeks ago when you weren't sure about how to proceed with her."

He licked his lips, which was going to dry them out. I would need to make sure I bought him some lip balm if he was going to keep that habit up for very long. "Right. I did say I loved her. And I do." He rushed to tack on that little bit of insistence as if needing to prove it to both of us. "So maybe getting married isn't a bad idea at all? Right?"

I almost felt sorry for Chloe. I wouldn't want to be dating somebody as uncertain and insecure about his feelings for me as Anders was for her. Which meant I had to be a good friend in all directions and weigh all options for him, since he was clearly unwilling to do it for himself. "But marriage is a big step. You're not that old. I mean, come on, you're what . . . twenty-eight?"

He nodded. "You're right. Twenty-eight is really young, isn't it?" His circular reasoning and feelings were making me crazy. I finally stopped in the middle of the path, turned to face him directly, and demanded to know the end result of his conversation with his girlfriend. "Anders, are you or are you not engaged to be married to this woman?"

"I think I am."

Chapter Three

"Beware the woods, for it is there that you will not meet up with dragons, trolls, or wolves. It is there that you will meet yourself, which can be the most terrifying thing of all."
— Charlotte Kingsley,
The Cinderella Fiction
(The "Know Yourself" Chapter)

"You think?" I'd playfully hit or punched Anders a gazillion times during the time that we had lived as neighbors. But never before had I actually wanted to slap him full on, hand opened, across the face, in a way that would maybe make him need to be checked for a concussion. How could a man not know whether or not he was engaged?

Rather than continue to seethe over the fact that my dear friend who was smart and clever and witty could be so stupid, I decided to ask him out loud why he was so stupid.

"It's not like I had time to figure it out, Lettie."

"How did you not have time? Were you beamed up into a spaceship or something in the middle of the conversation?"

"Sort of. I got called into work. She was in the middle of explaining how she'd been thinking about this for a while and she wanted to know if I ever thought about it, but then she never gave me a moment to answer what I thought about it because she kept talking, and then my pager went off. She was kind of ticked, but I told her I had to go because my not going would put somebody's life on the line."

Right. His job. Of course. How many conversations and movies had his job interrupted for the two of us? Plenty.

"Did everything turn out okay?" Even being mad at him, I had to ask because Anders saw things in his job every day that weren't great. Sometimes people died in his arms, and if that had happened, the emotions he felt regarding that would trump his confusion over a maybe engagement. Being his friend meant understanding that.

"Everything turned out okay. He wasn't responsive at first, but he came to. It was an allergic reaction to a new prescription."

I was glad the call had been fine. There was one time when he'd answered a call for a woman whose baby had stopped breathing. The woman met him in the driveway before they could even get the ambulance to a stop. As he jumped from the vehicle, the woman thrust the child into his arms and demanded he save it. The baby didn't live. Anders was a mute for several days as he tried to process what he might have done differently, before he finally understood there was nothing he could have done differently.

Once I felt Anders was sufficiently stable mentally, I asked the question again. "So how do you not know if you're engaged or not? Has she said something? What has your conversation been since then?"

He let out a long breath, long enough it was hard to believe he could hold that much oxygen in his lungs. "That's the thing," he said. "We didn't shake hands or anything, but she seems to think we've come to an agreement."

"And are you okay with the agreement she thinks you've made?"

He scrubbed his hand over his head and let out an exasperated noise. "I don't know! That's why I had to get you out here to come talk to me."

"What do you want me to do? I can't tell you if you're engaged or not."

"What would you do?" he asked, his voice a higher pitch than it had ever been during the course of our friendship. We'd crossed the Muddy River and made it to the James Kelleher Rose Garden entrance. Without asking if Anders wanted to go in or not, I pushed the wooden gate open. Anders went in, and I followed him, letting the gate swing shut behind me. We walked the graveled path and breathed in the scent of cold, wet earth from the evening's previous rainfall. My mind wandered to the oddity of it not having snowed for the last few weeks. I considered how the rain and the warmth felt more like spring than the end of winter. My mind pondered the weather while it also formed an answer to his question. *What would I do?*

I would have cut the guy loose way before it got to this level of emergency. But my commitment issues weren't in the playbook for Anders. My issues came from years of watching the married people in my life living in misery. My parents were divorced. Both sets of natural grandparents were divorced, and my aunts and uncles were all divorced. Sure, some of the second mar-

51

riages were doing okay, but not all of them. I wrote about happily ever afters in my fairy tales. But life had taught me not to believe in them.

"You know I'm the wrong person to ask, Anders," I finally said. "I don't think I believe in marriage."

He gave me a sidelong glance. We neared the fountain surrounded by creepy cherubic statues. Anders stopped walking and turned to face me. "I hate it when you say that. It's like when a person says they don't believe in fairies and a fairy drops down dead somewhere."

I laughed. "What? You think every time I say I don't believe in marriage, a married couple drops down dead?"

"Okay. So maybe you don't believe marriage always works, but don't you think it could? What if you found someone who completely understood you and couldn't live without you? And who you couldn't live without? What about then? What about for yourself?"

"You've clearly never met any of my past boyfriends, or you wouldn't ever ask me such a thing. Definitely not for myself. And I'm not saying no one should ever get married. Just because I don't think it's for me doesn't mean other people can't do what they want."

"You really don't believe, do you?" He looked surprised at the discovery.

"Anders. We've had this conversation dozens of times. Why are you acting like a five-year-old finding out about Santa?"

"I just thought you were being all bluster. I didn't think you meant it." He looked disappointed in a way I couldn't understand. Did he really want to marry Chloe, and my lack of belief was holding him back somehow?

He sort of had a point, though. Some part of it was all bluster. I wrote fairy-tale endings because the idea of true love inspired me. Not believing in something and still wanting it to be true was exhausting, but it was the place where I lived.

I broke away from his intense gaze and stared at the creepy cherubs. I'd once used them as inspiration for a nightmare scene I'd written into one of my darker fae novels. "I want to believe in it. Is that good enough?" My eyes drifted back to sneak a peek at him.

His shoulders slumped a fraction. So not good enough.

"Anyway," I said, "this isn't about me. This is about you." Even as the words fell from my mouth, it felt a little bit about me.

I shook the thought off, hating it when the fantasy worlds in my head collided with my reality. I'd made a fool of myself more than once when I'd allowed myself to believe in my own daydreams. "What are you going to tell Chloe when you see her next?"

His slumped shoulders shrugged. "I do believe in marriage. I believe being together is a good thing. Healthy and great if it's done right."

I liked that he said that. It gave me hope for the world in general. Nice guys existed. Nice guys who loved the idea of happy endings as much as I did. "I guess the bigger question is: Do you believe in marriage with Chloe?" The back and forth of my emotions was killing me. I wanted to see Anders happy. I wanted to be a good friend. But I also wanted him to stay the way we were: best buds and neighbors in the same apartment building.

"I'm seeing her tonight. But I think . . ." He looked at me, really looked at me as we stood there by the cherubs. The look was so intense it nailed me to the spot. My feet couldn't have moved if they'd wanted to. "Twenty-eight really isn't that young. And my *farfar* is getting old. I'd like him to have a chance to meet the woman I marry before he dies."

Farfar is what Anders called his grandpa. It means father's father in Swedish. I remembered him telling me his grandpa was in his eighties.

When I didn't respond, Anders nodded and straightened his slumped shoulders. "I do love her. And she loves me." He nodded. And that settled that. Anders was engaged. Not just in theory but in fact.

I took a deep, cleansing breath. Anders was my friend. And I would be cool with whatever choice he made. Besides, he was right. He talked about being married and having kids, or *kid* in this new situation, all the time. Family life was something he wanted, which was weird because he was from Sweden, and from what he told me about it, Swedes didn't care much one way or the other about actual marriage, but Anders was different that way. He talked a lot about his *farfar* and how much his family meant to him. Which made sense. His parents were still together. His one set of grandparents had been together until they died, and his other set had also been together until his grandmother died and left his *farfar* alone. His sister, who lived in Canada, was happily settled with a dentist. Anders came from solid family stock.

We discussed variables of his newfound

engagement after that. Things like where they would live after getting married, possible dates for the event, who his best man would be.

I tried to be the supportive friend I knew he needed, but I couldn't help the traces of sadness leaking into my heart. He would definitely have to move. His studio apartment was barely big enough for him let alone him with a plus one. He seemed relieved to have come to a decision, relieved to have moved past deciding and into planning.

I am glad for him. But as I thought that, the cherubs seemed to laugh at me. I glared at the evil little stone monsters and lifted my chin, determined to be as happy for my friend as I kept telling myself I was.

Back at my apartment, Anders leaned into the doorframe as we parted ways. "Thanks for coming out to talk with me, Lettie. I always have better clarity when you're around."

"We're friends, Anders. Of course I'm available to talk when you need it. That's what friends are for."

He smiled. I smiled.

He shoved off from the doorframe. "Well, I'd better go. You've got work to do."

He wasn't wrong there, but I didn't really

want him to leave. I opened my mouth to try to come up with a reason for him to stay, but the words clogged in my throat, and I swallowed them back down in much the same way Anders had swallowed down his words earlier.

Instead of replacing what I had wanted to say with something not true, I simply smiled and nodded and watched him walk away down the hall to the stairwell.

I stood there even after the stairwell door clicked closed before I shook myself out of the stupor and closed my own apartment door. Once alone, I shed my coat and paced my apartment for a few minutes to pull myself back into writer mode and to shake off the uneasiness that came with thinking of a future with Anders not being right downstairs anytime I wanted him.

I thought of his relief in making a decision, of how his shoulders stopped slumping as if a burden had been lifted from them once he had decided what the next chapter in his life would be.

As I settled back on the couch with my laptop over my crossed legs, I thought about Anders moving forward and all the ways it affected me. The sad leaked in some more, but I squared my shoulders and did my own moving forward by putting my fingers back on the keys and filling the pages of my new book. This would be the chapter about making decisions and moving forward.

I finished the book a week later, actually writing the words *the end* just because it felt good to write them. Of course, I deleted them a few minutes later so my submission didn't make me look like an amateur — but not until after I took a screenshot of the words and updated my social media account with a celebration GIF. I didn't include any of the actual words of the book in the screenshot except those words: "the end." I was not a read-the-last-page-before-the-first kind of girl, and no one else got to be while they were on my watch.

Several of the people I traded critiques with online left encouraging comments and virtual high fives.

I expected Anders to come up to my apartment and celebrate the completion with me when I texted him to tell him I was done, but he only texted back a jumping smiley-face emoji and a congratulations. He didn't show up. In fact, he hadn't been physically back in my apartment since that moment he'd agreed to let Chloe be right when she'd decided they were getting married.

I tried not to take it personally. Of course he'd be busy. Of course he'd be spending his time with her and not with his neurotic neighbor.

Only I did take it personally. I'd known I would lose him as a best friend once they were married, but I hadn't thought it would happen now, during the engagement part. Wasn't there supposed to be some adjustment period?

I almost sent the book to a few of my critique partners, the regulars who, with grabby hands, wanted everything I wrote. But this book was different and deserved to be unveiled all at once to everyone in a way that could be celebrated. Instead I ran a spell-check and let the book sit on my computer for two days. Then I went back over it again, reading each word out loud. After that, without even having to look up her address because I practically had the woman on speed dial as far as my email addresses were concerned, I sent the book to Jennifer Apsley — the agent of my dreams — crossed my fingers, and celebrated alone with more ice cream.

This time, I actually had some in the freezer because I'd decided to own the fact that fairy godmothers don't exist. In the real world, you had to learn how to make your own magic. And not only did I have ice cream, I had the raspberry fudge that felt fitting as a metaphor for the moment: smooth and sweet. A tingling sensation worked its way up my spine. The sensation felt like a premonition that my days of eating rocky road as a life metaphor were over.

With the book finished, there was nothing left for me to do except return to my day job at Frankly Eyewear. The unseasonably warmer weather turned to rain and misery. Even the skies mourned my return to the day job. Nicole Hall, my boss, was in my glass cubicle before I could get my drenched raincoat off my shoulders. Since she insisted on being in my personal space so early, I didn't feel too bad when shaking out my coat ended with her being splashed. Sometimes karma needed coaxing.

"Have a nice vacation?" The question would have been benign from anyone else. It might have even been friendly coming from a different mouth. But from Nicole, sarcasm and contempt dribbled out between the words.

"I did. Thanks." I scooted around her to hang my raincoat up on the human-sized fountain pen that decorated my cubicle. The five-foot pen had been a gift from my dad when I graduated college with an English degree and a confidence that I would be a writer. Dad wasn't around much, but he showed his solidarity where he could. He'd told me if writing didn't work out for me, I could use it as a jousting stick.

I considered that option as Nicole prepared to rant at me. She waited several moments longer than I'd expected before she finally exhaled her first dig.

"To take all of that time off at once was incredibly irresponsible," she said.

"I had the PTO to cover it."

"PTO isn't meant to be stored up and then taken all at once."

I imagined her, with her fake-baked leather skin and her dark shaggy hair, as a dragon blowing smoke and flame as she ticked off on her fingers all the reasons why my taking off so much time at once was an inconvenience to the entire office.

I settled into my chair and pressed the computer power button on, since it would likely take the entire time that Nicole lectured me for the computer to warm up to the idea of working. My computer was a derelict throwback from the first of the century. When I once denounced the machine as a contemporary of the dinosaurs, Nicole told me that as a writer, my work didn't require very much memory or speed. I complained that I still had to do research and be on the internet, which required speed, but she turned a deaf ear to my complaints, saying they had to save the nicer machines for the designers and web developers.

"The company allows PTO to accumulate over two years before they force you to take it," I said calmly. I stayed calm because she hated it when people didn't get worked up about things the way she did. "This means that company policy is fine with it being accumulated over that time and then taken whenever the employee needs it. It's in the employee handbook."

"You left everyone in a lurch!" she said, throwing her hands in the air. "It was selfish!" I pretty much tuned her out after she insisted on hashing through the reasons I had done everyone a huge disservice a second time. Instead, I imagined myself holding a shield with magical properties that blocked out the smoke and fire to protect innocent villagers, or, in this case, my coworkers, who were all watching through the glass dividers.

I might have been an eccentric, quasi-shut-in writer, but it didn't mean I didn't like my coworkers. They were actually pretty cool people for the most part. And if my absence really had left them all in a lurch, then I genuinely felt badly.

Except, based on the looks of pity they were casting my way, I didn't believe they'd been left in a lurch. They would have looked mad at me if they were upset. Besides, my files were accessible on the server, and there was enough generic content in those files that anyone could piece together pretty much any kind of content they needed without too much lurchiness taking place.

Regardless of my belief that Nicole was exaggerating the peril my absence had caused, her displeasure meant that I would hit the ground running. As she explained her vexation, she also explained the mountain of work ahead of me. While I was away, the company had decided to do a refresh on the website, so Nicole's declaration of being left in a lurch wasn't entirely false, just mostly false, since the only one really inconvenienced had been her. When I explained that she could have plugged in the content in my files from the server, she acted as if she had never seen those files before. I'd shown her the files at least once a month since I'd started working with the company four years prior.

Instead of telling her that maybe she

would have better luck finding things if she got her hair out of her eyes via the means of a haircut and a decent ponytail holder, I kept quiet, waited for her to finish ranting. Once she left, I got to work. The next week and a half would have to be spent zealously overworking to compensate for my time gone. I would write advertising copy and articles for Frankly Eyewear's online magazine with fervor and passion even if that passion came through gritted teeth. It honestly killed my soul to write for someone else after writing for myself for three weeks. But, writing for myself had yet to pay any bills. Writing for someone else paid for all of them. This was why showing up to work and playing nice was essential.

A refreshed website meant refreshed content, which was grueling work. Creating engaging content that was also informational, in order to induce the masses to buy eyewear they probably didn't need because the eyewear they purchased at their doctors' offices would do just fine, was a lot more difficult than one might think. Ali and Nate stopped in my office when it was apparent that the dragon had vacated and showed no signs of returning.

"I tried to warn you that she was on the warpath." Ali sat on the edge of my desk.

Ali was the company editor, which made her my editor. Nate remained standing and did double duty as lookout in case Nicole ambushed us. "But all my calls went straight to voice mail."

I cringed. "Yeah . . . I broke my phone and was out of the loop for a while."

"What did you do during your time off?" she asked.

Nate grinned. "Please tell us it was something amazing that involved a lounge chair on a beach and sunlight and someone massaging your hands from all the typing you do." Nate was the company photographer.

I laughed. "Almost. Trade the lounge chair for a couch, the beach for my living room, the sunlight for my really awesome moon lamp, and the massage for a workout — because I *was* typing — and you've got it right."

They both looked at me like I'd grown an extra eyeball in the middle of my forehead.

"That sounds like we weren't right at all," Nate said.

"Are you telling me you spent your *vacation* writing?" Ali asked.

"I did."

Neither of them much liked that confession. They were horrified to know that I'd pretty much never left my apartment.

They'd assumed that three weeks off meant I was backpacking Europe or exploring tombs in Egypt or ancient ruins in Mexico. To take that kind of time off for sitting at home and typing all day came across as pure blasphemy to them.

Not long after Nate and Ali left my cubicle, the entire company knew what I'd done during my break.

None of them could understand why I would stay in my living room and do what I did while in the office.

It became evident that the rumor had made it to Nicole when she showed up at my cubicle. Only this time, instead of looking cross, her bony arms were across her chest and her hair hung in her face, almost covering the sneer on her messy, lipsticked lips. "You stayed home to write?" she asked.

When I didn't respond, she said, "Don't tell me. Another book. Another, what? Three hundred? Four hundred pages that will never be read by anyone — not even your mother, since we all know how well you two get along."

I couldn't be mad at her for the mom-jab. It's not like that part wasn't true. But the rest . . . Didn't she have apples to poison or cauldrons to clean?

"I know you think I'm being mean to you,

but I'm just trying to keep you from being disappointed. You'll never earn a living writing books. You could have stayed at work, and we'd have paid you to write."

"Technically, Nicole, I did earn money writing this book. You did pay me to do it. Since I did it while out on my paid time off, I made just as much writing for myself as I would have made writing for you during these last few weeks. The only difference was my level of enjoyment. You're a smart woman. You figure out which I enjoy and which I don't."

She left, growling and grumbling about my attitude and human resources.

That altercation and the several others that followed left me excited when the weekend rolled back around, allowing me to go home and live my own life without Nicole using my dreams and goals for target practice, and my coworkers casting curious glances and shakes of heads in my direction. It didn't hurt that we had a company-wide early-out Friday. I was out of the office by noon.

The excitement of my weekend off died immediately upon opening my front door and finding that the lights were on. They weren't on because I'd been mindless regarding energy preservation and electricity bills, but because someone was in my apartment.

CHAPTER FOUR

"If you have struggles, you can't blame
the Evil Queen. At some point, you have
to make your own choices and stand
by them."
— Charlotte Kingsley,
The Cinderella Fiction
(The "Know Yourself" Chapter)

The noises of that someone rattling around
deep inside my apartment made the hair on
the back of my neck stand on end. How
many times had Anders warned me to lock
my door because Steve down the hall acted
creepy?

The briefest joy tumbled in my stomach
at the thought that maybe Anders had
finally come to visit. But he hadn't been by
in weeks. The chance of him being inside
now, especially when I wasn't there, was
absolutely zero. Besides, the noise was coming from my bedroom, not my kitchen. If

Anders had decided to ascend the stairs for a visit, he would've headed to the kitchen to sneak into the stash of chips and my home-made salsa.

My hand went slowly down, and my fingers wrapped around the rather large umbrella I'd just set down, which I'd taken even though the weather had been good that day. If Steve had decided to make a move, he'd find me to be a less-than-easy target. I held the umbrella out at the ready and made my way to my room, making sure not to step on any of the places where the floor creaked. Anders lived in the apartment directly below mine. He complained when I paced over and over the squeaky boards. And so I had learned to pace around them during my first month of residence. Who knew that such an education would allow me to apprehend a criminal?

It's not like anything in my apartment held any value or could be called special or important. There certainly wasn't much worth stealing, which was probably the reason I never bothered to lock the door. But there was my laptop, and my laptop contained everything I had ever written. If I lost that, I'd be ticked. And okay, I was smart about my writing. It's not like I didn't understand the laws of loss. With technology, there are only two kinds of people. There are those who have lost their information due to a crash or whatever, and there are those who *will* lose their information.

I'd already managed to make the list for the first group. Losing work was possibly the worst thing that could ever happen to a writer. It had taken me months to get my mojo back. I now kept everything up in the cloud. But that didn't mean I wanted whoever was rooting through my stuff in my room to get access to anything on my laptop.

If that meant bludgeoning the perpetrator to death with an umbrella, I considered that option to be a heroic act.

Based on the sound of my closet door closing, it seemed that the criminal was coming my direction. I stood outside my bedroom door with the umbrella held aloft, waiting to let fall a fatal blow. Okay, maybe not fatal. But hopefully a disarming blow. A normal person might have been afraid, but I couldn't help but consider the moment to be an exciting opportunity to get some hands-on research. I would absolutely write it all down in a book sometime. I was not a normal person. I was a writer.

The intruder darkened the doorway, prompting me to lift the umbrella higher.

Just as I was swinging down, the criminal exited and was . . . humming?

The tune was familiar enough and the voice was familiar enough that I managed to just stop the umbrella from connecting with a skull. "Kat?"

My standing in front of her with an umbrella held over her head must have startled her. Or possibly it was me shouting her name that startled her. Either way, she made a *yeeahh* noise, jumped several feet the other direction, and hit the wall.

"I nearly bludgeoned you!" I finally had enough control of myself to lower the umbrella without actually hitting her.

"Lettie, you scared me!"

"I scared you? Who's the one currently involved in a home invasion?"

"I left you a voice mail," she said. She was wearing my favorite elephant-print chiffon jacket, which explained what she'd been doing in my closet. Her naturally curly, long, dark hair and narrow elfin features made the jacket look better on her than it did on me.

"No, you didn't," I answered.

"Yes. I did. I swear you never check your voice mail."

She had me on that. I didn't always check. My voice mail wasn't one of those things

72

that I was actually good at keeping up with. "My phone broke. I had to order a new one, and it took a while to get here."

Not that my phone being on order meant I couldn't check voice mail, but the excuse still felt valid enough to let stand. With my heart coming off the adrenaline kick and finding a normal rhythm, I allowed myself to really look at my little sister. "Hey. Are you okay?"

Kat lifted a bony shoulder in a shrug.

"What did she do this time?"

"Nothing different from the usual. I just hit my limit; that's all."

I closed my eyes briefly in relief. I'd been on the receiving end of my mother's fun-sucking lectures and "reality blasts" for most of my life. But I worried sometimes that, without the blood bonds, she would take it further with Kat and do some real damage.

"So how long are you staying?" I asked.

We might not be blood related, and we certainly didn't look anything alike considering her dark skin and dark hair next to my freckles and red hair, but Kat was as much my sister as any that could have been born through my actual parents. Kat's great-grandparents had emigrated from Iraq in the fifties. Her mother was the first in her line to marry outside of the arranged marriage tradition. When I introduced Kat to people as my sister, we sometimes received odd looks, but I refused to introduce her as my stepsister. We solidly belonged to each other.

"At least a week, if that's okay. Our step-monster is just so . . . argh!" She made a growling noise. "If I stayed for even another minute, they would have to haul me in for homicide, and you know I look terrible in orange. Prison is so not for me."

"That bad, huh?" I always thought it was funny that she claimed my mother to be my stepmother, too. When we were younger, I argued the point, insisting that my mom was my actual mom not my stepmom. But Kat informed me that even though the woman gave birth to me, she still played the part of evil stepmother in my life. The logic was sometimes hard to dispute. I let Kat come crash at my house and empty my fridge into her belly whenever she wanted. It was cheaper and less trouble than psychiatric evaluations would be.

I had some friends who claimed that steps were only good for leg day, not for family. But it wasn't true, at least not in the case of my little sister. She was a delightful bonus that came from my parents getting divorced

74

and my mother remarrying my stepfather. The new stepfather wasn't a bad guy either. He was just a yes-man. To whatever my mother wanted, he said, "Of course, dear." Which was really annoying. But the daughter he'd brought into the family from his previous marriage was like a beautiful present given to me by a universe who must have felt apologetic for all the other crummy things in my life.

The downside was that sometimes Kat biased me against my own mother. Because, though my mom was difficult in the ways that she was difficult, she wasn't entirely evil either — no matter what my sister and I said about her. My mother genuinely believed she did her best in raising me and in raising Kat, too. She felt that by eliminating anything whimsical from our lives, she prepared us for the real world.

"How come you don't have any cookie butter?" Kat was the only person on the planet who put cookie butter on her ice cream. It was weird but still lovable.

"Because you ate it all last time you were here."

"Why didn't you buy any more?" she asked.

"Why don't you get a job?"

We stared at each other for a few moments

before we both burst out laughing. The go-get-a-job comment was one that my mother used on both of us during our teenage years. Since Kat was not yet out of her teenage years, she probably still heard it several times every day.

The thing was that Kat actually did have a job. It was our little secret from Mom. If Mom had any idea that Kat had found gainful employment, she would probably start making her pay rent immediately in spite of the fact that Kat had yet to graduate high school. Mom was a tough-love kind of woman. A long time ago, I'd decided that tough love meant that it was tough to love someone who didn't often seem to love you back. Kat went to work as soon as she was able so that she could save up enough money to move out immediately after graduation.

Both Mom and Kat's dad thought that Kat was doing an unpaid internship to earn college credit. And that was mostly true: all but the unpaid part. Kat was actually getting paid very well for her accomplishments, and everything she did was specifically for college. She worked for a fashion design company where she played with fabric swatches and a sketch pad all day. Since she fully loved clothing and had a natural understanding of how to create fashion out of anything, the job was perfect for her. A guy named David who was a family friend of her mother's had gotten the job for her.

"How did you get a whole week off of work?" I asked, thinking of my own work and all the grief Nicole had given me in spite of my work ethic and longevity with the company.

She looked abruptly away from me and turned all her attention back to the cupboard, which was painstakingly void of the cookie butter she'd been searching for. Her voice became suddenly small. "David felt like maybe I needed some time, especially for today."

"What's —" I almost asked what today was before the truth of it hit me. My life had been so crazy and full lately, I'd forgotten about my sister's needs. I exhaled a slow breath before asking, "Would you like me to take you to the cemetery? We can stop and get some flowers and a new night-light if you want."

Her eyes went shiny with tears. "I don't want to be a bother, Lettie."

I crossed over to her and wrapped my arms around her. "Kat, you will never be a bother to me. You're the best thing I've got going in my life."

Her showing up at my door now made sense. Catching the subway from our parents' house to mine was doable for her. Sure, there were about three miles of walking to get to the station, but Kat didn't mind stuff like that. There was no subway line to take her to where her mom was buried in Pine Grove Cemetery on Cape Cod. Not that such things had stopped her before. When our parents were first married, she'd gone missing. After hours of searching, her dad had found her curled up around her mother's headstone. It had been the second anniversary of her mother's death and, instead of spending the day with her, he'd spent it with my mother. Kat had rightfully felt abandoned, and had taken off. Even now, none of us could verify how she got there.

Her dad had promised her that he wouldn't forget and leave her to mourn alone ever again. But she was at my house today, which could only mean a broken promise.

"Let me get changed into normal clothes and we'll go, okay?" I said.

She nodded and blinked several times to keep the tears from falling.

Once in my bedroom, I hurried and placed an order from Bob's Grocery. Not having a fairy godmother didn't mean I couldn't *be* a fairy godmother. My sister wanted cookie butter, so there would be cookie butter waiting for her when we returned. I ordered a few of her other favorite things as well and left a note to leave the order at the door.

With that done, I changed clothes, grabbed my bag, keys, and sister, and left on a quest to salvage her emotional well-being.

We stopped for the necessary items: flowers, a solar-powered light-up dragonfly, and car snacks, because every road trip, even the short little two-hour ones, was worthy of good car snacks. And because it was my kid sister in her formative teen years and I cared about her health, I even made sure we had some healthy options. The last thing I wanted to be was a bad example.

The lack of snow days and the warmer weather meant a slight green had begun to overtake the cemetery lawn, throwing off the dead of winter. The day had been warm enough to mostly dry off the many days of rainfall New England had experienced, leaving the air smelling clean and the plant life eager to wake up.

At the grave, I stayed back to give Kat privacy while she settled the flowers and arranged the solar-powered dragonfly light. Kat regularly replaced the light she kept at her mother's gravesite so her mom always had a working night-light. She said it was because her mom had always made sure Kat had a working night-light when she'd been little.

Keeping myself busy while Kat took some time with her mom was easy. Her mom had been interred in my stepdad's family area. His family had chosen headstones with interesting funerary art, but the entire cemetery was interesting. I wandered through the stone tributes and considered the lives of the people tucked under the grass. Francis Moore, a humble baker who was also one of the revolutionary patriots, was buried in the Pine Grove Cemetery. His story intrigued me because he was one of the few men who threw tea into the Boston Harbor without disguising himself as a Native American. He went to that protest as himself, not as part of the mob, but as a man sending a message to the king that he would not stand for tyranny. He stood for something, and he stood for it in his own shoes. He owned his decisions.

After ten or so minutes, Kat looked up and caught my eye; she smiled and waved me over to join her.

When I reached her side, she took my hand and stayed quiet for several moments before saying, "You know, my dad didn't even mention it this morning. It was like he'd forgotten her completely — like he hadn't ever known her. And when I brought it up to him? He actually got mad at me. He told me to forget her. He told me it was time to stop mourning like a child and to grow up and live my own life because that was what she would have wanted. She'd want me to forget all this nonsense." She slumped down cross-legged on the grass in front of her mother's headstone. Her father's words sounded like my mother talking.

Kat stared at the frayed edges of her shoes, a pair of sky-blue hemp wedges, to avoid having to look up at me.

I lowered myself to the grass, ignoring the fact that it was cold and still wet enough from rain that it would leave a spot on the back of my pants, and ducked my head low so I could peer into her face. "Your dad *isn't* right, Kat. You *shouldn't* forget her. That's not the answer. I'm pretty sure, after everything you told me about your mom, that she would want you to remember her. She'd be glad that you come visit her grave and make sure she has a night-light and beauti-

81

ful things surrounding her." I took a deep breath, feeling pretty certain Kat wouldn't like hearing what I had to say next. "But your dad's not wrong, either."

Her head shot up, and I lifted a hand to quell her argument. "Your mom *would* want you to live your life. She would want you to be happy, not sad. Whenever I think of your mother and the person that she might have been, I always think of you and the person that you are. I bet you're like her. And you're the sort of person who would want someone to celebrate the fact that you lived, not mourn the fact that you're gone. Your mother would want you to live. She would want you to be happy. If she saw you all sad and mopey all the time, I think that would make her sad too. So your dad's not right, but he's not wrong either."

After a few seconds of her not responding, I added, "You see what I'm saying, right?"

She nodded. "Maybe. You've got a point, but it's not just about her. It's about him, too. It's like he never even loved her. He only thinks about Felicity now. And he repeats everything Felicity says and does like he's her pet parrot."

Kat only called my mom by her actual name when she was really mad. She called her the step-monster when she was mildly irritated, and stepmother the rest of the time. Hearing my mom's name made me cringe. "Your dad does love my mom." The fact couldn't be argued.

She deflated even more as the anger drained from her. "The weird thing is I think she really loves him, too. She takes care of him, you know? She does stuff for him — little things like making sure he has the pepper grinder on the table for all meals and always buying the chocolates with the almonds in them . . . that sort of thing."

Those facts couldn't be argued either. They might not be awesome as parents, but they were pretty good as a couple. And they weren't always awful as parents either. I could understand that when I was feeling fair-minded. My mom loved reality — even in all of its harsher shades. She felt that stable adults came from children who could face reality.

Kat rolled her eyes at herself. "It's fine that he loves her. You know? It's not like I don't want him to be happy. Of course I want him to be happy. I just want him to love my mom, too, so . . . you know?"

"Come on, Kat, you know he still loves your mom."

"How would I know that? People fall out

of love all the time."

"I don't think so," I said. "I don't believe people ever fall out of love. Sure, they might get bored, or they might get selfish, but I think if you ever really loved somebody, you don't ever stop." The bigger problem was finding people who were really in love to begin with. My own parents had married for reasons that still eluded me. I didn't think they had ever been in love, so it still baffled me to think that my mom could love anyone, but I didn't tell Kat that.

"Then why would he tell me to forget her?" She ripped grass blades out of the soil and tossed them away from her. "I don't think he loves her at all anymore, and if he . . ."

Man, I was dumb sometimes. How had I missed the bigger picture of her fears?

"He loves you, too, Kat."

She stiffened. "I wasn't saying . . ."

But she had been saying.

Why was today full of all the hard things?

"Maybe it's easier," I said. "Maybe moving on is the only way he knows how to handle his grief. If he stays in that past place full of grief and loss, how will he be able to have happiness in his present and future? How will he find joy in what he has — a daughter who is growing to be a beautiful

84

woman — if he is stuck in the grief of what he doesn't have? Everybody handles grief differently. It's not fair to him to say that he doesn't love her or to worry about him loving you. I've heard him talk about your mom. I've heard the ache in his voice as he drops into a reverential whisper usually reserved for deity. And sometimes when he's sharing a memory with me, he gets that smile that people get only when they are thinking of something perfect and wonderful. He gets that same smile when he looks at you sometimes."

"Does he?" So much need and hope in two words.

"He absolutely does. So let's not be too hard on him, okay?"

She nodded. Her eyes were still shiny from tears. But her fingers were no longer digging into the lawn to uproot helpless blades of still-brown grass, which proved she was trying to see the other point of view. That was important. Seeing the other point of view kept people from becoming villains.

I believed in villains. Every time a person failed to see how somebody else might feel or think, that person became the bad guy in every story. "What do you think we should read your mom today?"

"*Cinderella?*"

I gave her a smirk. "I think we're experiencing enough real angst against stepmothers for the day. Try again."

She laughed, which was good to hear. "Fine. How about the story of the boy who wanted to know what fear was? We haven't done that one in a long time."

We hadn't. I opened the book of fairy tales we'd brought with us and read the story to her while she lounged against her mother's headstone, and plucked a few of the flower petals from the roses we'd bought, and rubbed them between her fingers, bruising them enough to send their scent into the air.

The sun hung low in the sky, and the air had chilled considerably.

She grinned at me when I finished the story. "You should be an elementary school teacher or a librarian who does the storytime hour. You have a great reading voice."

I smiled back and stood, wiping grass clippings from my pants and inwardly sighing at the wet spot that definitely marked the back of me. Though the day had been warmish, it was cooling quickly enough that we needed to head back. "I was kind of hoping to use that great reading voice for doing actual readings for my books before book signings."

86

"Right. The books. How's that going?" She stood, too, and turned in the direction of the car.

"My employer told me I'm wasting my time and talent on dreams that will never happen."

"Wow. You went to work for your mom?"

I laughed and bumped her with my shoulder. "You have an evil side, little sister."

She laughed, too. "I learned from the best. Thank you, Felicity, for your grand education!" She raised her hands to the sky and brought them together in a show of humble gratitude.

"You're awful!" I said. "Anyway . . . work was less than awesome. But I did just finish a new book."

She whirled on me, her face twisted in the indignation of one who had been left out. "And you haven't sent it to me yet?"

"It's not a fairy tale. It's . . . something else."

"But I read everything you write. I'm your comma queen."

I gave her what I hoped was my most apologetic look. "I've already sent it in to the agent." I didn't have to specify which agent because we both knew who I really wanted.

She scowled but good-naturedly asked,

"Any bites?"

"No, not yet. But it's only been a few days." That was kind of a lie. It had been a week and a half. We walked to the car, and, as I was clicking the key fob to unlock the doors so we could get in, my phone pinged with the message. Without really thinking, I swiped the message open and then glanced down to see who was writing. My jaw went slack, and I had to lean into the car to hold me up because my knees no longer seemed to think they had to hold me upright.

"What's wrong?" Kat asked from over the top of my car.

I stared up at her, my jaw still slack, my heart slamming my ribs. My eyes had never seemed to stretch open so wide before. In one breathless sentence, my entire life changed. "I just got a bite."

CHAPTER FIVE

"Know what you want and dare to go after it. Bargaining your life away to a sea witch so you can lose your fins, get legs, and talk to the prince of your dreams might get you turned to seafoam. But it might not. And you'll never know unless you dare to try."
— Charlotte Kingsley,
The Cinderella Fiction
(The "Make Your Own Magic" Chapter)

"No way!"

"Way." I couldn't breathe. Was I hyperventilating?

"Well? What does it say?"

I was dreaming. I had to be. I'd been climbing the ladder to success for so long that it felt like this new development might really be me just falling off, not me arriving at the top. "It says she wants to talk to me as soon as possible and wants to know if right now or sometime in the next few hours would work for me."

Kat practically pole-vaulted over the hood of my car. She had to come to me because I still couldn't move from where the car held me in a stable, vertical position.

"No way, no way, no way!" Kat grabbed my phone from my hands so she could read the message for herself. "No way, no way, no way!" She shoved the phone back into my hands. "What are you waiting for, dummy? Tell her to call!" My sister was great at giving simultaneous positive and negative feedback.

"Now? We're in a graveyard." My hands shook. Maybe we were having an earthquake. Maybe I was about to pass out.

"Tell her to call!" My sister yelled through the fog and the black that was edging into my vision.

My fingers moved on the screen. I'm not sure what I wrote. It might have been, "I just wished hard on a star. Please don't make it explode." I felt delirious and happy and slightly sick all at the same time. If this was true joy, then true joy was weird. My finger hit send.

"What do I do if she does call?" I asked. The phone rang just as the question left my mouth.

I held out the phone as if it had turned into a scorpion with a wicked, twitchy tail.

Kat laughed. "Answer! You answer, Lettie. I'll go hang out with Mom some more." She slipped the Grimm's fairy-tale book from my arm and bounded off across the cemetery.

I obeyed my sister and answered.

The conversation was shorter than one would have imagined. Big things apparently didn't require lengthy conversation. I managed a few verbal grunts of agreement and maybe caught half of what she actually said because everything turned to static after her opening sentence. "We absolutely love this concept!"

They loved it.

Who *they* were in regards to the *we* she mentioned hardly mattered because *they loved it.* They loved what I wrote. They loved my words.

"I'd like to offer you representation. How do you feel about that?"

How did I feel about that? Was this a trick question? "I think that would be terrific," I said, instead of squealing and crying and saying thank you, thank you, thank you over and over and over again.

She talked some more about how our partnership would be fantastic and how she felt real excitement in finally getting the chance to work with me. Then she said she wanted to meet with me.

The agent of my dreams wanted to meet with me.

She gave me a proposed time to meet, and I must have said something that sounded like agreement because her next words were, "I'll send you the travel itinerary in the next ten minutes. Write back to confirm you received it and that everything checks out, okay?"

She was sending me a travel itinerary. They loved it.

"Okay, Charlotte?" Jennifer Apsley prompted me again as my mind started drifting away in the moment where day-dreams collide with reality. My reality-sucks-but-it-is-reality mother never pre-pared me for this.

"Yes. That's great, Ms. Apsley."

"Call me Jen."

"Jen. I look forward to meeting you."

"Yes. Bright and early Monday!" She made a salutation that almost sounded like a kissing noise.

"She wants you there Monday?" Kat said, when she realized my phone was no longer near my ear, and hurried over to discuss what had just happened. She didn't even try to pretend that she'd made it back to her mother's grave and hadn't been creeping back in my direction to eavesdrop. I grabbed her arms and let out a happy, scared, manic scream that should have awakened all the people in their caskets. Kat screamed with me. We jumped up and down and screamed.

Then I started crying. Because I was a ridiculous excuse for a grown-up. I'd finished my first novel not too long after my twentieth birthday. Six years of rejection and failure were wrapped up in those tears, and they released in a torrent I couldn't have controlled if I tried.

Kat laughed while I cried, but she stopped abruptly, her eyes suddenly serious. "We don't have time for this. We've got to get you home. We've got to get you packed. Got to get you dressed. Get you ready! Come on, Lettie. We've got to go!" She cast a look back over her shoulder in the direction of her mother's grave and said, "Bye, Mom! Gotta help my sister! Love you!"

Kat pretty much shouldered me out of the way after that so that she could open my car door and then ramrod me inside.

I don't remember driving home at all. It obviously happened because before I could comprehend anything, Kat was gathering up the delivery order left at the door, propelling me into my apartment, dumping the groceries on the couch, and talking a mile a minute about my wardrobe for the big meeting.

"And we should absolutely celebrate tonight!" she declared as she moved into my bedroom and farther still into my closet. "When does Anders usually come by? We should totally wait for him before we head out."

The silly smile that had occupied my face from pretty much the moment I ended the call with Jennifer Apsley slipped from my lips. I focused my attention on the bedroom and followed Kat's voice. How could such complete happiness crash around me in so little time? "Anders won't be coming by. It'll just be the two of us."

"Not coming? Why not? Oh, did he get called out? Did he text you or something?"

"No, he didn't text me. I don't know if he got called out or not. He just doesn't come by anymore. That's all."

"Why wouldn't he come by anymore? He's, like, your best friend. I mean, besides me. Obviously."

"He's engaged."

She dropped the several hangers of shirts she felt were possible candidates for the meeting. "No. He's not." She shook her head.

I nodded my head to counteract her shake. "Yes. He is."

"He can't be engaged when everyone knows you two are meant to get married. So unless he's engaged to you, and you're a jerk for not telling me, you're wrong." She actually stepped on the clothes she'd dropped as she exited the closet, still shaking her head. The snap from one of the hangers breaking under her weight felt like my emotions had been given a brief voice.

Snap.

Break.

I hadn't allowed myself to feel the sad that had been leaking in about Anders. I'd shoved it away every time its shadowy fingers reached for me, but now — in the stark contrast of the happiness over having the agent of my dreams call and declare me validated as a writer — his absence felt like a dagger twisted under my ribs.

"How could you let that happen?"

Her words carried such force, I actually backed up a step. I let out a stuttering laugh. "Oh, come on, Kat. It's not like that's something I get a choice in."

"But you do have a choice. All you have to do is tell him that you love him."

I laughed again, only this time it was in straight-up panic. "I don't love him. I mean I do but not like that."

"Yes, you do." She crossed her arms over her chest and gave me a look that reminded me of my mother. Whether Kat liked her or not, she'd managed to acquire a few of my mom's mannerisms during their time together.

"No, I don't."

With a grunt of frustration, Kat swept past me to the couch, where she'd left her backpack when we'd come in. She returned with her phone, her fingers moving over the screen until she found what she was looking for, then she turned the phone to me. On the screen was a picture of me sitting on the couch with Anders. There was a bucket of popcorn sitting on our laps. Half of the bucket was on his right leg and half of the bucket was on my left; that's how close we were sitting next to each other. I looked calm, relaxed, peaceful, in a way I never felt when I looked at myself in the mirror. Is that what people saw when they saw me with Anders?

"Yes. You do."

Yes. I do, my heart said.

Kat's voice softened. "And you should go tell him before you can't ever tell him."

I rolled my eyes at her and shook my head. "I'm not that girl. I can't ever tell him. Not now. Not ever. He's engaged, so that book is closed."

She harrumphed at me and flounced back to my closet as if I had offended her in the worst way. She picked up the clothes she'd dropped and then sighed. "We should still celebrate. This is all kind of a big deal."

I smiled, faking every centimeter that my lips stretched upwards. "Yes. We should definitely celebrate."

After Kat pretty much emptied my entire closet onto my bed in order to find the perfect outfit for my meeting on Monday, we went to dinner. Cicero's was the restaurant of choice because it was the nicest restaurant in my neighborhood. Besides, Italian was Kat's favorite food. She looked so incredibly depressed about Anders getting engaged, I knew I had to do something to lift her spirits. The nice thing about trying to make someone else happy was that usually made you happy, too. The evening turned out to be really good even with the prickling reminder that Anders was out of my reach. I tried to reason with myself, to make myself understand that he had never been within my reach, but his continued absence left a little hole in me that got bigger every day I didn't see him.

Kat's dad called her halfway through the meal. "You need to answer that," I said.

"No, I don't." She kept her eyes on the penne pasta drowning in marinara sauce.

"You absolutely do." It was the third ring. My phone went to voice mail on three, but having had experience with Kat's phone, I knew hers didn't go until the sixth ring.

"Why?" Fourth ring.

"Because you're still a minor, and he's your father — your legal guardian. And because neither of us want a policeman knocking at my door and arresting me for kidnapping you. So. Answer. The. Phone." I had to give her my stern look, though I didn't believe she ever truly took it seriously, because we'd made it to the pause between the fifth and sixth rings.

She answered, but glared at me. Just like she didn't take my stern look seriously, I didn't take her glare seriously.

Based on the hushed and angry hisses that came from her end of the conversation, and the loud noise that came from him through the phone, I gathered that the conversation didn't go very well. She explained to him that she was staying with me for a while. My stepfather and I didn't have the best relationship. It wasn't like I ever thought to

98

myself, "Man, I really wish I could go hang out with Edward for while . . . maybe catch a movie, go to a baseball game, or fishing, or whatever it is that dads do with daughters." But the relationship wasn't too awful either. I didn't do those things with my own father. Why would I expect to do them with Edward? What we did have was a mutual respect for one another. Edward was a pretty decent guy, all things considered.

Because of that mutual respect, Edward relented and said that Kat could stay with me for a few days. It didn't hurt her cause that she reminded him of the anniversary of her mother's death — the one he'd told her to get over. He must have had some time to rethink his words to his daughter. He didn't exactly agree to the entire week but neither did he disagree, which meant she would be staying for the entire time that she planned on and probably longer just out of spite. I was totally fine with that, especially in light of everything happening in my life. I would have someone to share my excitement with over the possible contract with an agent and maybe even a publisher, and I would have someone to mourn with over my situation with Anders. There was no downside to Kat spending time with me.

Except when there was.

The downside came while I was sleeping. At some point, Kat sneaked out of my apartment and stirred up a tempest.

No wonder stepsisters always got a bad rap in the fairy tales.

CHAPTER SIX

"Fairy tales teach us that family is not
always to be trusted. There's always
some stepmother ordering a huntsman to
rip your heart out, or a dad leaving you in
the woods with your brother — never
mind the fact that a gnarled little witch
with a house made out of diabetes and
stomachaches is out there."
— Charlotte Kingsley,
The Cinderella Fiction
(The "Love the Family You've Got" Chapter)

I awoke to the noise of excited chatter and
pans clanging around in my kitchen. I
would have thought it was the television
except I didn't have a television in my
kitchen. Did Kat invite friends over? When
one of the voices revealed itself to be
distinctly male, though muffled, I actually
felt irritated. Had Kat invited a boy over?
Because as much as I wanted to be the cool

big sister, I really wasn't okay with her inviting someone over without talking to me about it first. Because if she wasn't asking me if she could have friends over, she certainly wasn't asking Mom or Edward.

My sister would not end up as a teen pregnancy statistic on my watch.

Besides, she had the sort of stepmom who'd go all Mother Gothel on her and lock her up in a tower while shamelessly dropping Kat's prince out of the tower window into a thorn patch. I would've thought that would be enough deterrent.

I'd been a teenager before, which meant I knew that when a teenager had something to hide, there was probably a good reason to be hiding it. Sure, whatever was being cooked up in the kitchen smelled amazing, but that didn't mean responsibility could be thrown out the window along with Kat's would-be prince. I entered the kitchen prepared to be the stern grown-up.

But I was not prepared for what actually waited for me in my kitchen.

Anders.

I stared at him, a million questions on my tongue, but I was unable to ask any of them because as much as it had hurt to not see him since the day he'd told me he might be engaged, seeing him in my kitchen for the first time and knowing he was out of my reach hurt so much worse.

He looked up, and his face brightened into a smile so wide the dagger that had been living inside my ribs twisted just a smidge more. "Lettie!" He crossed the kitchen from where he'd been standing at the stove and gave me a hug.

In spite of how much I didn't want to, I breathed a sigh of relief at his touch. I hadn't realized how much I missed that physical contact from him.

"What are you doing here?" The words came out far more crisply than I had intended.

"Kat knocked on my door in the middle of the night and told me I missed a celebration. Lettie! How could you not tell me?"

"I . . ." How could anything be explained without making me sound pathetic or mean or both? How could I tell him that since he'd decided not to be a part of my life for the last few weeks, I'd childishly decided not to let him be a part of mine either? "I don't know," I finally said, because we couldn't just stand there staring at each other. "So what are you guys doing?" I pointed toward the oven and stove top, where things were both baking and sizzling.

"I missed the celebration dinner, so I

decided to make a celebration breakfast. It probably won't be as good as it would have been if you'd done the cooking, but we used your recipes, so there's hope. We've got lemon blueberry muffins, hash browns, fried eggs, and a fruit bowl."

When he mentioned the fruit bowl, he gestured toward my sister. Since I could not look at her without venom, I didn't look. I would deal with Kat later. Later when I'd decided how to deal with myself and all of my emotions tumbling around in a confused mess like an overloaded washing machine.

Happy, relieved, embarrassed, sad, and a smidge ticked off, too. How all of that could exist inside me all at once was a mystery. So I stood there in my kitchen in my Sleeping Beauty pajamas — in blue, not pink, since I was Team Merryweather — and bare feet and worked very hard to feel nothing at all.

"Breakfast smells good." My second lame attempt at conversation made me do an inward eye roll. And why wasn't Kat helping with the conversation? She could invite the guy over but she wouldn't help me talk to him? She and I were definitely going to have words when this was all over.

"It's going to be great!" Kat interjected from where she was chopping up fruit, if the sounds of the knife against the cutting board were any indication. Her first words of the morning, a motivational message on how I should feel, didn't actually make me feel any better and made me wish she'd go back to not talking.

I grunted some response that was probably less than friendly but also probably more of a response than Kat deserved at the moment.

It seemed I'd walked in at just the right time because breakfast was done and ready to be served. Kat already had the table set with three places, and Anders ushered me to one of the chairs. I sat. What else could be done?

Anders served up my plate. He put on all the things that he knew I loved, garnishing it in a way that I would have done if I had done it myself. He knew all of those little things about me. He knew what I liked and what I didn't like: two shots of Tabasco sauce over my potatoes, my syrup on the side in a dish because I like to dip my food, not drown my food.

How had he come to know so much about me when we were just neighbors?

Once everyone was settled, the questions came in a torrent. What did the agent say? Did she offer anything yet? Why is she wanting to meet you? Is that typical for an agency to fly you in for a first meeting before there's even a contract?

I wasn't able to answer all of the questions or even most of the questions. I had no idea if going to meet her was typical or not. I kind of thought all that stuff was done over internet and phone, but maybe I was wrong.

Somewhere halfway through the meal, I must have forgiven my sister. How could I be mad at her for giving me this moment with Anders that was so calm and peaceful and comfortable? Anders in my space might only last for this one moment longer, but I would enjoy the gift for what it was for as long as it belonged to me.

Having him within reach and out of reach all at the same time wasn't easy, but I couldn't complain.

Until I could complain. At the end of breakfast when it became apparent we were all finished eating, Kat jumped up and said, "I'll scrub everything up. You guys go for a walk. I know you have things to talk about." She gave me a meaningful look that I returned, I hoped, with slicing daggers.

And I'd forgiven her? Well, that forgiveness was now revoked. She had been returned to the evil-stepsister list.

Anders was also on his feet. "Yes," he said.

106

"We do have things to talk about." The look he gave me was meaningful as well. Immediately I went from hot anger to cold fear.

Had my sister already told him that I cared about him in a way that was not appropriate for a friend-neighbor? Had she gone over there and spilled my guts to him? Was he now furious with me for being so ridiculous with my own emotions?

Was he going to give me a lecture about how the thing I felt for him wasn't real, and he was taken, and he had somebody, and blah blah blah?

Why hadn't anybody warned me that siblings could be dangerous?

Of course, the fairy tales all warn about stepsiblings. Yep, Kat was definitely on the evil-stepsister list. She was going to have to slave like Snow White did for those seven messy dwarfs in order to get off that list.

I made a growl low in my throat and stood as well. If Anders had a lecture for me, I might as well get it over with. After years of living with my mother, I had become a rip off the Band-Aid kind of person — even if that Band-Aid had princess decor.

"You'll have to give me a moment to get ready," I told him. "Obviously, I can't go out in my pajamas." Which wasn't strictly true. I'd gone out in my pajamas lots of times, maybe not in that particular night-gown, since it was my most childish one, but definitely in others. Regardless, I'd be darned if I was going to be trapped in pajamas while Anders lectured me.

Changing into suitable clothing also meant brushing my teeth, jerking a comb through my hair, and pulling it up into a ponytail. There was no reason for me to look like a feral red fox.

I grabbed a coat to ward off the cold, and we exited the building. We turned in the direction of the Muddy River and the rose garden with the cherubs. Of course we would go that way. That was where Anders always went when he wanted to think, when he wanted to talk, when he had something he needed to work through.

He stayed silent for the first part of the walk. The silence killed me. My mind ran over and over all the things he might have to say to me about my feelings and how misplaced they were. Unable to take it any further, I broke the silence. "I'm really sorry about Kat. I had no idea she'd gone to your place. Believe me. If I'd known, I would've duct-taped her to a chair."

He seemed startled by that. "Why? I thought we were friends. Why wouldn't you want me to know the cool things happening in your life?"

That caught me off guard. Admonishment had been expected, but I hadn't expected him to admonish me over not telling him about the agent. "I knew you were busy."

"Busy? Too busy to be a good friend? You must not think much of me if you think that I'm too busy to care about what's going on in your life."

The conversation wasn't going anything like I had expected. "Well, with your engagement and everything, of course you'd have a lot going on. And of course I was going to tell you. But I wasn't going to waste a weekend evening when you probably would be with your fiancée. I would've told you on Monday after it's all gone down because, honestly, I don't even know what there is to tell right now. The agent seems excited. She wants to meet me. I don't really know much else. Monday's a better time to be telling anybody anything because then I'd have real information." I hated how defensive I sounded but kept going because I didn't want him to think we weren't friends. I would always be Anders's friend. "For all I know this is another dead-end situation. And wasting your time on a weekend when you would be with your fiancée, over something that might not be anything, seemed . . . absurd."

"I'm not engaged." He said it like a shrug, an afterthought, as if the words weren't the most powerful things ever uttered in human history.

I stopped dead on the sidewalk and stared at him. "What?"

"I'm not engaged."

The eyes that stared back at me were clouded with uncertainty. Was that uncertainty because he was sad about his engagement break-up?

"Why not? What happened? I have a shovel and a pretty decent knowledge of the surrounding woods. If she broke your heart, all you have to do is say the word."

He laughed. "No. It's nothing like that. I was technically never engaged. When she wanted to talk about it, I told her I needed some more time. In that time, I really paid attention to who she was and who we were when we were together."

"Who are you when you're together?"

"We're friends. Really good friends but only friends."

"I thought you loved her and that you were ready to take her home to meet your *farfar.*"

"I do love her. She's an amazing woman. She's just not the amazing woman for me.

We've been officially unofficial for about a week."

"Wow," I said. "That's rough." Part of me was deliriously happy to hear this news. But the other part of me worried about him. A breakup is hard regardless of how it goes down. "So, are you okay?"

"Yeah. I really am. Better than I've felt in a long time."

We'd made it to the garden. Anders held the gate open for me.

Once we'd stepped inside, I stopped and shoved lightly at his chest with the heel of my hand. "Hey! Wait a minute! You're out here lecturing me about not telling you about the important things happening in my life, and you waited a whole week to tell me news like this? Seriously?"

I moved to shove at him again, but he caught my hand and grinned like he found my irritation hilarious.

"I needed a breather for a bit, some time to think about what I really want."

"Oh? What you want? And what's that? A smack to the side of the head? Because that's kind of where we're going here."

"You can't be mad at me. You held back information, too."

The cherubs looked smug today. It figured they were on his side.

111

"At least I had a good reason. Your reason is lame. You don't need a breather from me. I'm your friend."

"I know. And it was friendship that got me thinking. It was friendship that made me decide to not be engaged."

"Circles, Anders." He usually talked in circles. It was how he communicated. Most guys were choppy, incomplete sentences. Anders was a run-on sentence. He'd once asked me to use the code word *circles* if he got out of control. I swiped at a rosebush, since he'd just catch my hand again if I swiped at him. But the plant swiped back as a thorn dragged over my open palm. I cringed but didn't cry out, because such an alert would sidetrack Anders, who turned to paramedic professionalism whenever blood was introduced to a situation. Even a tiny scratch would make him turn around so he could fetch antibacterial ointment and a bandage.

"Friendship is important to me. What I want is for the woman I marry to not just be any old friend. I want her to also be my best friend. Don't you think everyone should have that? To be married to their best friend?"

We sat on a bench facing the cherubs. I closed my fingers over my palm to press

112

away the sting of the rose thorn cut. The bench held the cold of the season, which seeped through my jeans. I did my best to ignore both the frigid bench and the stinging cut.

"Of course," I said. "If someone's going to actually go to the trouble of getting married, they should definitely marry the best person for them."

"Right. And I want that for myself."

"And she's not that?"

"No. Not really. You know I'd like to move on in my life. I feel like I'm ready for that stage of settling down and putting down roots. And I know that makes me weird in comparison to our generation — in comparison to you, specifically. But just because I want to be settled doesn't mean I want to be stupid about it. I don't want to do it wrong. I want to be married to somebody who is my best friend." He turned his whole body so he was facing me.

"You keep saying that, Anders. But we're back to circles. Who's your best friend?"

He paused at that, looking toward me and away from me and toward me again as if not sure how to proceed. I'd asked the question to help him get to the point, but the question rolled around in my own brain for a moment before it occurred to me what

113

I'd asked and what his sudden nervousness might mean. Was he saying . . . ?

"I don't know yet," he finally said, making me exhale a disappointed breath I hadn't realized I'd been holding. "But I think . . . I hope . . . what I'm trying to say is: I would like to go on a date with you."

Anders scrubbed a hand through his hair and rolled his eyes. "I have never asked anyone out in such a way that made me look so awkward and ridiculous before in my life."

"You want to go on a date?" The words came out slowly, every syllable attended to because I needed to be absolutely clear on what he was asking.

"You *are* my best friend, Lettie."

I *was* his best friend. And he was mine. His saying that he was ready to settle down should have terrified me. It should have. But it didn't. Anders had declared himself ready for marriage at the same time that he declared he deserved to be married to his best friend while at the same time declaring I was his best friend. Why didn't that terrify me? What kind of hypocrite did that make me? Since my fifteenth birthday, at the time members of the opposite sex had become interesting to me, I'd decided the whole trouble of them was more than I cared to deal with no matter how interesting they might be.

Yet, a man stood in front of me talking marriage and friendship and *me,* and the shiver down my spine didn't come from fear, it came from anticipation of something great. Did that make me a hypocrite? Or did it make me a romantic? Or did it make me hopeless? Maybe a hypocritical, hopeless romantic? But I didn't mind or care.

Because maybe I didn't just *write* fairy tales. Maybe I believed in them as well. I would argue how I felt about actual marriage later when Anders wasn't looking at me with that blue-eyed intensity and waiting for a response.

I gave him the most attractive smile a woman who'd been caught by surprise and had barely managed to run a toothbrush over her teeth could manage. "I think a date would be a fantastic idea."

His vulnerable expression fled, replaced by relief and a bit of satisfaction as well.

I grinned. "Were you afraid I was going to say no?"

He made a *psh* noise. "Of course not. A woman would be crazy to turn me down."

He was more right than he knew. He scooted forward and reached out for me — the friend who had reached out *to* me a million times but who had never reached *for* me. This wasn't a grab for the chip bowl or a playful tug on my braid as he made jokes about Scottish tempers and redheads in general.

His hand slowly moved my direction, a slight tremor in his fingers as he trailed the back of them down my jawline.

My breath hitched in my throat, and my eyes briefly fluttered closed at this foreign contact between us. What was he doing? What were *we* doing?

He was so close, his breath washed warm over my lips. He smiled. "Does Wednesday work for you?"

"Wednesday?" What were we talking about? Why were we still talking at all?

"Yeah. For our date. We can celebrate the contract you're getting with an agent when you meet her on Monday. And celebrate our friendship. All the new things."

"Our friendship isn't new." I would have rolled my eyes at myself for sounding so breathless, but breathing suddenly felt like one of those impossible quests, like when the rebel leader asks the young princess to beat the evil mage with nothing more than her wit and a short sword.

"But it's taking a new direction." He smiled wider and gently took my hand, bringing it between us to his mouth, where he pressed a kiss to my knuckles.

His lips were soft as he smiled against my fingers and then leaned in close to my ear. He whispered softly, "Charlotte Kingsley, I think this is going to be the beginning of something incredibly good for both of us." His lips brushed my earlobe briefly — so feather-light, I might have just wished it instead of feeling it. He pressed another kiss to the place just behind my ear.

Another shiver coursed down my spine.

He moved away then, getting up and keeping my hand in his so he could help me up.

I finally remembered to breathe. The beginning of something incredible, indeed. We hadn't shared our first kiss, but if that little bit acted as a teaser of things to come, I had a lot to look forward to.

Anders and me. Who would have guessed? Well, my sister, obviously. How did I get here? How did I get to this place where the agent of my dreams was paying for a plane ticket for me to go meet her in New York and my best friend was looking at me with such intensity in his eyes?

Dear Fairy Godmother, I thought, *I apologize and take back every mean thing I ever said about you. Clearly, I was wrong. I'm sorry I said you were lazy. I'm sorry I accused you*

117

of stealing, instead of actually replenishing, the ice cream in my freezer. I apologize for calling you an audacious flirt who probably was spending all of your time with my also-nonexistent tooth fairy. Clearly, you were watching out for me the whole time. I was wrong. I can admit that.

Fairy tales were coming true.

CHAPTER SEVEN

"Most of us imagine ourselves to be the Cinderella character as we stumble along waiting for a fairy with a wand (and probably an ulterior motive) to save us from the ugly stepsister holding us back in life, which is why it's hard to discover that we might just be the ugly stepsister."
— Charlotte Kingsley,
The Cinderella Fiction
(The "Honesty" Chapter)

Anders did not kiss me. Maybe it was because he was a don't-kiss-a-woman-before-the-first-date kind of guy. But I certainly hoped he wasn't a don't-kiss-a-woman-*on*-the-first-date kind of guy because, after some consideration, nothing sounded better.

Anders spent the rest of the day at my apartment. When he discovered I had a cut on my palm, he did exactly as I had predicted and went into paramedic mode, complete with triple antibiotic ointment, bandages, and the confidence of a true professional. After that, he became full-on nervous. His embarrassed half smiles and quasi-stammers when he asked me to hand him something or conversed about my upcoming meeting with the agent made him decidedly awkward. The awkward wasn't bad. It was actually kind of adorable.

Kat's behavior, on the other hand, was unbearable. She spent the day giving the smile of the smug.

That girl belonged out in the rose garden with the evil cherubs.

Even with Kat being smug and Anders being awkward, I could not have asked for a better support team to help me get ready for my meeting. Kat showed Anders the outfit options she had picked out for me.

"I don't know," he said. "You've made her look too runway model. This is a business meeting, not *Vogue.*" Anders then invaded the private space of my closet and picked out what he thought I should wear. It was a black pair of slacks and a blue button-up I'd actually forgotten I owned.

Kat, whose dark hair had been put up into a twist and held in place with chopsticks from my kitchen drawer and who wore my elephant-print chiffon jacket again and who looked every bit the part of a fashion designer, gave Anders, who wore jeans and an EMT shirt that declared him a saver of lives, a flat-eyed stare. "This," she began, "looks like a uniform worn by someone employed at a reform-school cafeteria."

He looked back at the clothes he held up. "No, it doesn't."

She rolled her eyes and tugged the hangers out of his hand. "Totally does." She discarded his choice to the pile of definitely-not-in-a-million-years that occupied the reading chair near my bed. They squabbled over clothing until they both agreed on an outfit that landed at that professional space between reform-school cafeteria employee and runway model.

I watched the entire process, recognizing that my opinion was entirely irrelevant. But if I couldn't trust my little sister and my best friend to pick an outfit for me to wear while chasing my dreams, then I was doing life wrong. Besides, anxiety chewed away at my nerves and short-circuited pretty much any shred of reliable decision making I possessed. My raw senses would likely misfire entirely and leave me dressed in a clown suit for the meeting if I were left on my own.

Together, the three of us spent the rest of

the evening doing Google searches on questions that were important to ask an agent making an offer.

I almost went to my online writing groups for guidance but felt . . . apprehensive. What if my telling other writers about this new situation jinxed the whole thing?

But even without those peer relationships, which might have helped me know what to do, Anders, Kat, and I spent our time at Google and YouTube University and learned everything I needed. Well, at least enough that I felt I had the information necessary to make a good showing at my meeting with Jennifer Apsley. We figured out what questions to ask and what answers to be on the lookout for. All of the online articles insisted that I treat the meeting as if I was employing her and not the other way around. *Knowing* that and *doing* that were probably going to be two totally different things. Because, in my heart, I knew the agent was the cool one, the one everyone wanted at their party.

Anders had to work that Sunday, so when it came time to say goodbye Saturday night, he hugged me extra tight, holding me longer than he'd ever done before. His cheek was warm against mine as he whispered, "You're going to be great, Lettie. Remember, you're the one doing the interview. You're the one with the product they want. Be smart, be confident, and remember how amazing you are."

As Anders pulled back from the embrace, he let his mouth trail across my cheek and dropped a gentle kiss there before pulling away entirely.

With that kiss still burning against my cheekbone, it became my turn to stammer out a farewell parting. I think I might have told him to have a good time at work. Which was entirely blasphemous being that he was a paramedic.

"A good time at work?" I said out loud after I shut my door and turned to face my sister. "Why do I say things like that? What would that even mean? Not having anyone bleed on him?"

Kat shrugged, not looking up from her phone. "I guess a good time at work to him would probably mean no one ever calling them out for an emergency. It might mean that he gets to play video games all day. That's a good time at work for most people."

Her point saved me from embarrassing myself further by texting an apology for saying the embarrassing thing in the first place.

A text from Anders came almost directly after my decision to not text him. "I expect notification as soon as you are done with the agent and as soon as you are back in this apartment building," he texted. "We can celebrate and first date at the same time. Knock 'em dead, lady. You're going to be amazing."

I must have sighed and grinned stupidly because Kat returned my stupid smile with her smug smile and said, "Did you really try to tell me last night that you aren't in love with that guy?"

"Shut up." I threw a throw pillow at her and felt no guilt because, by their very name, that's what those pillows were made for. "You shouldn't have gone over to his apartment in the middle of the night," I added after a few moments.

She threw the pillow back at me and hit me square in the face, knocking my head slightly to the right. "Shut up," she said, mimicking me. Her satisfaction with herself did not end with that night but continued into the whole of the next day. Everything she talked about was in regard to Anders and I being a couple. She talked about needing a chaperone for her senior trip. And wouldn't it be fun if Anders and I would be willing to do that with her? Kat basically had my wedding dress, my colors, and all of my bridesmaids picked out. And, of course, she would be the maid of honor. She said if I got chummy enough with my agent, perhaps she could be a bridesmaid as well. I laughed; that idea was ludicrous. It was even more fanciful than anything I could have ever concocted. Maybe the wrong sister was writing books.

I awoke Monday morning an hour and twenty-three minutes before my alarm was set to go off. Of course, my body needed sleep. But no matter what I did, my mind would not stop racing with all the possibilities and probabilities and actualities the day had in store for me. My overnight needs were already packed in a small carry-on. My e-tickets were downloaded and ready on my phone. My clothes were hung up in the bathroom waiting for me to get ready for the day. All I needed now was more sleep. If I showed up at this meeting having missed nearly an hour and a half of sleep, there would probably be bags under my eyes. Or worse. What if I fell asleep during the meeting? What if I missed some important information that would help me seal the deal because I was too tired to pay attention?

These worries only added to the stress of my already racing heart. They did nothing to help me go back to sleep. So, recognizing a losing battle, I pulled my exhausted-but-not-at-all-sleepy body out of bed to get in the shower and ready myself for the day. Anxiety proved to not be a very helpful companion there either.

After my shampoo ran down into my eyes and I nicked my knee while shaving, it occurred to me that anxious, exhausted people should never be allowed in the shower. Where was the warning label for that sort of thing? My owner's manual for my car came with a warning label regarding operating the vehicle while drowsy. Why didn't my shampoo and razor offer me the same courtesy?

After rinsing out my eyes, drying off, and bandaging my knee, I dressed carefully in the black slacks and gray tunic with flouncy sleeves and an asymmetrical hemline, making sure that all the zippers were zipped and all the buttons were buttoned. I didn't have lots of experience with wardrobe malfunctions — such things were hard to achieve when wearing only jeans and T-shirts — but I certainly didn't want today to be the first. The outfit was graceful in a way that made me grateful for my sister and her fashion sense.

My hair was in a loose-enough-to-be-whimsical-and-tight-enough-to-behave bun at the nape of my neck and pinned with way more pins than probably necessary to make sure not one strand moved out of place during my meeting. A final glance in the mirror startled me.

I didn't look like me. Not really. It wasn't just the clothes. It wasn't just the hair. Or even just the makeup. It was all of it together. Considering the lack of success I'd enjoyed in the past, maybe looking like someone who wasn't me would prove to be the lucky charm I needed.

With the usual traffic, a drive from Boston to New York City would have taken just over four hours. If you included the time needed to get through airport security and taxi down the runway for takeoff and landing, it almost took that long to fly. It would have been better for me to drive. At least then, my nerves wouldn't have had idle time to send me into full panic mode, which is where I was when I found myself exiting the security area and looking at a woman waiting for me, holding a sign with my name scrawled on it.

I stepped up to her and tried not to act ridiculously excited or ridiculously panicked. "I'm Charlotte Kingsley. Are you Ms. Apsley?"

The petite, blonde woman smiled at me. "You can call me Jen. After all, we're hardly strangers, right? We've been exchanging emails for quite a while now." She lowered her sign and held out her hand. She had a strong handshake, not the limp-wristed quasi-squeeze of the insecure or disinterested and not the vice grip of the overeager or overbearing.

I laughed, wishing she hadn't mentioned the email exchange that had been taking place for several years. The reminder of my many submissions and subsequent rejections did nothing to quell my nerves.

She indicated for me to fall into step beside her as she said, "I have so many things planned for today, but let's get the work out of the way first so we can enjoy everything else comfortably."

Knowing how much more comfortable I really would be once the details of the book were settled made me nod my agreement. I wanted the meeting done and over with so the anxiety of questions could finally be put to rest.

Only the fear of sounding like an amateur kept me from asking her if bringing me to New York for this meeting was normal.

Once we were in the backseat of an honest-to-goodness limousine and moving through New York City traffic, Jen turned to me and smiled. "It is so good to finally meet you, Charlotte," she said.

I almost told her that she could call me Lettie in the same way she'd told me that I could call her Jen, but I waited too long to say the words, and the moment passed where such a thing would be anything but awkward.

Instead, I said, "It's nice to finally meet you, too —" I closed my mouth with a click of my teeth and swallowed down the other words I'd wanted to add to that statement. Like *I didn't think this would ever happen,* or *took you long enough to finally see my talent,* or *will you pinch me to make sure this is real?* I smiled. She smiled. And the driver drove.

When it must have become apparent that I had entered the silence that was self-preservation mode, Jen swished back her blonde hair and smiled wider. "I love your tenacity. Most people give up long before they get to this place." She patted the luxurious seat we occupied. "It's like the prisoner you wrote about in your book, the one chipping his spoon at the walls of his escape tunnel. You are the writer who keeps chipping away at the work that needs doing so you can get to where you want to go. It's a very admirable trait."

Something like joy tightened in my chest. She had quoted me, well not quoted exactly, more like paraphrased — okay, not paraphrased either, but Jennifer Apsley, top-of-my-list agent, just referenced my book. The story was of a prisoner who stole a spoon from the cafeteria and used it to tunnel his way to freedom, going deeper and deeper until he was certain the entire thing was going to come down on him and he'd die buried under tons of rock and debris. Full of fear, he gave up. He hung his head and slumped back to the tunnel entrance, where he covered it back up so no one would ever know he tried to escape. He never discovered that if he'd just chipped away another inch, his rusty, bent little spoon would have thumped against the door to freedom. It was from the "Fear Sucks" chapter.

She had referenced my work. I wanted to grin stupidly, maybe squeal, and possibly stand up through the sunroof of the limo like people in movies did, and cry out that today was the Best. Day. Ever.

Instead, I said, "Thank you. That's nice of you to say."

The life of Manhattan swished by in the form of tall buildings, busy streets, and traffic. The horns and sirens coming and going and passing by felt familiar.

Jen followed my line of sight out the window and asked, "Do you come to the city very often?"

She said this as if the words "the city" could only mean Manhattan. As if my living in Boston could be paralleled to living in the quaint outskirts of some little town or hamlet somewhere. Not that she'd offended me. To those who truly loved a place, that place became the center of everything. I felt the same way about Boston. My dad felt the same way about San Diego. Anders felt the same way about Sweden.

"I come here every once in a while," I answered, making it sound like visiting Manhattan was an experience that happened far more often than it actually did. The reality was that I only showed up in Manhattan when Kat begged me to take her to whatever new trendy play happened to be premiering. Kat loved all things pop culture and contemporary.

"Well, hopefully I'll be able to show you a few things you haven't seen while you're in town."

I nodded some more and refrained from saying aloud that the only thing she could show me that I hadn't seen before was a book contract.

Jen smiled encouragingly when the limo

pulled over to the curb. She waved toward the building outside our window and said, "We're here!"

The driver handed us out of the car and then winked one of those very pretty blue eyes at me as he handed me back my carry-on that he'd fetched from the trunk. The wink seemed to say he could tell a limo ride was not a usual day-to-day activity for me. If I hadn't already decided that Anders was a person of interest, and if Anders hadn't already asked me out on a date, I might have worked in a way to get the driver's name and phone number.

Instead, I winked back. Why not? I had just been in a limo with an agent I had only dreamed about actually seeing in person. Weren't these the moments that required the cocky reaction?

Well, maybe they weren't.

But the confident reaction . . . Surely, the confident reaction was appropriate. I had to be confident. I couldn't let them see my desperation. Nothing smelled worse than desperation.

I squared my shoulders and lifted my chin, not enough to be cocky — because cocky really wasn't good for the current situation — but enough to be confident. Jen Apsley invited me here; that had to mean she saw worth in me and my writing. Agencies didn't spend money flying people around and picking them up in limousines just for fun. I turned my focus away from the driver to face my future. The city felt dense with cold. The smell of whatever was wafting up from the subway grates embedded in the smudged sidewalk crowded together with the noise of traffic in a way that made me feel claustrophobic. *Don't do it,* I thought. *Do not throw up, Charlotte Kingsley, not now, not when you're in the last stretch of this crazy race.*

Jen greeted the doorman, who stood waiting for us to approach. They obviously knew one another and were on friendly terms. While they exchanged casual banter, I reminded myself to square my shoulders again.

And then did so a third time because I couldn't seem to remember that I was going for confident.

Then we were in the building. A shock of recycled cold air — in direct denial of the chill outside — made me shiver. What kind of mutant ran the air conditioner with the sky clouded over and the day's temperature not peeking up over fifty degrees?

Jen's high heels and the carry-on that I wheeled along behind me clicked through the marble lobby to the elevators. Once we were in the elevator, Jen looked at my carry-on in a way that said she'd only just remembered I still had it. "I'm sorry," she said. "I should have given you a moment to drop off your bag and relax at your hotel, but the way schedules worked today . . ."

Then we were going up. We exited the elevator, walked down a short hall, and through some glass doors into the reception office of — my jaw dropped open — no! No way! I'd assumed I was meeting with Jen. Just Jen. Just Jen at Bennion Literary Agency.

But Jen wasn't taking me to her agency's office. We were standing in the offices of Mirror Press — if the black Helvetica sign above the reception desk was any indicator. Jen had not escorted me to her agency to talk over the places she would send my book for submission. She had brought me to a boutique publisher well-known for its best-selling nonfiction.

Maybe Bennion Literary Agency shared office space with Mirror Press?

Jen announced us to the receptionist, who then invited us to have a seat while we waited. Announcing us to a receptionist meant it wasn't a case of shared office space. This was happening. We were meeting with Mirror Press. Which prompted me to remind myself to not throw up all over again. I had to keep my hands stiff on my legs to refrain from yanking out my phone and texting a digital squeal to Anders and Kat.

The receptionist spoke into his earpiece. I heard him say Jen's name and then say mine as if my name was worth noting. I wasn't just Jen's tagalong. Before we even had a chance to sit, a heavy wooden door swung open and a dark-haired woman swept out with her arms open in greeting.

"Jen! It's so good to see you." They shook hands.

Jen stepped to the side. "Melissa, I'd like to introduce you to Charlotte Kingsley. Charlotte, this is Melissa Norwood, head editor of Mirror Press.

Melissa shook my hand. Her hand was cool, her grip confident. I wasn't sure my fingers remembered to grip back. Everything seemed to be happening so fast. An agent *and* an editor? All in one day?

I owed my fairy godmother big time for what she'd managed to pull off for me in spite of all the grumbling I did about her. But maybe my dreams were getting ahead of themselves. Just because an agent and an editor stood in the same room I occupied

135

didn't mean anything. Better not count my glass slippers just yet. No offers had been made. No promises given. It almost felt like the beginning of a joke: an author, an agent, and an editor are in the same room together . . .

"It's nice to meet you, Melissa." My voice didn't crack, squeak, or quaver. I could do this.

Melissa led us through the heavy wooden door, down another hall, and into a boardroom. Bookshelves full of books lined the walls on one side, and windows looking out over the city lined the other. Several titles on the shelves were books I'd read and loved. Mirror Press might not have been one of the big New York players of publishing, but they knew what they were doing and had a level of respectability that made them hard to ignore. Melissa motioned for me to take a seat in one of the plush chairs tucked into the polished wood table.

"Can we get you anything?" she asked. "Water? Coffee? Soda? Are you hungry?"

Just the mention of possible food or beverage made my stomach churn. "No, thank you. I'm fine." I said this while sitting in a chair that was every bit as plush and comfortable as it looked. I would've actually written at a desk rather than at my couch if a chair this comfortable had existed in my apartment.

Jen took the chair next to mine, a physical reminder that she was with me — on my side. Melissa took the chair across from us.

"Well then, let's get down to books."

It was certainly a different take on the phrase *let's get down to business* that was said at Frankly Eyewear at least a dozen times a day. It made me smile. These were my people.

Melissa had a file open in front of her, with several sheets of paper fanned out over it. "At an expo, Jen and I happened to be seated at the same table for dinner, and she told me she had read the most amazing book by a new, up-and-coming author."

Up-and-coming. Jen called me up-and-coming.

Melissa paused, clearly knowing the power of those words. "She told me all about this book and how it could be life changing for a lot of people if it was marketed properly and given the exposure it deserved. Obviously, she had me intrigued, so I asked her to send it." At this point, Melissa sighed and closed her eyes as if reliving the joy of the finest food she'd ever tasted. "What a read! I called Jen back and said I had to have it!"

Was someone sucking the oxygen out of the room? Why couldn't I get air in my lungs?

"When we discussed potential marketing for the book, we came to a small snag." Melissa squinted her eyes and tilted her head, with her mouth twisted in that way a person does when offering a strange sort of sympathy.

Someone definitely sucked all the oxygen out of the room. What did a snag mean?

"You have an idea that's fantastic, and you've executed it perfectly. But what do you know about image and brand?" Melissa asked.

"Image?" I had to repeat her word, had to clarify. Lack of oxygen made it hard to think.

Melissa smiled, the indulgent sort of smile that one might give a small, adorable child when handing them a sucker. "Yes. Image. A certain sort of personality needs to accompany a work like this. Our marketing department scoured your online activity and aren't sure you're up to the task."

"What makes you think I'm not up to the task?"

She took a deep breath, but it was just for show. She was clearly prepared to say whatever she felt needed to be said to me.

"You wrote a book that exudes confidence and authority. I applaud your very real talent. You did a spectacular job."

"Thank you?" I hated myself for the question in my voice.

"The problem is that your social media tells the story of an insecure woman who requires validation."

Her comment made me hate the question in my voice even more. "I'm a writer. The only writer I know of who can tell you that they don't require validation is the one who's lying to you."

Melissa laughed. Laughed but didn't back down. "And the other concern is that the woman in my presence right now is not the same woman presented online. Your hair isn't in a halfhearted ponytail but a bun that was carefully planned to look messy with your red curls but that was likely scolded quite severely with sprays and gels into behaving. You're not wearing comfortable sweats or other loungewear but an outfit that is both tasteful and powerful. I am prepared to offer you a very nice deal — a deal that also comes with a catch."

"Catch?" Was this where they revealed that Melissa was a faker-name and she was really Rumpelstiltskin's sister, the sister that expected me to hand over my firstborn unless I could guess her real name? I shot a look at Jen in an effort to remind myself that she was on my side.

"Your book is titled *The Cinderella Fiction,* but you're living the life of a swamp witch. That can't continue if you want to see this book published."

"Excuse me?" Did she call me a swamp witch? To my face?

Jen must have gauged my reaction because she jumped into the conversation. "That's not an insult."

I gave her a glare that demanded she explain how she'd figured that.

"It's a reference to one of your chapters, where you specifically mention that people don't have to live in palaces, but neither does that mean they should be living in the mud under trees."

"And you think the real life — emphasis on *real* here — I've been posting online is akin to the lifestyle of the swamped and cursed?"

Melissa laughed again, as if we were all merely telling jokes as friends and I wasn't on the receiving end of her insults. "Please understand I'm coming from a marketing perspective. You can have a book that is fantastic but released with a small print run that ends up mostly remaindered and sold in bulk bins in dollar stores but have the gratification of knowing your name is on the cover; or you can have your words read widely and be available in every bookstore and library from here to the West Coast."

"And you think my Instagram pictures are so plagued that my book wouldn't be read from here to the West Coast?" She was just offending me now.

"I do. If we're going to publish this book, we're going to need it to have a different face."

CHAPTER EIGHT

"The ambiguity of 'once upon a time'
really just means the storyteller is
completely unreliable. If they can't
pinpoint a date to be fact-checked, then
the event probably never happened."
— Charlotte Kingsley,
The Cinderella Fiction
(The "Honesty" Chapter)

"Seriously?" Were they filming me on some crazy reality show? "What? Like hire someone to pretend they wrote my book so they can be the face?"

"No. Of course not. You will still be the author of your book, but . . . It's a book that empowers people to be their best selves."

"Right." We could at least agree on that.

"But people don't want the sort of life advice you're offering from someone who displays pictures of clothing finds with thrift store tags on them. And they certainly aren't going to pay the cover price for that kind of life advice. Cinderella didn't get her dress from a thrift store."

I frowned. "So what are you saying here?"

"We're asking you to be your best self."

If a frown could go deeper than the Mariana Trench, mine did at that moment. I'd kind of thought I was always, or usually anyway, my best self. "And that means?"

"We have a publicity firm that we work with frequently. The self-help business often requires a little help itself, and a good publicity firm offers that for our authors. If we choose to purchase this manuscript, we need *you* to be willing to put the kind of effort into it that *we're* willing to put into it."

She slid a sheet of paper across the table to me. "I am not here to insult you," Melissa said, even though subtle insults still counted as insults. "That's the reason Jen and I have discussed extensively all the ways in which you will be compensated. Because I am prepared to make an incredible preemptive offer on the purchase of your book, Jen has allowed us to have this meeting."

I looked at the paper and counted the commas. Commas. As in more than one. I had never seen two commas placed in a string of numbers on anything that had to do with money that would come to me. Those kinds of numbers existed in math problems and in hypotheticals for other things but never as a possibility for an upcoming bank deposit. This was the deal. This was the moment I'd dreamed about since Mrs. Brown's creative writing unit in seventh grade.

"Of course," Melissa said, "this is for North American rights only. Jen has plans for selling foreign rights. She's a shrewd agent. She's negotiated a good contract. She's told me about your fortitude and tenacity in continuing to submit and improve your writing. She wouldn't settle for anything less than the best for you."

Tenacity. Both Jen and Melissa had used that word when describing me. And I hated how much I liked hearing it. The work to get to this point had been hard. The struggle had been very real. But now, here I was. What did being here mean? The moment had been imagined a million times, but it had been imagined differently. I had never anticipated being made to feel validated and invalidated at the same time when offered a publishing contract. I looked down at the numbers and commas that were being offered to me as an advance for the words that I had written.

Those numbers meant I could quit my job at Frankly Eyewear and focus solely on my writing. Those numbers meant I could take a trip to Europe and take Kat with me. If things with Anders worked out, maybe I'd take him too. I shook my head, clearing my thoughts. A million questions swam through my head, fighting for attention, demanding to be recognized, and making it impossible for me to actually ask any of them.

Melissa fell silent, clearly placing the ball in my court and waiting to see what I would do with it.

Jen uncapped a silver pen and laid it out over the papers. "This is the door. You've been tunneling yourself out of your own creative prison for a long time now. But this is the door to everything you've wanted. All you have to do is open it."

She would have to use my own metaphor against me.

By signing the paper, I would establish myself as a legitimate writer.

How much could a social media makeover hurt? Unless . . . "Who's paying the publicist?" I asked.

Melissa smiled. "I love that you're looking at all the angles. You'll be footing the bill for the publicist. They will be working for you, but don't worry. Although the public relations firm we're referring you to isn't cheap, they are excellent in a way that almost guarantees you'll earn out your advance before Christmas."

"Almost?"

"The only thing that is an absolute guarantee is that nothing is a guarantee." Her eyes dropped to the still unsigned papers.

Mine did as well, providing me a view of the numbers and commas.

I picked up the pen and signed.

There were congratulations, smiles, and celebrations to be had all around.

I felt . . . well, I knew I was happy. After all, this was the moment so long waited for, dreamed about, wept over, worked toward. But knowing you're happy and feeling happy are apparently not the same thing. It's just that it all came about in a way that left me doubting myself. I'd never envisioned this moment being tainted by the knowledge that my book was sellable as is, but that *I* wasn't. And I'd never envisioned my first contract to be for a nonfiction book.

My moment of triumph was supposed to come from a work of my heart — not a work born of frustration.

But there was still celebration to be had, so I joined because it was a beginning. It was *my* beginning. Melissa and Jen discussed timelines, because Melissa planned on having advanced reader copies of the book available by several book expos scheduled for the beginning of summer. They cast several glances at me and waited for me to nod in agreement to the dates before they continued on.

I honestly could not recall one of the dates mentioned. Was it for a photo shoot? I couldn't remember. By the time we shook hands to say goodbye, I wondered if notes should have been taken. Was there a secretary who would send me the minutes of the meeting? Would someone think to give me a CliffsNotes version of all that had transpired?

Instead of taking me to the hotel to drop off my suitcase or to have a few minutes to text Anders and Kat, Jen took me straight to the public relations firm.

Outside the building that stretched farther into the sky than any of Jack's beanstalks, I gripped the handle of my bought-secondhand rolling luggage and stared at the fading-into-the-distance limo and wished I was still on it.

I didn't mind when my sister did movie-makeover moments with me. I could wash those off, brush them out, step away from

147

the frivolous. Melissa and Jen acted as if they'd anticipated me embracing whatever new look this agency handed me. I glanced at the business card. HNT Media Group. Somewhere inside the fortress of a building was this media group, and they would tell me all the things that were wrong with me. And I had signed papers declaring I would agree with them.

Jen looked back, only just realizing that I hadn't followed along behind her. "Ready?"

"Let's do this." I smiled, worrying that this smile would be the first of many lies I would have to tell about myself. *Be positive!* A social media makeover didn't mean lying about *me* any more than makeup meant lying. A little lipstick and mascara enhanced what was already there.

That settled it.

I fell into step alongside my agent and went to get the eyebrows of my social media plucked.

I don't know what I expected from a PR firm. Maybe some castle-like façade with a waterfall cascading from somewhere out of view. All things considered, HNT Media Group was minimalistic enough to make anyone not already in the know wonder what the company did. The vinyl sans serif font displaying the company name could have marked the doors of any place, from a janitor supply company to a secret branch of the government.

Jen glanced at me as she reached for the handle. "Hey! Don't look so nervous. They already have your file, and they're expecting us. They'll be guiding this whole meeting. Besides, I'll be here with you through all of it, so there's nothing to worry about."

Her declaration of solidarity offered little in the way of comfort. What did it mean that they already had a file on me? What could possibly exist in such a file? Maybe a PR agency really was like a secret branch of the government.

Before I could ask Jen more questions, we were already in the reception area, where a man and woman who looked to be my age sat behind a granite counter. Before Jen could do much more than smile a greeting, the woman pointed down the hall to the right and said, "She's already waiting on you, Jen."

"First name basis with the PR mafia?" I whispered as we made our way unescorted down the hall.

She laughed. "Mafia?"

"They have a file on me."

"They'd better, or they won't be worth the money you'll be spending on them. And we're on a first-name basis because they help several of my clients. They're the best at what they do."

Jen knocked but entered the room before being invited, since we'd already been told they were waiting for us.

Inside the big-enough-to-be-impressive and empty-enough-to-drive-home-the-minimalistic-theme room, a woman with sleek black hair sat behind a desk. Her eyes didn't so much as flicker up to acknowledge our entrance. Her thickly mascara-ed eyes stayed trained on the blonde, curly-haired woman sitting in front of the desk. The blonde tapped her foot impatiently.

"I'm not going to apologize," the blonde said, in a tone that left little doubt of her sincerity. If she owed someone an apology, they were never going to receive it. Her accent seemed southern; though, from the little she'd said, I couldn't pinpoint what state she might have been from.

"Lillian . . ." The dark-haired woman said, her tone reasonable and calm.

"Don't you *Lillian* me. It isn't my job to care if a small group of people turn a joke into a political opinion."

"But it is *my* job to care," the woman said. "We've told you that getting political on social media could be damaging to your career."

Lillian's foot stopped tapping as she sat up and scooted to the edge of her seat. "I didn't get political. Besides, the royalty checks that keep coming and keep getting bigger say you're wrong."

"Can you talk some sense into her, Jen?" the dark-haired woman asked my agent.

Lillian turned in her seat and moved to her feet when she saw Jen. "I'm so glad you're here." She crossed the room to give Jen a hug. It was hard not to notice the contrast in our appearances. This woman was fair-skinned to my pale, freckled face; blonde hair to my red; and slightly heavier than my fairly average-sized frame.

Our outfits were similarly styled — basic slacks paired with a tunic that flowed whimsically around the waist and hips, but their effect was decidedly different. Her top was a bold red, not the neutral gray I wore. She'd paired her black dress pants with red heels so glossy they could have been used for mirrors. Based on the ruby shine of the woman's footwear, the Wicked Witch of the West might have mistaken this woman for the person who'd dropped a house on her sister and then stolen the family shoes. I wore dull black flats.

151

She was truly a beautiful woman. Classy, while also being vibrant. Where I worked hard to blend into my environment and go unnoticed as often as possible, she clearly didn't mind standing out.

Jen smirked at Lillian. "Are you giving Toni grief again?"

"Other. Way. Around." Lillian tossed back a glare to the dark-haired woman, whom I could only assume was Toni.

Toni cleared her throat and stood. "Protecting the L. M. Christie brand is not the same thing as giving you grief."

My head snapped back to the blonde they'd called Lillian.

Only a miracle kept me from gasping aloud.

L. M. Christie!

I'd read all her books, and not just read them but actually owned them. All of them. Her complete works sat in a lovely line tying up almost three full shelves in my living room. She'd written thirty-plus novels and an instructional book on writing. Her mystery series was one that both my sister and I loved. And her fantasy series was unparalleled.

Now here she was in the same room with me. Would she think it inappropriate if I fished my phone out of my purse and snapped a selfie with her?

I didn't do that, of course. The calm, cool, and collected points all went to me.

"What did you do?" Jen's casual tone and slight smirk said she didn't think whatever Lillian had done could have been too bad.

I followed L. M. Christie religiously on social media. I hadn't seen anything.

"She didn't think my vegan joke was funny." Lillian shrugged.

"The one from this morning?" I burst into the conversation without meaning to. "I loved that! I laughed out loud on the plane!" I stopped there, leaving off the fact that I'd even put three hearts in the comment section. L. M. Christie received thousands of comments on every post. Mine was a drop in an ocean.

"See?" Lillian crossed her arms over her chest and gave Toni a look of sheer triumph before she uncrossed her arms and turned back to me. "It was hilarious, wasn't it? I was eating breakfast this morning and it just came to me, and my husband and I both laughed ourselves sick over it, and —"

"And it offended people," Toni interrupted.

"People have got to stop taking themselves so seriously or there won't be anything left to this world except offended people. It was a joke, Toni. And it wasn't directed at humans. It was directed at plants. I doubt, I really do, that kale is going to file a lawsuit against me."

"Some people who eat a plant-based diet felt like you were making fun of their life-style."

I interrupted again. "The guy next to me on the plane was vegan, and he peeked at my screen because I'd been laughing. He thought it was hilarious, too. He took a picture of the post with his camera and sent it to his friends."

"There." Lillian waved at me. "You see? You can pat that mountain back down into a molehill because my friend here has proven my point." She waved in my direction and then frowned. "I'm sorry. What was your name?"

I put out my hand. "I'm Lettie. Lettie Kingsley. I just signed on with Jen this morning." I knew that Jen represented L. M. Christie because on the acknowledgments page of every book she wrote, there was a special paragraph to her agent. That had been one of the reasons I'd persevered in submitting my manuscripts to Jennifer Apsley.

Lillian took my hand in hers, showing off her red-polished, glossy nails, and then pulled me into a hug. "Welcome to the family!"

L. M. Christie was hugging me and calling me family. Now would definitely be the time for me to snap a selfie, but I felt the cold shadow of Toni's disapproval from over Lillian's shoulder. I stepped back and cleared my throat. After all, I was the interloper in the situation.

"I think that's everything," Lillian said to Toni. "We'll finish up through email, since I have an appointment I need to get to."

"What appointment?" Toni asked.

"The one I plan on making as soon as I leave your office," Lillian said.

I barked out a laugh that had to be swallowed back down at a single sharp look from Toni.

"We are going to be such friends, Lettie," Lillian said to me. "You call me if you ever need anything. You can ask pretty much anything."

Ask anything?

It was a credit to me that I didn't ask whether or not Maggie Wood, heroine of the *Silent Dust* series, would ever find the source of the mountain's magic to defeat the evil heir apparent. Lillian was probably under contract and unable to share that information anyway. Besides, she was gone before anyone else could get another word out of their mouths.

"That woman is far too flippant for her own good." Toni did not sit back in her chair but, instead, picked up a file, crossed the floor, and circled me in a way entirely unlike a vulture might circle its next meal.

Unlike because the look she gave me upon inspection was one of *meh.* A vulture would have at least looked interested.

Toni shrugged. "You clean up well enough. Your online presence didn't give me much hope, but you're well-dressed and tidy enough today. It at least gives me a better baseline to work from."

Ouch.

I kept to myself the fact that I was only well-dressed because other people had dressed me. No reason to throw wood on the fire she planned on using to burn me at the stake.

"So is her contract signed?" Toni asked, talking around me instead of to me by asking Jen.

Jen nodded.

"Yes, I signed my contract," I interjected, making it clear that I could answer my own questions.

"Good. As soon as Jen gets you the first check and it clears your bank, you need to

156

go shopping." She pulled a list from the binder in her hand and held it out to me.

I looked down at the list and realized something more than the Mariana Trench would be needed if I intended to frown as deeply as I wanted.

"What kind of crazy person made up this list?" The list was double-columned and two pages long. It included a camera, a whole column of equipment needed to accessorize the camera, curtains, a coffee table, books to go with the coffee table, a couch to go with the coffee table, and clothes. Next to each item were suggested brand names and website URLs to stores no self-respecting person on a budget would ever shop at unless there was a clearance sale.

Toni smiled the kind of smile that said she thought I was legitimately funny. "I made the list."

I shook my head. Not that I didn't believe she was a crazy person, but that what she was suggesting went way beyond mascara and a different shade of lipstick. "But I already have all this."

Toni also shook her head, starting the motion before I'd finished speaking. "You have the hazmat version of these items. The secondhand, scratch-and-dent version."

"Ouch." This time I said it out loud. "Be-

157

ing thrifty does not make my life a hazmat crisis."

She gave me a look that might have seemed like patient understanding to the average onlooker but had all the marks of an eye roll. I had a hyper-controlling mother and a teenage sister. I knew an inward eye roll when I saw one. "You're right," she said. "There's fashionable thrifting, and then there's the thrifting one does out of abject poverty."

"I'm not impoverished," I said.

"I know. You do well for yourself. But your social media looks like the life of one who is impoverished."

"But the things I own are already on my social media. It's not like I'd be fooling any of my followers."

"We will be scrubbing your social media and starting over."

"Starting over? I have more than a thousand followers on Instagram. It took me four years to build that."

"I can get you that in a day. It's important that we bury your previous social media so that it can rest in peace in an unmarked grave and we can move on to something better."

"But I follow people, too."

She ignored that comment as she pushed

forward with what she envisioned as my future me. "Yes, we'll have to start fresh with your social media. We need to capitalize on your nickname."

My head spun at her rapid-fire list of things to do. "But my social media already uses my nickname, and if the name is already in use . . ."

She gave me a look that made her appear to have just walked into a room full of teenage boys who hadn't showered in over a month. "Yes. I know. *Lettie.* That's not the nickname I mean. Lettie is the name of a ten-year-old who does what her mother asks without needing to be asked twice. It's the name of the girl who never skipped piano practice and always did her homework the moment she got home from school. It's boring. It leaves no lasting impressions. So that isn't the nickname I meant."

I tried — and failed — to not flinch at the insults she flung. I glanced at Jen for some kind of intervention, but Jen was looking at her phone — likely to avoid having to look at me. "I don't have any other nickname."

"That's why we're here. To give you a fresh start. Your name has so much potential, I don't know why you cling to a childish nickname."

I clung to it because it was what my father

called me when he came into my room at night to listen to me tell him the stories I made up. Princess Lettie, or sometimes even Queen Lettie when my stories were extra special. It was the name of the creator — the girl who told stories.

"Charlotte . . . Charlotte . . ." She clicked her pen, flipped it over, and clicked it again in the same way she seemed to be mentally flipping my name. Her eyes widened and she straightened in her chair. "Char."

She said it like she'd come up with something unique. Lots of people who didn't know me personally shortened my name to Char. It felt abrupt and lazy all at the same time. It was the name used by someone who hadn't taken the time to get to know me. "You want me to be associated with images of seared meat?" I asked.

"Not seared. But sizzling. It's perfect. It's what's happening now."

"I just don't think —"

"I know this seems harsh and you likely think I'm being a bully, but I am your advocate in every way. Jen got you a contract because you're a good writer and you deserve a contract."

Without intending to, I straightened under that praise.

"But no one will know you deserve that

160

contract if you can't appear to them as someone they should admire. If you want to keep your old couch and coffee table, that's fine, but for your social media pictures, we have to start fresh. Your pictures need to look like someone who is flawed and willing to show those flaws."

"I don't understand." I needed to sit down but didn't want to draw more attention to myself by actually moving. "Isn't everything you just said about me a flaw?"

"Charlotte, living within a budget is not a flaw. I'm not criticizing your life. But we need flaws that make you a leader — someone who can take others to the places they want to go, not just by the words you wrote but by the walk you walk. People don't want to aspire to live in a world where they require a budget. They don't want to aspire to a reality they already live in. Your flaws need to be carefully manicured so that they aren't pitiable but adorable instead."

That made sense in a twisted, uncomfortable sort of way — uncomfortable enough I had to interject. "The book is about accepting yourself as you are. It's about being the authentic you. Shouldn't I be my authentic self?"

"Mm-hmm. Yes. It is, and you should. But people tend to need heroes they can look up to, heroes who can show them a better way. You can still be authentically you. But outfits like this need to be restructured." She produced a picture from my Instagram out of her binder. In the picture, I was wearing my six-impossible-things-before-breakfast shirt.

"But that's my lucky rabbit's shirt." My voice cracked with the heightened protest. The picture on the T-shirt was of the White Rabbit holding a pocket watch. He was framed in the words the Queen had said when Alice told her it was impossible to believe impossible things.

"I wear it when I feel like I'm coming close to the end of a book."

"And that detail is adorable, likeable, follow-able. So instead of wearing this faded, worn-out shirt that you've likely had since you were twelve, you can wear this." She retrieved a box from her desk and handed it to me.

"What is *this*?" I asked.

"It's a gift to welcome you to the HNT family and to wish you a well-earned congratulations for snagging an amazing book deal. And I read the book. You have so much to be proud of. I want to help you shine. I want people to see you for the genius you are."

162

I pulled the ribbon from the box, lifted the lid, and stared at the shirt inside. There was the same *Through the Looking Glass* quote and almost the same image, but this was *not* the same shirt. It was a Cora original with Swarovski crystals sewn into the picture of the pocket watch, each crystal marking an hour on the watch face. I would have been too pedestrian to know the brand except Kat wanted to own a Cora original.

Toni had done something unexpected. She'd given me a gift I loved and a compliment my heart couldn't ignore.

"You see?" she said. "You're still your authentic self. I'm not here to change you. I'm here to help other people see the diamond that you really are."

I gave a single nod of assent. "Okay. I'm ready. What do we need to do?"

She set me up with new accounts on social media and got me an appointment for my hair and makeup and then a photographer for when I was back home. Like a fairy godmother, Toni wielded her pen and laptop as if they were magic wands. She showed me how to transform myself from the household servant to the woman in the ball gown.

The first consultation with Toni had been painful, and the idea of an exhausting routine that required me to keep up with the world made me regret in the tiniest bit signing the contract, but I reminded myself that I had a fashion-designer sister and a photographer best friend. The level of engagement wouldn't be too hard to maintain once it got going. And Toni knew her business. I trusted that she could do what she said.

Jen, who had said she would stay with me for the whole ordeal, had remained quiet for most of it, so it almost startled me when we exited the office and she spoke up. "Lillian asked if we'd like to join her for an early dinner."

I glanced at the clock. Had we really been in that office so long that it was now dinnertime and, wait —

"What?"

"Lillian, the woman in Toni's office when we arrived, wanted to get some dinner with us. If you're too tired, I can tell her it's not a good time." Jen positioned her phone to cancel the coolest dinner date I would ever be invited to in my entire life.

"No!" I wanted to reach for her phone and throw it to the curb to keep her from declining. "I'd love to!"

Jen tilted her head and gave me a look that said she wanted to make sure; when I nodded, she did as well, settling the matter.

We met Lillian at a nondescript cafe that served anything but nondescript food. It was there that I sat at a table with my hero author. Lillian asked all about me, about how I'd come to know I wanted to be a writer, about how I'd gotten so lucky to be catching my big break so young, and how I was lucky to have Jennifer Apsley as an agent and Melissa as an editor.

"You haven't mentioned how lucky I am to have Toni as my publicist." I'd waited until Jen excused herself to use the restroom before approaching the topic of the PR firm.

Lillian hooted at that. "Ah, yes. Publicists. They are a necessary evil."

I thought about the list burning a hole in my future bank account total. "Are they?"

"We aren't supposed to talk over the details of contracts, but it's obvious your deal came with a publicist clause or you wouldn't have been in Toni's office."

I nodded that she'd hit the mark.

She sighed. "Writing is such a difficult thing. To finally get the validation that we all crave so much it's basically oxygen to us is exciting. We want people to know that we did what we said we were going to do. We want our friends to know. We want our family to know. We want all of those people who told us that our dreams were silly, ridiculous, and a waste of time to know that they were wrong. Don't regret this day, Lettie. Toni and her group will make sure that everyone knows. And if I know Toni, she'll probably rub their noses in it while making you look humble and sweet in the process."

I groaned. "I love the idea of people loving my books, but I'm not so sure how I feel about standing in the spotlight with those books."

"Ah, you're the recluse writer, huh? Well, you'd better get used to the spotlight because that is where they need you to be."

"I do trust her to do what she says."

"Good. You should. She's the best." She leaned forward. "A little change is good, Lettie. But don't let her change everything about you. Be stubborn enough to push back every now and again. When it really matters to you, don't give in. It's the thing that's kept me sane."

The advice was good. I tucked it away to use in case Toni crossed a line I didn't want crossed. I thanked Lillian and then really looked at her. "I'm confused. Why does your brand need a publicist? Not to sound like the stalker fan-girl that I unabashedly am, but you're already famous."

Lillian laughed. "Oh, honey, you really don't spend enough time on the internet if you have to ask questions like that. The comment section of any article or review will tell you that people think their opinion matters more than anything else on the planet, and any minor indiscretion ever committed in your life will be ripped open and put out there for everyone to judge and stamp an opinion on. I got death threats when I killed off Carmichael. Death threats! Because of a *fictional* character. So when my real life gets sticky, I need a publicist to save me from the public."

Lillian made sense. Before we parted ways, she asked if we could get a photo together. She had Jen snap one with her phone as well as with mine. We did a selfie with all three of us. Back in my hotel, I immediately forwarded the photos to Kat with a million exclamation points and a GIF of Cinderella going from her peasant garb to her gown. "I met L. M. Christie! And it's official! I have an agent, and I can't wait to tell you everything when I come home tomorrow!"

I sent a similar message to Anders, who was working a graveyard shift at the station. We texted back and forth until I couldn't keep my eyes open.

My phone dinged with his last message. I pried my eyes open long enough to read, "Go to sleep, Cinderella. You deserve this dance at the ball more than anyone I know, which means you deserve to finally rest."

I smiled even while doing as his text directed and drifting off to sleep.

CHAPTER NINE

"No one recognized Cinderella at the ball.
If she'd passed a mirror while walking into
that ballroom, would she have recognized
herself? Look past the gown and glass
slippers. Look past the peasant clothes.
See the person."
— Charlotte Kingsley,
The Cinderella Fiction
(The "Know Yourself" Chapter)

Kat was downstairs and out the front door
of my building to greet me, which meant
she'd been waiting by the window to see
when the driver of the hired car dropped
me off. She slammed into me in a huge bear
hug, nearly knocking me off the curb and
back into the street. She tugged the handle
of my carry-on out of my hand to help me
up the stairs outside my building. Her help
wasn't exactly help, as she used the trolley
handle to lift the bag up rather than the

carry handle, but I had a check coming to me soon enough that meant if the handle broke, I could afford to buy a new suitcase.

"Your building manager is an idiot, by the way."

"Shannon? Yep. She really is. But what did she do to prove it this time?"

"She spoke Spanish to me and then became incredibly offended when I told her I don't speak Spanish."

"Why would she think you speak Spanish?" I asked.

When Kat turned to shoot me a look of incredulity, I realized I was much more preoccupied with all my news than I'd thought. "Right. Sorry."

Similar scenarios had happened to Kat before. People assumed that with her dark hair and dark skin, she must be from Mexico. They didn't often guess her true heritage.

"I should've responded to her in Arabic. Seriously, the next person who assumes I speak Spanish simply because my skin is darker than theirs, I'm going to respond in Arabic and see what they do. What do you think your idiot building manager would do?"

"Shannon's a wild card. Her response to anything is anyone's guess, but if she messes with you again, tell me."

"And you'll what? Make her attend a sensitivity training meeting or something? Anyway, forget her and tell me everything!" she insisted. "I want to know what other people wore and if we picked the right outfit for the meeting. Where did you eat? What did they say? How soon will they have the book sold? Do you think they'll make it into a movie?" She stopped and made a breathy sigh. "A movie. I could be related to someone famous soon!"

Kat the dreamer. She would never know how close to right she was. The movie deal would probably not happen — not with a nonfiction, self-help book. But the famous part?

Well, I didn't know about that either. But if Toni had anything to do about it . . .

Kat started walking again, forcing me to walk as well so she didn't run me over with my own suitcase. I took a deep breath of my own just before we moved into the entry of my building.

I could now afford to move to a nicer apartment building — a building without a Shannon. But then I'd be forced to live in a building without an Anders, which would mean it wouldn't be nicer at all.

"Have you texted Anders?" Kat demanded

to know even before I could get through my doorway.

She turned and gave me a narrow-eyed stare that she'd most certainly picked up from my mother. "You haven't." She let my suitcase fall to the side with a thunk against my coffee table — the one I'd be replacing. "Why do you insist on sabotaging yourself?"

"I wanted to wait until I was home."

My sister stared at me until I pulled out my phone. I sent the text announcing my arrival home and then showed her the screen. "See? Sent."

"It's disturbing that a high schooler has to help you manage your love life when you're the adult here. Especially when your idiot building manager asked all sorts of questions about you and Anders once she found out I was your sister. Well . . . I mean . . . she argued the fact that there was no way that I could possibly be your sister because you look like an Irish temper tantrum — her words, not mine — and I look —"

"Did that cow say something else to you that was racist? I swear I'm going to have her thrown off a balcony."

Kat laughed. "Whoa! That was way darker than making her attend sensitivity trainings. I can take care of myself, you know. Did you not catch where she said something rac-

172

ist about you? She called you an Irish temper tantrum in spite of the fact that you're Scottish. Anyway, she didn't actually say anything else to me because Anders was entering the building at that moment and that creepy crush she has on him wouldn't allow her to look bad in front of him. All I'm saying is that you need to keep that monster away from Anders."

On cue, Anders replied to my text by bursting through my front door, taking a picture of me with Kat, crossing the room, handing the camera off to Kat, and wrapping me up in his arms so he could lift me off the ground and whirl me around. It was a movie moment, the kind that never happens in real life.

Except that it did.

It happened in my real life.

"Tell me everything!" he insisted as he put me down.

Get your head out of the clouds. This was what my mom always said to me when I was little. She still said it pretty much every time we talked on the phone if I mentioned my writing and career plans as a *book* writer and not a copywriter.

Get your head out of the clouds. But my head wasn't in the clouds. It was so much higher than that. I had the agent of my dreams, a publishing contract that opened up all my possibilities, and a man I cared for looking at me like *we* had possibilities. My head had passed the clouds entirely and gone straight to the stars.

Both my sister and Anders stared at me expectantly, so I pulled back from Anders's embrace and sat on the couch. Kat sat in the armchair across from me, and Anders seated himself next to me.

I told them everything.

They were an amazing audience — full of excitement and genuine happiness for my happiness. Kat begged to know every single detail about my meeting with Lillian and begged me to take her the next time I had the chance to see Lillian. Two sets of eyes widened into super-moon proportions when they heard about my advance. "You can take me to Europe!" Kat squealed aloud the very thought I'd already entertained. "You can take Anders, too!" My sister really did know me.

When I got to the part about the publicist, Kat confused them with the publisher. Anders didn't.

"Wait. What's this list?"

I pulled the folded list from my purse and handed it to him.

"I don't think I understand." He frowned

174

at the list, looking at it with the same expression I likely had when looking at it for the first time. "What's wrong with your curtains?"

I sighed at my curtains. I loved them. I'd snagged them on an eBay auction for seven dollars. That included shipping. Sure, they were used and had a small hole that I'd sewn up, but I loved the midnight blue panels with the glittering stars on them. They were as close to fairy-tale decor as an adult woman could get without having to explain herself too much to her dates. "I guess they're too dark. They want my living space to look bright and minimalistic in a trendy sort of way."

"Are they going to be parading prospective book buyers through your apartment?" Anders asked.

"This is for my social media. It's part of the marketing. The bad news is they expect me to help with the marketing. The good news is that I have you guys!"

He flipped to the second page. "What do you need all the camera equipment for?"

"Like I said: the good news is that I have you guys. Want to be my photographer for a while? At least until I get the hang of this?"

He looked at me over the top of my lists. "What, and support you in your lifelong dream of being a published author? Who do you think I am?"

I tugged the list from his hands. "My best friend."

He gave a dramatic sigh. "I guess, when you put it that way." He lunged at me, crumpling the list between us. "Congratulations, Lettie. I'm so proud of you!"

Kat joined us by turning our embrace into a dogpile. I only got her to get up by mentioning the Cora-original Alice in Wonderland shirt. She nearly wept with joy when I promised she could borrow it whenever she wanted.

Anders left my apartment to get ready for the night shift, but he already had our first date for the following night planned.

The next day, he picked me up around 7:30 for what he called a "late dinner," late meaning dinner after eight. Not that I had rules on when dinner ought to be, or *where,* but when we arrived at Independence Wharf, I raised a protest. "There's food here?"

"What?" He pulled the door open. "You don't trust me?"

"Of course I trust you." I laughed and entered through the door he held for me. "I just didn't know there was food here." I didn't ever have a reason to be in this part of town, so the few occasions when I'd passed the red-brick and glass building that from a certain angle looked like a red capital L with a glass box sitting on it, I'd pretty much ignored it. It was a financial building and didn't really hold much interest for me.

As I passed through the doors, I saw the sign that said there was an observation deck. Things were starting to make sense. A nice view. Anders loved a good view of the world. When he handed his ID over to the guard at the reception area, his plan solidified for me. We were going to the observation deck.

The guard escorted us to the elevator and hit the floor button for us as we got in. The guard moved out of the way, tossed a wink to Anders, and told us to enjoy ourselves. The elevator doors squeaked closed as I leaned against the silver bar and gave Anders a smirk. "The sign downstairs says that the observation deck closes at five. It is now 8:12. My math isn't awesome, but even I know that 8:12 comes after five. So how did you get him to let us in?"

"I helped do an emergency delivery for his baby."

"You've delivered a baby?" How did I not know that about him?

"I've delivered three babies. This one was even named after me."

"Well, there is a thought I've never had before." I swiveled to stare at the numbers dictating our ascent to the fourteenth floor. "There's another person running around with your name."

Anders gave me his half grin — the one I'd always thought of as endearing. How had the steam of that single facial expression never provoked a full-on fire in my belly before?

"There are actually hundreds, probably thousands, of people running around with my name."

I had to center my thoughts on his words, not his mouth. "Didn't you say you've only delivered three babies?"

"I'm talking about Sweden. In Sweden, my name is as common as the name John is here."

"So can I start calling you John, since we're not in Sweden?"

"Sure. You can call me John if I can call you Charlotte the harlot."

I rolled my eyes and made a *psh* noise. "How long have you been holding in that extra lame and entirely unoriginal joke?"

"Pretty much since the day I met you. But I'm a nice guy so I never used it until you decided to mess with my heritage." He smirked. I laughed. *This comfortable banter is why I love him,* I thought.

And then I blinked.

That word again. Love. I could not seem to stop using it when thinking about Anders.

The elevator suddenly felt like too small a space for the both of us. But for the first time in my life, claustrophobia wasn't an issue. I pushed off the side of the elevator to put myself directly in front of Anders. "I'm sorry," I said, finally coming to terms with the fact that I couldn't pay attention to what he was saying when so much was new between us.

"For what?"

"For not seeing you before the way I see you right now."

He leaned in and turned his face down so close I could feel the warmth of his skin and the energy flying between us. "You are most certainly forgiven," he whispered.

My eyes fluttered closed of their own accord in anticipation of the kiss that had to follow such a moment, but a bell dinged, and the elevator doors squeaked open. I had expected the doors to open out to the observation deck, but they opened to a hallway, which, thankfully, was empty.

Anders stepped over the gap to keep the elevator door from closing on us, which meant I had to stop thinking about kissing the man and move forward. He held open the door that led to the observation deck. The initial chill of wind made me glad he'd told me to dress warm. My mouth fell open when I saw what waited for me. "Oh my," I said. "How did you do all of this?"

All of this consisted of a table complete with a white, perfectly pressed tablecloth and china and crystal place settings. Cloth napkins were folded into the shape of a swan and placed on top of each plate. A silver chafing dish had a silver dome over it to hold in the warmth of the food. And a few of those fake flickering candles stood on a glass pedestal surrounded by rose petals in the middle of the table.

The two chairs had been pulled out from the table and set to the side as if the table had arms to welcome us into its embrace.

The whole thing was crazy romantic.

Romantic.

It had never occurred to me to think of Anders as romantic. Funny, friendly, fantastic, all of those. But not romantic. Until now.

"Wow," I said again, only this time the word was whispered in reverence.

Anders must have felt pleased to hear the approval in my voice because his shoulders squared and his chest puffed out. He put his hand to the small of my back and led

180

me to one of the chairs.

"This is a lot."

"A lot meaning overkill?"

"Overkill would be if you made these napkins out of real swans. But seriously, how did you pull all this off?" I took my seat.

"Baby delivery, remember?"

"That must have been one cute baby."

"Obviously. No one would want to give an ugly baby such an awesome name." He slid onto the chair across from me and barely scooted it forward so he could still tuck his long legs properly under the table.

Even without Anders lifting the lid from the chafing dish, I knew what hid underneath it. He knew me so well. "I wasn't aware The Thai Guy delivered all the way out here. Did you deliver a baby for Pravat, too?" Both Anders and I did enough business with The Thai Guy to be on a first-name basis with Pravat, the owner. We'd spent as much time in his restaurant as we did in our own kitchens. Or at least we had until Pravat implemented the delivery service. Now, not only did I not go to Pravat's restaurant, but I could barely be convinced to leave my apartment. Bob's Grocery and The Thai Guy were enabling my agoraphobia.

"No, not a baby. But I did treat a nasty cut on his head."

"Oh yeah? How did he get that?"

Anders's grin widened. "That was the reason he had me do the stitch work instead of going to a hospital like he should have. He didn't want to talk about it, and he didn't want anyone asking questions."

I frowned. "And you agreed to this plan that sounds incredibly shifty?"

Anders busted up laughing. "What he was involved in was not so much shifty as it was him doing something stupid, and I think it involved him not wearing a helmet while taking his new motorcycle out for a spin even though his wife told him he could never drive the motorcycle without the helmet."

Anders pinned me with a knowing look that was easy to interpret. I'd been present the day Pravat's wife told him that he was, under no circumstances, to purchase the motorcycle in the first place. So the fact that he'd bought it and then chosen not to wear the helmet she'd asked him to wear . . .

Anders nodded at my new understanding. "Right? Nothing hurts more than admitting to someone that they're right and you're wrong. If there was a hospital bill, he would have to explain to his wife why he wasn't the smart man she thought she'd married."

I lifted the dome from over the food. "So can we base what kind of stitch work you do on how good the food tastes?"

"If that's how this all actually works, then I can guarantee you will never have a better meal than you will tonight because I do the kind of stitch work that's so good little old ladies come to me for seamstress advice."

I started dishing up a plate for Anders. "Sweet!" I said in response to his declaration of sewing skills. "You can help me make my Halloween costume then." The words brought a sigh of relief to my lips. Anders would probably be around for Halloween. He wouldn't be engaged or worse, already married. He'd be available to be my . . .

I wasn't sure exactly what of mine he would be, but whatever it was, he would be mine in some capacity or another. We would watch scary movies, perhaps go to his work costume party — which, based on the time I'd gone with him before, was where the best costumes could be found.

He accepted the plate I prepared for him with a thanks and a grin. While I'd prepped his food, he'd prepped mine. I grinned back as I thanked him for my plate. Pad Thai for him, yellow coconut curry for me.

"We're like one of those old married

couples," he said with a laugh at the way we knew each other well enough to prepare plates with the right amounts of rice and sauces.

It wasn't that he was wrong. He drew an accurate picture of us. But the way he called us a married couple made me hesitate, my fork hovering over my food.

I gave myself a shake. His statement didn't qualify as a proposal, meaning I had nothing to freak out over. I focused on enjoying his company knowing that no one would interfere with that for at least long enough for me to figure out how I felt about us on this new level.

We ate, talked, laughed, and watched the planes descend over the Boston harbor. No topic was too small or too large. His blatant and unashamed theft of my streaming accounts, how wild rice was harvested, politics, the state of the world, and our goals and dreams: all subjects served to entertain us. We discussed at length Anders's work as well as an award he'd received for a photo of a child with a blanket watching intently as a paramedic gave the child a shot. The scene was tender, and the little boy had the biggest eyes I'd ever seen on a kid.

And Anders, with his artist's soul, had caught the image. He gave a face to a job

184

not many people ever thought about.

We talked about my writing, my agent, my publisher, how much it meant to me to have met one of my hero authors. And with every word, I hated that we were kept separated by the table. The lower timber of his voice buzzed in my head. My focus moved more and more from the words he said to the mouth he used to say them. The planes slid by silently, cutting the darkened sky with intermittent flashes of light. The moon crept up among the stars.

The setting was just so perfect. And the table stayed solidly between us.

As I was formulating a plan for getting Anders up and away from the table, it occurred to me that my dilemma had been handled before. In so many of those movies, one part of the couple asked the other to dance. It got them both up, removed the obstacle of the table, and allowed them to get closer. Anders interrupted my thoughts. "Just don't ever write any of those lame books, okay?"

His comment made my wandering thoughts hit the brakes. "What do you mean by lame books?" Anders had read my last few books. Had he not meant it when he'd said he liked them?

"You know the kind: the kind that keep

185

me always buying print instead of digital just in case they need to be chucked across the room and into the wall."

"You buy paperbacks so you can chuck books against the wall?" I made sure my expression carried the appropriate amount of horror.

"Well sure. I can't do that with my tablet or my phone. You're the one who throws phones at walls, not me." He leaned on his elbows over the remnants of his meal. Then he grinned.

I rolled my eyes and got up. "I cannot listen to such blasphemy for another second."

Anders, actually looking slammed at my abrupt change in the conversation as well as by my declaration of leaving, also stood. "It's blasphemy to mention you throwing your phone?"

"No. It's blasphemy that you throw books."

"You're not really mad at that . . . are you?" His eyes were wide, his expression worried.

For all the months of teasing and pranking, his fear that I might actually storm off really amused and baffled me. He knew me well enough to dish up my food for me but was insecure about what he could joke about? We really were in a new place for us. Not that I gave up the teasing immediately.

"You actually throw books? Perfectly benign, and even innocent, books at walls? I don't know if we can be friends now that I know such horrible things about you. I speak softly to them, whispering words of love as I tuck them back into their shelves at night. Throwing them at walls makes you a monster."

I'd moved closer to him with every word, pulled by the promise of something that created a fire in my belly. A good chance existed that sharing any kind of physical contact with Anders would ruin the friendship — the near perfect synchrony we had when we were together. But I could no longer deny the shiver in me when he was close. To not move toward him would be betraying every nerve in my body.

How we were close yet not touching — not connected in any way — baffled me. The energy between us crackled and sparked like it was being pulled too tight, stretched to its limits.

Even without him reaching for me, the warmth of him flooded my senses.

"You think I'm a book-throwing monster, huh?" He finally caught that I'd been teasing before, that the only emotion between us was that of a need to be closer.

"After the statements you just made, I'll need some evidence to the contrary if you want me to believe otherwise."

He leaned in and whispered, "What kind of evidence?"

My eyes fluttered closed at the feel of his breath against my cheek. And I knew what kind of evidence was needed. I turned my face toward his, where our eyes locked, and the energy between us turned to the sort that stars are made from.

This was it — the point of no return where Anders would go from neighbor and friend to something more. Did I want to cross that point? Did I want to change what we were? What if it ruined everything?

His lip quirked up to the side on the right, as if he saw the conflict in my eyes. He made no move to close the distance between us. He simply stood there.

I leaned in closer. His eyes dropped to my lips, but he didn't move so much as a flinch in my direction.

It seemed Anders was all tease and no kissing. Or, more likely . . . he was leaving this decision to me. He wanted me to be sure about this, about him.

He knew my dating track record. It wasn't like I was a novice at the first kiss. One could even go so far as to call me an expert. But I also never went beyond that by very much because relationships expected things from me that I never felt prepared to give. Anders waiting for me to make this move was also Anders asking me a question. He wanted to know if this was what I really wanted. We both knew this relationship was different for me. It wasn't a movie or dinner with a casual acquaintance or an almost stranger. This was a step forward with something more. Anders was asking if I wanted the more.

I tipped my head back, pushed up on my tiptoes, closed my eyes, and closed the distance.

Warmth — no, *fire,* flooded me.

He cradled my face with one hand, and the other went to the back of my head, where his fingers threaded through my hair. My fingers curled into his shirt, pulling him closer. Heat and heart tangled together into something tangible. For a moment, I felt more real than I'd ever felt before.

People talk about puzzle pieces and being completed by someone else. I had never imagined something like that for me. Those fairy tales belonged to . . . well, the fairy tales.

Or at least to other people. They'd never

even belonged to people I knew.

And yet, here I was, feeling *completed.*

Anders pulled away slightly and rested his head on my forehead. "I can't believe we're here," he said.

"Me either," I agreed.

He stared at me with the same wonder I felt. Neither of us had expected our friendship to bring us to this place. And the fact that kissing Anders elicited a visceral reaction in me meant something even more.

He kissed me again. With the urgency gone, his lips moved slowly over mine and then strayed over to my cheek, along my jaw and back to my lips in a trail of kisses that were light as breath and intense as lightning.

We stood a long time in each other's embrace with the moon rising on this new chapter in our lives. Contentment wrapped around me. Whatever the future held, it promised to be fantastic.

CHAPTER TEN

"Getting the last word in during an
argument isn't everything you hope it's
going to be. Take a page from Cinderella
and try getting the nice word in instead.
It'll likely go further in your aim to irritate
the opposition in your argument and will
leave you with nothing to regret."
— Charlotte Kingsley,
The Cinderella Fiction
(The "Be a Good Person" Chapter)

The couple of days that I'd been to work
since coming home from New York, Nicole
had made my life sheer misery, even going
so far as to say that the company wasted
perfectly good money paying my wages.
Thursday morning, when my alarm went
off, I wondered why I continued putting up
with her perpetual abuse.

I called the office to let them know I
wouldn't be coming in. Ever again. When I

hung up from the rather tense conversation with Nicole Hall, where she informed me how I was leaving all my coworkers in a lurch and being unprofessional by not giving two weeks' notice and by being unwilling to train my replacement, and where I informed her that I just didn't want to waste the company's money on my wages any longer, I let out a gleeful laugh that probably sounded like a cackle as I dropped the phone to my bed in mic-drop fashion.

"What are you doing?" Kat had come into my room quietly enough to take me off guard and make me jump like I'd been caught doing something illegal.

"I . . . was just calling in sick to work." She'd interrupted me just before I'd gone into what would definitely have been a victory dance of embarrassing proportions.

"It sounded to me like you were quitting." She smelled of apple-scented shampoo from her shower.

"Yes, well, I'm calling in sick permanently."

She stared from me to the phone on my bed and back to me again. "Lettie, how long will it be before you get the first check for your book? What if it takes months? You can't just quit your job. You'll have to move back in with Dad and your mom if you jump the gun on something like this. Trust me. You don't want that."

"Have some faith, Kat-astrophe. I'm a responsible adult with enough savings to float me for a while."

"Really?"

"Sure. Have you met my boss? I've been socking it away, knowing that, at some point, the crazy woman would push me over the edge. Why do you think I live what my mom calls paycheck-to-paycheck?"

She flopped down on my bed. Water droplets from her hair speckled my arms and hands as she went. She propped her head up on her hands. "You better be sure. The life of a homeless woman is only marginally better than a life with your mom."

I swatted her with a pillow. "I'm not going to be homeless."

The pillow connecting with her head flicked more water in my direction and pretty much everywhere else as well. The pillow didn't bother her.

"So explain to me your book. I don't think I get it. You say it's not a fairy-tale story, but the title sounds like one."

"It's really more of a self-esteem book."

She scrunched her nose and curled her lip. "Ugh. Seriously? Lettie, why? Isn't there enough of that in the world? I'm so tired of uninformed people telling me how to feel about myself. I can't be the only one to be sick of it."

She rolled over to her back and stared at my ceiling.

"Who are the uninformed people telling you how to feel about yourself?" I asked.

"Oh, you know. People at school and stuff."

I had the feeling that it was more of the "stuff" than school. She was tired of her dad and my mom telling her how to feel. She had to go home in a day or two. Her dad had already called and said she'd outlived her welcome at my house, even though I had assured him the exact opposite was true. He wanted her to come home. She wanted to stay forever. He'd later called me privately to plead for my assistance in talking to her. And I'd agreed.

I sighed.

It was time to make good on that promise. "School huh? What? With the no-bullying campaign, or is it some other program they've established to make them feel better about the jobs they're doing?"

"You know I'm in the Hope Squad. Mocking anti-bullying campaigns is a hit to me."

I settled next to her and stared up at my

ceiling with her. "So you're one of those people telling other people how to feel?"

She gently knocked her head into mine. "Hopeful is a good thing to feel."

"Right. So who's telling you to feel otherwise?"

"No one."

"Not the school?"

I felt her head give a shake next to mine.

"Certainly not me, since you haven't read any of my riveting thoughts on self-esteem."

She blew out a breath that managed to sound exhausted, furious, and resigned all at the same time. "My dad thinks I'm wasting my time on fashion design. They say it's not practical."

Though she'd started out saying it was her dad, she'd ended it with *they*.

That meant my mom was involved.

"What did she say?" I asked.

"She said that matching outfits is an accomplishment worthy of mastering when you're six years old. She said no one takes a grown woman seriously if all she can do is pair a jacket to a handbag, and it's certainly not a career choice with any weight to it. I don't even know what that means. What is weight, and why am I supposed to care who takes me seriously?"

I briefly closed my eyes. What a disappointment both Kat and I must have been to my mom. Her natural-born daughter chose a literary arts career instead of being a scientist or the first woman to walk on the moon or something equally as history-book-worthy. And then when she had a second chance to raise up a girl to be a realist and a historically relevant woman, she ended up with a fashion designer.

I opened my eyes again and blinked away the image of my mother standing in my bedroom doorway and scolding me for reading "silly books" instead of the serious ones she bought me. Her short hair, which was meant to look businesslike and be easy to care for but in reality took a good forty-five minutes to be forced into looking like she'd spent no time on it, would stay rigid even while she was shaking her head at me.

"Kat, design is what you love. It's what you're brilliant at. You would be miserable doing anything else. So, although I don't doubt they have your best interests at heart, and they just want you to be secure financially as an adult, what they don't understand is that you can be secure financially and do what you love at the same time. Just because they both have jobs that pay well doesn't mean they know everything about the job market. I do what I love and what

I'm good at, and I am financially secure — secure enough that you caught me quitting just now. If I can do it, you can do it."

"Right? Dad really hates his job, you know? If he could do what you just did, he totally would."

I nodded. He was an accountant. He made good money working on corporate taxes, but he sighed on his way out the door and scowled for at least an hour when coming in again.

"They'll probably give me a big lecture about it when I go home. A lecture that will never end until I move out for good."

"And they might. But you and I know those lectures don't matter. You are free to choose your own path in life. This isn't the fourteenth century; your parents can't sell you off to apprentice for a boot maker. You're going to be good whether they lecture you or not."

"I could live with you."

And there it was. Edward had worried about this very question coming up and had asked me to say no. The reality was that I wanted to say yes. Kat had such a hard time with my mom. Her life would be easier, better, with me. But the fear that I was wrong, that I'd make things worse for her, tied me in knots. Maybe my mom's methods weren't

197

so terrible. After all, she'd raised me, and I liked me. And she'd had a hand in raising Kat, and I liked Kat.

Would I screw everything up?

I didn't know, and the not knowing paralyzed me. "Try going back home with your dad for a while. Just see how it goes. If things are still bad in a couple of months, then yes, you can absolutely come and live with me."

"A couple of months?" The whine in her voice hit puppy-dog proportions. "Lettie, they might have murdered me by then."

I smiled at her dramatics and turned my head on the pillow so I could see her directly. "I'll make you a deal; if they start investing in cutlery or firearms, pack your bags, and take the next train into town. But really, I think everything's going to be fine. You are a talented young woman with a brilliant career ahead of you. My mom and your dad are not enough to quash the brilliance that is inside of you."

She turned her head so she was looking directly at me as well. "Do you really think so?"

"I absolutely, one hundred percent know so." I tugged lightly on a strand of cold, wet hair.

She grinned, half of her mouth disappearing into the folds of the pillow. "You know, Lettie, I think you just might be great at writing a self-esteem book."

Warmth flooded me. "I hope so," I said. *Because here I go,* I finished in my head.

Kat helped me buy the clothing indicated on my list, though we both cringed at the price tags, and she kept saying, "Are you sure you can afford this?"

I wasn't sure, but *geronimo!*

Anders had told me not to buy any of the camera equipment or the camera because he'd let me use his. What he meant by *use* his was that he would take the pictures, because he didn't like people touching his camera.

I'd almost forgotten about the social media expectations except that Lillian Christie tagged my new account with the picture of us. She'd captioned it with a, "Hey guys! Check out the new, up-and-coming awesome to the literary world!" My new account gained over a thousand new followers. Lillian sent me a direct message with a smiley face and a "You're welcome!"

I drove Kat home at the end of her allowed time with me. It was the least I could do after not letting her live with me. I owed her that much.

In the driveway, Kat turned to me with her big eyes. "Come in with me."

It wasn't a demand but more of a plea. A plea I could not refuse, even though I hadn't intended to go in. I unbuckled my seat belt and offered her a shaky smile. "Of course."

We both exited the car with the same hesitance one has when walking up the wooden steps to the gallows.

Maybe she wouldn't be home. Maybe the tremor in my hands and the race of my pulse were for nothing at all.

I hope. I hope. I hope.

Kat opened the front door, and all hope was extinguished. "Well, look who decided to come home. Not a word or a message on how you're doing." My mother's voice hit an octave that made me inwardly shudder, just like it did anytime it took me by surprise. An article in *Scientific American* had once reported that when a woman hears her mother's voice, her stress levels go down immediately. If her mother hugs her, her stress levels disappear altogether. I say it depends on the mom. My mom wasn't the hugging type. And her voice did nothing but heighten my stress levels. Would this turn into a lecture on how I never visit?

But she wasn't addressing me. She wasn't

even looking at me. Her pale blue gaze had fixed itself to Kat.

Kat's dark brown eyes didn't waver from my mother's gaze.

Mom lost the staring contest and turned to look fully in my direction. "It's nice to see you again, too, Charlotte."

"Thanks, Mom. It's nice to see you again as well."

"I find that hard to believe when you never return my calls and never come to visit."

Ignoring the argument she clearly wanted to have, I asked, "How's work?"

Her less-than-enthusiastic greeting of us turned to something different with this change in topic.

"I got a promotion." The evident pride in her voice compelled me to smile and actually mean it.

"That's great. What will you be doing now?"

She frowned and looked at me like I wasn't paying attention. "Obviously, I'll still be an accountant, Charlotte. I will just now be overseeing all of our firm's newer employees."

"Great. I'm happy for you," I said, though in truth, I felt sad for the newer employees. They likely had no idea what they were in for when they were placed under the care of this particular taskmaster. Kat must have been indulging in the same thoughts because, under her breath, she said, "Has anyone broken the news to them yet?"

I lifted my arm to elbow her for the comment, but she'd already moved to head up the stairs.

"After you drop off your things in your room, I'd like you to come right back down, Kat," my mom called after her. My sister visibly deflated, which guaranteed she heard even if she didn't respond.

"You're far too lenient on that girl, Charlotte. How is she supposed to grow up to be a responsible adult when you're always there to clean up after her and coddle her through the hard things?"

I laughed. "Since when does loving a kid count as coddling, Mother?"

She sniffed at what she rightly interpreted as a jab at her less-than-loving parenting demeanor. "The anniversary of her mother's death is going to come every year. Missing her mother is going to happen every minute of every day for the rest of her life if she's allowed to wallow in it. You jumping in to, let me guess, drive her to the cemetery and hold her while she cries, cripples her from addressing her feelings and overcoming the stagnation that comes from such wallowing."

A familiar insecurity settled over my shoulders. Because, like it or not, she might have been right. I might have been making things worse for Kat.

I made my way to the living room off to the left. I didn't want Kat coming down the stairs and overhearing my mom being callous.

My desire to shield my sister made me worry all the more over the idea that my mom might be right about me coddling.

She's not right.

But what if she was?

She followed me. "But I guess if Kat had to run away in order to get you to actually visit, I can't complain."

And yet, she was doing exactly that.

"What did you do to get your promotion?" I asked, continuing on through the living room and into the kitchen, knowing she would keep following.

"I worked. Obviously. Haven't I always taught you that if you received an education and worked hard, you'd achieve great things? Haven't I always said that?"

"Yes. You've always said that." I pushed on through the kitchen to the French doors leading out to the patio. The garden really was the most pleasant place of my childhood home. My mother loved flowers, and I loved them too, so even when my punishments came in the form of weeding out the flower beds, it didn't really feel so much like punishment as it did a good chance to reflect and think and make up stories in my head.

If I had to talk to my mother, I wanted to be in the garden where there was peace to be had visually even if I could not enjoy any kind of verbal reprieve and even if it was still too cold for the flowers to be blossoming.

"Speaking of working hard, how are things at your job?" She didn't really approve of my job, so it was a surprise to me that she'd asked about it. She felt like it was dead-end employment, kind of on the level of working in fast food. Since I *had* worked in fast food during most of high school and college and even for a while after college, I clearly understood her feelings on that subject.

"Things with my chosen profession have never been better." How I wanted to tell her everything, to tell her how I was accomplished and successful in a way that would make her proud of me but also make her feel that she had been wrong about me and I had been right about me my whole life. I wanted her to be proud of me, and I despised myself for being so needy as to crave that approval. But I wanted to tell her on my terms, with Edward present, and while I was buying them a nice dinner.

"What? Did you quit?"

I started at that. How did she know I —

"Because that's the only way that job could actually be improved on."

"It's a multimillion-dollar, international company, Mother." It was kind of absurd that I was defending the company I had been dissing for so long. Especially when my agent assured me that I would be a multimillion-dollar entity all on my own. Especially when I'd quit the company and owed them no loyalty.

But really, what had Frankly Eyewear ever done to my mother that could possibly deserve her ire?

"No need to get defensive. You know I'm only looking out for you. It's my job to want the best for you."

"I know." And that was exactly the problem. I did know. It was the reason I was caught between never wanting to see my mother and wanting to give her a play-by-play of my every minute of every day just to see if I could win her approval. Because her approval meant that I had achieved the best for myself even if the best was only defined by her terms.

"Your father and I could really use your help with Kat." She slid to the new conversation without as much as a backward glance at the old one.

"Edward has already talked to me, and I've already talked to Kat. She won't take off again unless she's provoked to do so. And I know that you know what things provoke her, so could you try to just ease up a little?"

"I'm not a monster, Charlotte. I just want to see her prepared for the world. Do you think her future employers will ease up on her when they need things? Do you think her future coworkers will go easy on her when the team is required to do something that is hard? How about her college professors? Will they go easy on her?"

I was about to agree that, no, they probably wouldn't go easy on my sister, when my mom continued her train of thought.

"Of course, how hard can a fashion design professor actually be on a student?" How often had she said the same thing about an English professor? Which meant she'd never spent enough time in English courses; otherwise, she'd have the answer to that for herself.

206

The conversation didn't really improve after that. She felt vexed, and nothing anyone said or did could pull her out of that mood. When Kat, who was equally vexed, came down from her room, it was more of the same. Our time spent together was absolutely delightful, if delightful could be defined as ice picks being stabbed into the brain.

Kat tried several times to bring up my good news but finally caught on that I didn't feel like a show-and-tell with the parents. Not yet.

I stayed until Edward came home, not wanting to leave my mother and sister without supervision. When Edward did return, I jumped up, ready to leave the circus that was my family. But Edward insisted I stay for dinner, so the torture continued. It would have been a betrayal to leave Kat alone anyway, since Edward and my mom were intent on wringing her out for taking off without telling them and for staying at my house even when she was given direct orders to come home.

The only thing that kept the situation from becoming a full-on war where Kat packed her bags and ended up back at my place was me trying very hard to play the voice of reason.

I sighed at the lot of them and cut through my quinoa-stuffed avocado like a woman intent on murder.

Kat jumped up to walk me to my car when the opportunity for me to escape presented itself, but Edward beat her to the punch when he said, "Let me walk Charlotte out, sweetie. She and I haven't seen each other for a while, and I'd like a minute to talk."

He was probably worried she would end up in my car and refuse to get out again.

Kat shot me a look of apology. It appeared that we would both be lectured by the other's parent.

I returned that look of apology. After all, I got to leave. She had to stay.

"I appreciate you watching out for Kat for the last little while," Edward said as soon as we were out of earshot of the others. "And I'm sorry if her turning up causes any conflicts in your life. I know that being single and living on your own means that having a teenager around could cramp your style."

"Not at all," I assured him. "She actually makes sure I get a social life. She's no trouble."

"That's nice of you to say, but a social life for a teenager isn't the same as a social life for an adult. You can see how it's better if she's here at home."

I laughed, more comfortable with Edward than with my mom. At least with him, I could counter comments without it turning into the cold war. "If you believe that, then you have the wrong idea about my social life."

He raised an eyebrow, apparently not humored. "If your calendar has some holes in it, then maybe you could pencil in a visit every now and again to your mother."

"Edward . . . I —"

"She really loves you, you know?"

Kat had the same habit of affirming all her words with the tacked-on "you know."

"Do I know?" I lifted my eyebrow to match his.

He nodded. "Of course you do. She only wants the best for you."

I sighed. The same old cyclical conversation. She loved me, wanted the best for me, made me miserable, toughened me up for the real world, made me so insecure that the real world terrified me, and on and on, around and around we went.

"Anyway, thanks for bringing Kat home."

All things considered, the lecture was small and no promises for visiting my mom were extracted. It felt like a victory.

I escaped to my own corner of the world

in my own apartment and found myself sad to not have the companionship of my sister. I immediately texted her. "Hey, sis. Sorry about the awkward."

"Would it be family dinner without the awkward?" The text alert chimed immediately.

I laughed. No, it wouldn't. "Maybe." I texted. "Are things good there now?"

"Meh."

Dang. I'd hoped for better. "Remember. At the first sign of cutlery investments . . ."

"Haha! You know it! Love you, sis!"

I felt better knowing she was in good spirits even with the *meh* response.

With Kat gone and with Anders scheduled to work odd shifts for the next several days, boredom seemed inevitable.

But my editor had other plans for me. The phone call came early Monday morning. Before offering me a legitimate greeting, Melissa dove into the reason for her call. Marketing wanted ARCs ahead of some sort of book convention. Cover mock-ups had already been created, and Melissa had emailed them to me, and had I checked my email? Because if I had, could I please respond to her?

I hurried to comply by sitting down at my laptop and clicking open the email. Four attachments with different cover ideas awaited my approval.

Another email popped up in my inbox. That one was from Toni, saying she wanted to do her job and boost my posts, except the only post to work with on my Instagram account was the one Lillian had tagged me in. She wanted to make sure I was keeping my appointment for the hair, makeup, and photographer so she had pictures to work with. I checked the clock on my laptop. I sighed. At least I didn't have to get ready for the appointments, since the whole point of them was that someone else would be getting me ready. I was going to be late if I didn't leave soon.

Except that another message appeared in my inbox. Melissa now had a publication timeline. The manuscript would be turned into an actual book and be able to dance at the ball far sooner than I'd imagined. They expected it to be out this fall. The people in several of my online writing groups always said publication dates were at least a year out, and often two, once a manuscript had been accepted. For me, it was all happening in a matter of months. In just over seven months, my book would be available to buy in bookstores, both online and in brick-and-mortar stores. Was it normal for it to all happen so fast?

I didn't have time to contemplate actual time because I was definitely going to be late to my appointments. I grabbed my phone, figuring I could answer emails from the road, and hurried out.

When the "artists" were done with me, I glanced in the mirror and had to look a second time. And it wasn't because I was so staggered by the beauty they had found in me. I liked how I looked on an average day. What was so staggering was the fact that I didn't recognize the girl in the mirror. She wasn't better looking than me or worse looking than me. She just *wasn't* me. The photo shoot went well enough, with the photographer who'd introduced himself as Thomas moving me and angling me into positions that felt unnatural and stiff, though he assured me they would all look natural.

I finished and was about to leave when Thomas the photographer said, "I'll see you tomorrow, then."

"What?" I turned back to him. "Tomorrow?"

"For the location shots." His confirmation did not clear up my confusion.

"Location shots?"

"Yeah. We'll be coming by your place

tomorrow to do some environment shots. You know, with you in your own space. It's part of the schedule we have for you." He checked his phone. "Yeah, it's on the schedule."

"Oh. Right. Schedule. Tomorrow." Hadn't I skimmed through the emailed schedule Toni had sent me? Probably. Maybe. "What time?"

"Nine in the morning."

Of course it was first thing. Why wouldn't it be? "Cool. Do you know where you're going?"

He checked his phone again and rattled off my address.

Thomas and his photography team were coming to my house.

Upon considering what that meant, I thought about the mess the apartment was in.

The day my mother had warned me about had finally come.

CHAPTER ELEVEN

"Mice are not to be counted on for
housework purposes. Neither are birds or
other woodland creatures. If you have a
real aversion to housework, hire a maid.
Let's be real. Do you really want rodents
doing your dishes?"
— Charlotte Kingsley,
The Cinderella Fiction
(The "Own Your Own Space" Chapter)

"Keeping clean is easier than playing
catch-up clean," Mom always said. For a
few years, when I was very young, I'd
thought she was saying *ketchup clean* and
could never figure out how ketchup could
ever be considered clean. I'd spilled on
enough shirts to know that it never came
out again, and the shirt was ruined. By the
time I'd figured out she was saying *catch-
up,* I'd also figured out why she had repeated the words to me over and over. She

hoped to motivate me to keep my room tidy. She always used the argument, "What if one of your very important friends came over to visit and saw your room looking like this? Wouldn't you be embarrassed?"

I always responded that of course I wouldn't be embarrassed, because cleaning could be easily done as soon as they let me know they were on their way over.

"Tidying up is easily done. Cleaning requires time that is never available when company wants to drop in with little to no advance warning."

I hadn't picked up everything on the list Toni had given me, which meant I had to go shopping as soon as I left the photographer's studio.

By the time I arrived home and had taken multiple trips to lug up the various required items to my apartment, the digital clock read 10:42. In fewer than ten and a half hours, a camera crew would come in and record all the details of me. The apartment required at least that amount of time to be made friend-or-family presentable. It needed to be do-a-photo-shoot-for-the-public presentable.

I hated it when my mom was right.

It's not that I was a slob. But when life became busy, I prioritized, and cleaning never made the short list. With writing the book, catching up on work, being with my sister, and getting the new contract and a new relationship, my apartment had paid a heavy price. The basics got done: the dishes and picking up. But the deep cleaning: scrubbing the toilet, cleaning the shower, actually dusting . . . *That* stuff had gone the way of neglect and decay. Literal decay in some instances.

The tunes went on as loudly as the late hour allowed. Upbeat tunes were the fuel housework ran on.

I swept, mopped, scrubbed, and dusted every surface in my home. I reorganized my bookshelves so they were tidy and elegant instead of haphazardly thrown together with books crammed in to fit in every direction available. Since I didn't actually have enough shelf space for all of the books I owned, the less-impressive titles went into a cardboard box that was stuffed in the back of my closet, where the hanging pants could cover them up and keep them hidden until the people with cameras left. Surely, they wouldn't be taking those cameras into my closets, would they? Unfortunately, not all of my spare books fit in the box.

The extra book excess ended up being used as decoration. Books went above the cupboards in the kitchen in that weird dead space that people usually reserved for fake plants and empty baskets they didn't know what to do with.

I stacked a few on my coffee table and on the side table in a way that looked artsy and fun. I stripped the bed and put on my newest sheet set that was in the best condition and felt grateful that the comforter was relatively new.

I took down my curtains and had a moment of silence while I mourned the loss of them before I hung the new white curtains.

Though the coffee table was purchased and on site, as dictated by the list, the couch had become another issue because it wouldn't fit in my car, and to have it delivered meant waiting three business days. I knew Toni would never accept crummy excuses, so I called the only person capable of helping me.

"You want me to use an emergency vehicle to pick up a couch?" Anders asked when I had explained the problem.

"I don't have access to any other truck besides this one," I said.

"Lettie, you don't have access to this one either. First, a couch would never fit in it. Second, it's ethically wrong."

"We really couldn't make the couch fit?"

"Did you even hear the ethically wrong part?"

I slumped down to the comfortable couch that I loved but that had somehow offended Toni. "I just don't know what else to do."

Anders was quiet on the other end of the phone call. "You've already bought it?"

"Yes."

"Lettie, it's the middle of the night. I'm working a shift right now. Furniture stores are not twenty-four-hour establishments. We couldn't pick it up until morning anyway."

I hadn't thought about that part. Tired brains caused so many issues. "How do we know they aren't open all night?"

"Why would they be?"

"I don't know. Maybe if a member of the Mafia murdered someone on a couch, they'd need a quick replacement."

"Sometimes, you are a dark and scary person, Charlotte Kingsley."

"I'm not trying to be dark. I'm trying to get a new couch." I mouthed an apology to my old couch.

Anders sighed dramatically. "What time do they open?"

I looked it up and found out they opened at eight in the morning. I gave him the information, and he promised I'd have the

218

couch before nine. I hung up, trusting he'd do what he'd said. He was Anders. He always did what he said.

At three in the morning, the place looked pretty good — a happy coincidence of timing because my body ached for sleep and I had nothing left to give. I set my alarm for eight-thirty. Five and a half hours of sleep would be more than enough.

At least it would have been if I'd been able to get that much. At three minutes after eight, the prickly feeling you get when someone's watching you brought me to consciousness. My eyes popped open. Anders stood over me, his smile warm and gentle.

"You're beautiful when you sleep," he said.

This was, of course, a lie. I had it on the good authority of my sister that I snored. The drool I swept off the side of my mouth acted as a second witness.

"How did you get in?" I asked, though the fog of sleep cleared from my brain fast enough that I knew the answer even as Anders presented me with the key I kept hidden in the hall.

He grinned when I rolled my eyes at him. "If you don't want me to use it, then hide it somewhere else." He picked up my legs, sat on my apparently unlovable couch, and settled my legs over his lap. "Why are you sleeping out here?"

"I made my bed and didn't want to mess it up."

He glanced around. "You got all this done last night? I've never seen your place look like this!"

"I had a burst of energy. It helped."

"Wow. When you get that burst of energy again, feel free to come scrub down my place."

"Whatever," I said. "We both know you're the better housekeeper of the two of us." Anders kept the kind of housecleaning schedule that my mother would approve. He was the kind of guy who even pulled out the refrigerator from against the wall every couple of months to sweep out the stuff that sneaked under it.

He called himself tidy.

I called him OCD.

Anders shrugged at my comment, not arguing it because he couldn't — not even to save my ego. "Well, this place looks amazing."

"Thanks." I scooted myself to more of a sitting position and considered running my fingers through the tangles of my morning hair, but he'd already seen me and didn't seem too horrified at the red dreads of morning. "It's early."

"I have a couch all ready and waiting for you in the hall. Don't ask how I got it up the stairs. The railing may or may not have some damage, but if you don't tell Shannon, I won't."

I threw my arms around him. "I can't believe you were able to get it here this fast."

"As it turns out, when you gave me the name of the company, I remembered I had a friend there who owed me a favor. I got him to let me in early."

"Did you deliver a baby for him?"

"Nope. I did a photo shoot for his sister's wedding for free because his mom and dad were tight on funds after an unexpected layoff."

Anders really was a good guy.

"And technically, Chad from work was the one who actually got it. He had a truck and didn't mind leaving straight from work to pick it up." Anders didn't seem to mind accepting my enthusiastic embrace, even if he was giving Chad the credit.

Anders didn't stick around to cuddle. He maneuvered out from under my feet. Between him and Chad, the new couch was moved in and settled in its place. The old one that had been with me since I moved into the apartment now sat on the back of

Chad's truck. Chad said he needed a couch for his basement, so I offered him mine in trade for the service he'd rendered. Everything was done before the photographers came. I even managed to get myself dressed and ready.

Anders didn't stay long because he'd worked all night and needed sleep. They'd had a call in the night for an old man who'd fallen and shattered his hip. "Go home and call your grandfather," I said when he told me about his night. The photographer was taking pictures of the knickknack things Toni had made me purchase, so I had a few minutes alone with Anders.

"I'm sure he's okay. A guy falling in the States doesn't mean a guy is falling in Scandinavia."

"But you're thinking about it. You're worrying about it. I can see it in your eyes." I gave Anders a gentle shove toward the door. "Go call him and then go to sleep. Lack of sleep makes you a worrywart."

He went to the door without further shoving. I followed him. He turned in the open doorway and I tugged at his shirt as I went up on my toes to kiss him goodbye. "Thank you for helping me with the couch."

He looked over to where the new couch stood in all its beige, vintage-1950s, and therefore modern, glory. He gave it the stink eye. "We are never going to be able to spill anything on that couch because there's no way it'll come clean if we do. Maybe I'll bring in a camp chair for movies."

"I plan on keeping it covered with a big blanket. Consider movie night saved."

"I love it when you save movie night for me." He agreed far too readily to be actually agreeable.

"And that means what?"

He turned his stink eye on me. "If we're talking about you making me watch a ten-hour run of *The 10th Kingdom* with you, then maybe don't worry about it. I still don't get what you see in that wolf."

I laughed. "Wolf will always be my Hollywood crush. Be glad he's not real because if he were, you wouldn't get to do this." I kissed him again, a slow meandering kiss that made me really hate the three people with camera equipment in my apartment. "Because he'd be doing it instead."

Anders grinned in a way that looked wolf-ish enough to make me laugh. "You do know that the actor from that is probably in his late fifties by now, right?"

"Not on-screen. On-screen, he is trapped in youth forever, so I'm free to sigh over him."

Anders looked back to where Thomas had said he was ready for me. "You know I could have done these pictures for you, right?"

A twinge of guilt stabbed me. I had asked for his help, but Toni had made her own plans. "I didn't know this particular photo shoot was happening. I think this is just a jump starter thing for Toni to have material to work with immediately."

"We're ready for you, Char," Thomas said again.

"Char?" Anders snorted at that.

"Yeah, it's my new identity online, I guess."

"According to whom?"

"According to Toni."

"Miss Kingsley?" Thomas was apparently not a man of patience.

"I'll call you when I wake up . . . Char." Anders let out a guffaw, dropped a kiss on my lips, and was gone.

"I'm really going to hate that name," I said under my breath as I shut the door and turned to the madness in my apartment.

It was right to get my space cleaned up because they took pictures of everything. They wanted several of me in my "Everyone Needs Something to Believe in; That's why Fairy Godmothers Believe in Chocolate!" apron that Kat had made for me after we'd had a late night debating whether or not mythical creatures believed in anything. They wanted pictures of me working on my laptop everywhere: in the bedroom, on the new couch, in the kitchen, on a chair near the window with my new curtains. I changed clothes a dozen or more times and had to restyle my hair several times because it "gave a feel of time passing."

They had me holding mugs of cocoa and laughing. Laughing. Seriously. As if I found myself to be hilarious all the time when I was alone in my apartment. They had me reading, putting my feet — in the freaky wool socks from the shopping list — up on the coffee table, and flipping through Lillian's writing handbook while holding my pen ready to take notes. I actually did take a few notes, since pretending to read didn't make any sense when I could actually be reading. Thomas the photographer didn't just take pictures of me. He took pictures of things in my apartment — most of them things that had been purchased days earlier . . . or last night. I wondered if Toni had sent him a list as well.

At the end of everything, Thomas sent the pictures to me and to Toni. She sent me a list of her favorite pictures along with dates and times to post them. "You're a writer," her email said. "Give each one a Pinterest-perfect caption."

It sounded like something Nicole from Frankly Eyewear would have said to me. I shook off the negative feelings that Nicole evoked and did as Toni told me.

Anders showed up unannounced in my apartment a few days into my new social media me. "Should I be offended that your new online identity isn't following me back?" he said as he sat on my new couch and scowled because he didn't think it was very comfortable.

It wasn't.

I squeezed my eyes shut as if I could make his question disappear by not looking at it. "Sorry. It's not my fault."

"Not your fault that your account that you control isn't following me? What, is Char too good for me?" He squiggled around in an obvious effort to snuggle into the couch, but the cushions weren't made for snuggling. He pulled out one of the blue and green pillows from behind him and dropped it on the floor.

"Toni's in control of that account right now. She's given me a list of people I'm allowed to follow."

"And the man who kisses you good night doesn't make the short list?"

I sat down next to him so we could snuggle into each other. The couch might not be comfortable, but we were comfortable to each other, even if Anders didn't like Toni's list of things I must do and must be.

He relaxed against me, our closeness taking the edge off his irritation. "The pictures that guy from the other day took aren't bad."

"Of course they aren't. They're of me." I flipped my hair back and batted my eyelashes.

"But they don't really look like you."

"Ouch." I pulled away from him and turned so he could see my full glare.

He rolled his eyes and pulled me back towards him. "They don't look like you, which is why they're only not bad rather than absolutely brilliant."

"Nice save from my resident medic."

"So are you really never going to follow me?" he asked, resting his chin on my head.

"Toni said after the book releases, my account will be free to do those sorts of things. She told me family and friends would be understanding about the need to establish the accounts for professional reasons and not personal ones."

He grunted, obviously not loving my response, but he dropped the subject.

Unfortunately, Anders was only the first of several people who weren't happy to not get follow backs.

Kat was next, along with several of my friends from writer's groups and from Frankly Eyewear. Luckily, my mom wasn't aware of the new account, or I would've heard much more than basic grumbling. Wanting to make sure my mom found out about the book deal from me and not an online source, I invited her, Edward, and Kat all to dinner — my treat.

We went to Mistral, a nicer French restaurant in the South End. It was my mom's favorite, so the setting felt perfect. We arranged to meet at the restaurant. Breaking bread with the family did not mean I wanted to be imprisoned in a vehicle with the family.

I arrived early, mostly because Mom hated tardiness, and if I was there before her, it would add another point in my favor. While I sat at the restaurant, absently smoothing out nonexistent wrinkles in the tablecloth, a text from Kat made my screen glow. "Your mom just asked my dad if he knew why you were taking us out to dinner. When he said IDK, she said it was probably to announce that you're pregnant. I wanted to be the first to wish you congratulations."

I let out a loud-enough-to-be-embarrassing guffaw and checked to see if anyone had been disturbed by my outburst. A few heads turned my direction but turned away almost as quickly upon finding me not all that interesting.

"What did you say?" I texted back.

She sent me a smiling-devil-with horns emoji. "I didn't say anything until she asked if I knew anything. I told her that your news definitely started with the letter *p,* but that it wasn't my place to share your news. She's now fretting."

I kept my laugh quiet this time as I texted, "You are evil."

"But in the best way, right?"

"Of course."

They arrived several minutes later. Mom, who wanted her daughter to be the first woman on the moon, not just another number for unwed mother statistics, was definitely fretting. She rushed to our table, the staccato beat of her high heels on the floor. She pulled me up and hugged me hard. "We'll get through this," she said before I could say anything.

Kat looked amused, Edward looked horrified, and I couldn't say what I looked like.

But I felt somewhere between the two. "Mom, there's nothing to get through. I'm fine. Sit down. Let's order dinner."

The waiter gave us a moment to be seated before he approached us for the drink order. My mother had been pummeling me with questions but fell silent at his approach. She wasn't the sort of woman who handled family matters in a public setting. She immediately picked up again as soon as he'd moved out of earshot.

"Mom, calm down," I said. "Whatever you're thinking is wrong, so relax."

"I just cannot believe that in this modern day, where women have so many options —"

"Mom!" I had to interrupt before she went too far down that road. She fell silent. "I brought you all here to be with me so we could celebrate my good news. I'm published."

She opened her mouth in what was sure to be a lecture on how I'd failed my family, my gender, and my liberal education when the words actually made impact with her brain. "You're what?"

"My first book is being published. It releases in October."

She waited a moment before responding — long enough to allow Edward the time to give me a hearty congratulations and a one-armed hug that nearly pulled me out of my seat.

"Someone is actually publishing one of those fairy tales?" she asked.

I sighed but tried not to take her words personally. It was how she communicated. "Well, not exactly. The book is called *The Cinderella Fiction,* but it's nonfiction."

"How does a nonfiction book have the words *Cinderella* and *fiction* in the title and still qualify as nonfiction?"

I explained it as best I could, but the explanation never hit its mark. She asked me how much I paid the publisher, to which I replied that the publisher paid me. She asked me who sent the book in for me, to which I explained that the entire submission process had been done by me, not by favors friends owed me. She wanted to know who was going to buy a nonfiction book with the word *fiction* in the title, to which I explained that I didn't know but that I'd been paid enough to assume that a lot of people would be buying it. She wanted to know why anyone would be taking self-help advice from a woman who had an apartment full of hand-me-downs.

I didn't give an answer to that question. She didn't need to know that my publisher had ordered me to get a publicist because they had the same sort of concern. She didn't need to know that the new couch and coffee table and drapes in my apartment had been purchased for the purpose of marketing, not because I had finally figured out how to make grown-up purchases from places other than Goodwill.

She didn't love hearing about me quitting my job.

I would have thought she'd be glad about that. She hated where I worked and took every opportunity to slam it and my wasted potential. Instead, she seemed perturbed that I dared do something so boldly irresponsible as leave secure and gainful employment. She told me to go to them and grovel to get my job back.

Kat's focus was in her lap. I understood why when my phone buzzed with an incoming text. "You doing okay? Want me to kick her under the table?"

I smiled but texted, "That might not be the best idea."

"If you change your mind, just say the word."

"Kat, please don't text at the table." Mom's voice cut into the digital conversation with my sister.

I jerked my head up from where I'd been

looking at my phone, even though the reprimand wasn't for me.

"Sorry," Kat said without looking, or sounding, sorry at all.

As my mother opened her mouth to probably acknowledge the fact of Kat's empty apology, I hurried to interject. "I truly hope you'll all be at my book launch. I managed to talk them into having the launch in Boston instead of New York. That way, you won't have to go far. And, considering what a big deal this is for me, I would really love your support."

"Sorry," I texted Kat and meant it. I hated it when we were both doing the same thing wrong and Kat was the one who ended up getting chastised.

She shrugged.

The conversation then went to the date of my launch and the difficulties it would present to my mother to actually attend, what with all her new responsibilities at work, even though the release was months away, and where was that waiter to refill my mother's water glass.

Overall, though, the evening went well, even if the only one who promised to be at the book launch was Kat. I hugged my sister extra tight when we parted and was surprised when my mom hugged me as well. It was a limp sort of gesture but, considering that such things hardly ever happened, it might as well have been a death-grip embrace.

As I walked up the stairs to my apartment, I received a text from Toni.

"The photographer took several pictures of you with someone I assume is your boyfriend. He didn't send them to me until now, since I asked him for specific shots and these were different from what I'd requested initially. He finally decided to pass them along, however, because he thinks they turned out nice. The guy in the photos looks like a nice guy, but I want to make it clear that I vet all of those pictures for your social media sites. It's best for you to appear to be flirty and single, not in a serious relationship. The pictures are telling me it's a serious relationship. Please do what you can to keep him at a distance — at least until a couple of months after the book releases."

I stood in the stairwell trying to understand what she was trying to say. Did she want me to dump Anders? Because that wasn't going to happen.

I wrote back. "I don't think I understand. How would my relationship affect anything?"

"It could hurt sales. Available, free women

offer more to admire. A relationship might make you appear boring instead of adventurous."

"Boring to who?" I said out loud to the empty stairwell. I texted, "I'm not breaking up with him just for sales."

"I'm not asking you to break up with him. You can keep him and keep it private. But it's important you earn out your advance. If you don't have the sales to cover what they've paid, you might never get another book published."

I frowned at my phone and stomped the rest of the way to my apartment. The door hadn't even been closed long enough for me to put down my purse when Anders texted. "You're alive!"

"Barely!" I texted back. "How did you know I was home?"

"It was either you or a yeti with the way you thumped up the stairs."

"Right. Well, you know, family functions." I didn't tell him about the new directive handed to me from the publicist. Lillian's words to push back if Toni ever asked too much of me echoed in my head, and I'd done that. I'd pushed back.

"How did they take the news?"

The discussion about my family was easier than the one about my PR firm. I texted,

"My mom seems like she's still on the fence about whether or not to believe me. Edward is supportive, and Kat is still thrilled. I could use a mental distraction. Want to play video games with me?"

"Lettie, you don't own any games."

"But you do. We can play in your apartment." I tried not to think about why I suggested his apartment, but some part of me felt like we'd get caught together if we were in my apartment.

"But you don't really like playing games like that unless Kat's with us."

Why would the man bicker now for us to not play when he usually took the other side of this argument and begged me to play? His favorite was *Sorcerer's Guide to Winning,* which was a full-on adventure quest game that he loved. I appreciated the game's storytelling and the beautiful graphics, but it took way too long to solve all the quests. I honestly believed the creators of the game never intended players to stop playing. You finish one quest and there was a new one waiting to be solved.

I texted with what I was sure would be the decision maker. "We don't have to play anything. We can watch *The 10th Kingdom* instead if that's what you want."

Which was how we ended up in his apartment with controllers in hand, helping the game's local villagers figure out who had stolen their rune stone. We sat on the floor with our backs against the couch and our legs touching.

With my eyes on the game because, for whatever reason, I was a completely co-ordinated human in real life and a total klutz in the gaming world, I asked Anders how work had been.

Asking after the job usually didn't require much conversation because, according to Anders, the job was 95 percent mundane. On occasion, interesting things happened. On occasion, terrible things happened.

Which meant that up until now his odds for interesting conversation trumped mine every time because 100 percent of the job at Frankly Eyewear had been mundane.

But still, it always surprised me when he started with, "It was an interesting one to-day."

"Oh? Why?" I asked.

"Had a rookie with me. The kid spent the entire morning checking the ambulance because he didn't think I was thorough enough when doing safety checks. We got a call, and the kid looked like he'd just had Christmas handed to him in a puke bowl."

I looked from the screen to Anders. "Ew.

The imagery of what you just said. What does that even mean?"

He snorted. "It means what I said. The kid looked excited and like he was going to throw up all at the same time."

"You keep calling him a kid as if you're some sort of ancient creature. It's hard to play the mature card when we're playing video games."

"Says the woman who likes fairy tales. Anyway, this kid is just barely twenty. And so we take the call. I'm driving. And I remind the kid, when we're driving sirens, his job is to check all the traffic coming from the right of the intersection because he's the passenger. I swear, Lettie, I told him a half dozen times that he had to acknowledge an all clear. There were a few close calls. I was afraid we'd end up needing the ambulance."

I laughed and also felt relieved because Anders was still here next to me. He hadn't needed an ambulance. "So how did the call go?"

"It was a teen. The boy was cold and stiff. Dead on arrival. It looked like he'd been gone for a while. His sister had found him in the backyard and immediately started compressions. We took over, but I honestly didn't have even the smallest hope."

"Oh, Anders, I'm so sorry." He hated to lose anyone, but he hated it most when they were young like that.

He shook his head. "Don't be. The kid lived."

I fumbled the controller. "What? How? Didn't you say he was cold already?"

Anders shrugged. "I'm calling it rookie luck. There was no reason for that monitor to start beeping, but it did. We got him to the hospital, and they were able to keep the monitor beeping. It made for a good ending to what started out as a cursed call."

He placed his bare foot on top of mine.

It wasn't exactly a show of intimacy. He would have done that same thing a million times before we had decided to try this new place in our relationship. But Toni's warning rolled around and around inside my skull.

You might never get another book published.

Was kissing Anders a tactical mistake? Should I have stayed single? How did we recover from moving forward? Could we go back?

No.

Going back would mean losing him entirely — even more entirely than when he was supposedly engaged. I didn't want to go back, either. I wanted to move forward, not backward. I wanted to be in his life. And I wanted him in mine — all of mine. How could I recover from wanting to share all the things inside my head with him?

I heard the click of his camera and turned to catch him taking pictures of me.

"What are you doing?"

He shrugged. "Can't help it. You're too beautiful to not acknowledge."

His compliment should have made me smile. Instead, it filled me with unease. I slid my foot out from under his and began playing the game again but ended up getting my character killed.

"So why are you being weird, Lettie?" Anders asked.

"Me dying in this game is not exactly weird, Anders. I do it all the time."

He paused the game and turned to face me in a way that ended up with him resting his elbow on my knee. "You know what I mean."

I did know.

But I couldn't tell him that Toni wanted to scrub my social life as well as my housewares.

But I had to tell him something. "I just . . . worry about losing this." I motioned through the space between him and me.

"You don't have to worry. I've never been

so sure —"

I wanted to stop him before he got that far into the sentence. Stop him because I hadn't been so sure about anyone either. But I was also sure about my career finally being what I'd worked so hard to achieve. "I only want us to take our time. To keep the friendship part going. I don't know that I'm ready for us to be more than we are."

His entire body went still, like the boy he'd thought was dead on arrival in his earlier call.

That boy's heart had found a beat, but mine had stopped.

The words were in exact contradiction to what my heart wanted. And if the way Anders held himself rigid told me anything, my words were also an exact contradiction to what his heart wanted.

"Okay." He dragged the one word out, likely gathering his thoughts. "Lettie, I thought us together was something you wanted, too. Are you having second thoughts?"

No. None. But what I said was, "I just want us to be best friends without making it complicated."

"Okay. Well, that translates in my head to you not liking the idea of us as a couple. So I would love to hear an alternative translation if you have one."

"Of course I like the idea of us. I *love* the idea of us."

"Like it and love it in theory, but not so much in reality? Is that where we're going with this?"

He sounded hurt, which hurt me and left me flustered.

"Anders, I like it and love it in theory *and* reality. I just . . ." *A relationship might make you appear boring instead of adventurous . . . You might never get another book published.* "Just want us to take things slowly. That's all."

"But you're good with this? With us?"

I wanted him to be okay, to feel assurance. I put my bare foot over his. "I'm good with us."

The muscles on his face relaxed. His lips curved into a gentle smile. "You don't have to worry, Lettie. I won't let anything hurt you."

I smiled back and wondered how I would do the same favor for him.

"So nothing to worry about?" he asked.

"No. Nothing." I was determined to let that be the truth.

Anders didn't reach for me throughout the rest of the night. He didn't reject me taking his hand or resting my leg on top of his or leaning my head on his shoulder. He didn't pull away when I kissed his jawline, but none of our physical contact originated with him.

Part of me felt grateful. Part of me felt irritated. Irritated with myself, not with him.

Which was why, when I kissed him good night, I forced myself to forget Toni's words and book sales and the importance of earning out my advance. His hesitation about kissing me at all was enough for me to know I really couldn't go back to being just friends.

Anders had said it. Nothing to worry about.

So there wouldn't be.

CHAPTER TWELVE

"An apple a day keeps the doctor away.
Unless it's a poisoned apple. Then you
might feel bad that you didn't spend
enough time cultivating a better
relationship with the guy you're going to
need to save you from dying."
— Charlotte Kingsley,
The Cinderella Fiction
(The "Be Healthy" Chapter)

Aside from that brief time during his false-alarm engagement, Anders had always been a part of my daily life. Fortunately, that continued after our little talk. Things went back to normal. Nothing really changed. Yet, everything changed. When we were together, my stomach filled with the fluttering people always talked about when describing a significant relationship. When we weren't together, my brain could only think about being with him. Or planning the time we'd spend together when I was with him. Or texting him. Or thinking about what I wanted to text him.

Even better was the fact that he didn't act needy. He gave space where space was needed. And it turned out I needed a lot of space. I had thought — and hoped — that once I'd crossed off all the to-dos on Toni's first list, that would be that. It wasn't. She made new lists. She made new lists all the time. She spent months making me feel like her social media slave. Hundreds of advance reader copies had been printed and distributed at the book expos Melissa had talked about and the final edits had been turned in, but my plans to start writing a new book during all the free time I'd acquired by quitting my job had been put on hold. Lillian, who had become my direct messenger voice of reason, kept telling me that this time before the book released was the eye of the storm — the only time I'd have to myself until after my scheduled tour was finished. She reminded me to push back when needed. Toni, however, seemed to have absolutely zero concern about my personal time. Thankfully, Anders was patient. He acted like he didn't mind the time Toni occupied in my life. He affirmed over and over that he understood how important this book's success was to me.

I stole moments where I could, managing to sneak away every now and then to go with Anders on one of his photo shoots. He loved taking photos and then manipulating them digitally into art. Several of my writer friends who were going the indie route for publishing had seen Anders's work when I'd linked to it, back when my social media accounts really belonged to me. He'd taken quite a few jobs from them and had produced some amazing cover photos for their books. He didn't take on all the work offered to him — only the jobs that spoke to him on some artistic level.

One of those jobs required photos with a woodsy fantasy feel. His client had been on my short list of dependable beta readers for years, so he'd asked if I'd like to come along for the shoot.

"What are you wearing?" he asked when he appeared in my doorway to pick me up.

"Oh." I looked down at the shirt, which had a British flag emblazoned across it. "Toni picked it out. It's the newest Cora original."

"Did you need me to take pictures of you today?" The slow way those words exited his mouth revealed apprehension.

He'd taken lots of photos of me over time,

but, lately, it seemed like we ended up arguing whenever I asked him for help with pictures. What Toni wanted and what he felt showed the real me were not the same thing. The worst fight we'd been in had ended with him calling Toni the "used car salesman of humanity," which made me ask if he'd really just compared me to a used car. We didn't talk for almost a week, before I apologized for being overly sensitive.

Since then, anything having to do with Toni had been a carefully avoided conversation piece. Until now.

I swallowed hard. "Do you not like it?" I asked even as my mind screamed that only stupid women ask questions they don't want honest answers to.

"It's fine. It's just . . . you should put on a long-sleeved shirt. The mosquitos will be out thick tonight. It's not like you need to market your book to them. They don't know what a Cora original is. The only thing that shirt is marketing is your blood to the Massachusetts state bird."

I lifted my chin, not liking his implication that everything to me was marketing. "I don't want to change. I like this shirt."

His lips formed a thin line while he surveyed me. He likely wondered if this was a fight he wanted to have. He decided against the fight with a shrug. "Fine. Good. I guess I didn't know you were into waving the flags of other countries."

"Well, I am." The words weren't meant to sound snippy and snobby all at the same time. But they did.

"Good to know." He looked away and said, "God save the queen. I'll get you a shirt with the Swedish flag sometime just for variety."

Thawing the ice between us took almost the whole drive to the shoot. "Sorry," he said. "It doesn't matter to me what you wear. If it makes you happy, then it makes me happy."

His apology took the wind out of my sails of indignation. "Sorry if I seem sensitive. My mom keeps giving me angst about the amount of makeup I'm wearing now. She says I'm becoming a Barbie. You know how my mom puts me on edge."

"I don't think you're becoming a Barbie, but you also don't need the makeup to be beautiful." When I gave him a withering look, he added, "But it doesn't matter to me what makeup you wear. If it makes you happy, it makes me happy."

We moved to other topics that didn't include anything Toni had changed about me. I felt the need to defend her choices because she'd done what she'd promised: my social media engagement and following had become something epic. I had become a strange sort of online-famous. It didn't hurt that many of Lillian's followers had taken a liking to me. Several other authors had followed me based on the media buzz surrounding my book. The advance reviews had been stellar and had earned me respect I'd never imagined.

Even my mom was proud of me, though she acted completely devastated that none of my social media accounts would follow or friend her. Kat didn't act devastated over the friend-follow debacle, but she rolled her eyes every time it came up. Anders hadn't brought it up since that first conversation.

We arrived at the spot Anders had chosen for the shoot and unloaded his equipment. We hadn't strayed too far out of suburbia to find a great place to set up, which meant that when an ice cream truck's music floated our direction, I sat up straight from where I'd been lounging against an elm tree. I dropped the jagged-edged leaf I'd been shredding and said, "Tear Jerker Bomb Pop or Choco Taco?"

His camera had been set up on a tripod to get various shots of a row of moss- and ivy-covered sycamores. He straightened from where he'd been squinting into the camera and laughed. "It's gotta be a mile away. You'll never find it."

"Don't doubt the woman who's buying you ice cream. Just give me your order."

He looked to where the sun was setting. We were in what he called the "golden hour," where the lighting on those moss- and ivy-covered trees looked positively magical. There would be little to no digital manipulation needed to make his images incredible. "Fine, but if you don't find the truck immediately, come back. I don't want you wandering around in the dark."

I grunted. "Look at you being all primeval. I live in the city. And I'm usually wandering around after dark."

"It's not primeval. It's smart. Even I don't wander around by myself after dark when I'm alone, and I outweigh you by a good —"

"You seriously don't want to play the guess-Charlotte's-weight game. Just tell me what you want me to get you."

"Choco Taco."

"Got it!" I sped off, racing through the trees until I hit pavement. I stopped for a brief second to listen and ascertain the direction of the truck, and then I sped off again.

I returned before the sun could even think about setting and handed off the Choco Taco with triumph. Then I opened the original Bomb Pop I'd bought for myself.

Anders watched me instead of opening his Choco Taco. "Didn't you once tell me you always got the chocolate eclair ice cream bar?"

"This has fewer calories."

Anders ate his Choco Taco in relative silence before making a grunting kind of noise. "Lettie, you didn't change what you were going to get because of what I said, did you?"

It took a moment for me to figure out what he might be referencing. "Oh! No. Not at all. Tour is starting soon, and I want to look my best."

He didn't respond, but the tension I felt from knowing what he wanted to say made me grind my teeth together until they ached. When he spoke up again, I stiffened, expecting a lecture.

"You know, when I was a kid and we'd first moved to the States, my parents told me that the ice-cream-truck music only ever played when the truck had run out of ice cream."

I stared at him; the horror of such blasphemy and my own gratitude that he hadn't

251

lectured me soaked right down to my bones.

He stared back, tilting his head so the light from the still-sinking sun caught the ends of his blond hair and turned it to gold. "You have nothing to say to that?"

"I'm paying my respects to your stolen childhood with a moment of silence."

He laughed and sat next to me. "My sister told me they were lying and that if I'd just look at them with sad eyes, we'd both get ice cream out of the deal because I was the baby, but I believed them and couldn't see the point of crying over an empty truck."

I swallowed a cold bite and shook my head. "I can't tell you how sad this makes me for you."

"What? Your parents never told you something that wasn't true?"

"You've met my mom. You know that's not how she rolls." I thought a minute longer before adding, "But my dad told me that avocados were crocodile eggs, and that he had to sneak around the crocodile nests while the crocs were sleeping just so he could make my mom's sandwiches magical. I totally believed him and thought he was a really tough guy for being brave enough to sneak around crocodiles."

"I'll bet your mom loved that."

"She didn't. At all. Especially when I cried

one morning because I thought she was being selfish to put him in danger just so she could have magical sandwiches. But she loved it even less when my dad convinced me that paintings were windows into other worlds and that if you stared at one long enough and believed hard enough, you could travel to wherever the painting was. The trick was that the picture had to be done on canvas and painted with oils. Then Dad placed the most beautiful, fantastic paintings he could find in my room. My favorite was one with a little girl on a swing out in space among the stars and planets."

"With that kind of story, I'm surprised you didn't become an artist instead of a writer. Were you disappointed you couldn't ever get into a different world?"

"Actually . . . no. I would look at the paintings and imagine what life would be like inside them. It was almost like actually going. At night, I'd tell my dad the stories I came up with. After a while, he started writing them down, and that was how the writing thing started."

"It's funny that the make-believe things you were told as a child were charming and sweet, while the make-believe things I was told as a child are the reasons I have a therapist."

"You don't have a therapist," I said.

"Not technically. But you listen to my rantings often enough that you kinda count. You care that I bought into the biggest ice-cream-truck lie ever. What other therapy could I need than that?"

"If that's the worst thing you were ever told as a child, then you had a pretty good time of it."

He finished his Choco Taco and folded up the wrapper into a tidy little square that kept any of the sticky stuff inside the wrapper so he could put the wrapper in his pocket. "See. That's the thing. The ice cream truck wasn't the half of it. My sister told me that if she pressed the little 'diet' or 'cola' buttons on the top of plastic lids from fast food restaurants, it would magically turn my drink into something else. She did it all the time, and no matter what my parents told me, I believed she'd really ruined my root beer. I started drinking water because of her."

"So that's where your aversion to soda comes from. I knew there had to be a reason."

"Now you know. It was childhood trauma." He ran his hands down his jeans and looked back through the viewfinder of his camera. He snapped a few more shots, using the remote control so he didn't have to touch the camera while taking shots in the much lower levels of light. The sun had completely escaped the sky while we'd been talking.

I slapped at my arm. "The blood suckers are out." I didn't believe in vampires, but I had a healthy conviction about their insectoid counterparts.

Instead of giving me grief about having told me to bring a long-sleeved shirt, he pulled an old long-sleeved pullover out of his camera bag and tossed it to me. I didn't try arguing that I was fine and didn't need the protection he offered. My wounded pride was not worth having wounded arms as I scratched at the many bites that would have been sure to follow. "I'm going to work at not ignoring good advice in the future," I said as I pulled the shirt over my head and stuffed my arms inside as quickly as possible.

He snorted, which was likely as much sarcasm as I'd get from him over the whole thing. The guy knew me. He understood my quirks and faults and shrugged them off like they weren't that big of a deal. What made us good together was that I understood his quirks and faults as well. I understood that conversations with him sometimes felt like being on a merry-go-round that just never ended because he always circled back to the same ideas over and over again. When I was with him, I often found myself doing the same thing, which made me laugh. It was what made *us* work.

I thought we had wrapped up the picture taking for the night, but Anders didn't remove his camera from the tripod or start to gather up his camera bag and the sand-bags he'd placed on the tripod to keep it solid during the shoot.

"Are we waiting for something?" I asked.

"Mm-hmm," he said.

That was the whole of his answer, which wasn't like my Anders at all. I was waiting for him to expand that answer into something understandable when the first flickers of fireflies appeared in the foliage around us.

"Ohh," I whispered.

He put his eye to the viewfinder without touching or bumping the camera and tripod. His finger clicked the remote, and in quick succession, several shots were taken.

"Hey," he said. "Do me a favor?"

"Sure."

"Go stand in the path by the third tree down. Face away from me."

I did as directed. He gave me a few other

instructions to adjust where and how I stood and then the click of his camera signaled he'd found what he was looking for.

I turned, expecting to be done, but he said, "Wait a second. Do that again."

"Do what again?"

"Turn, but do it slowly and lift your arms out, with your palms up like you're catching rain, and lift your face up."

I laughed at that but did as directed. After a few turns, he finally said, "Got it. Come on back to me."

"Happily."

When I met him back at the tripod, he caught my hand in his and spun me into him. He tilted his face down and whispered, "You are the most beautiful thing I have ever seen." His thumb traced over my palm before he brought my hand to his lips, where he pressed a kiss to the center of my palm.

I hadn't expected the contact. He was working, after all, and Anders had a way of being able to focus. He didn't allow much deviation when he was working. His lips moved to my wrist, and then he pulled me closer and covered my mouth with his in a slow, exquisite moment.

"What was that for?" I asked when we

broke apart.

"For inspiring me to be a better version of myself. You . . . well, Lettie, let's just say I love you."

I blinked.

I almost fell over except he was holding me.

Anders loves me.

Anders loved me!

He said it, and there were no givebacks.

Few people in my life used those words with me.

My father. My sister.

Once, Edward-the-stepdad had given me a one-armed hug and said, "You know I love you, right?" And he often told me my mother loved me, though she never said the words.

So much power in three words.

They were a magic spell bigger than curses from witches, bigger than wolves, bigger than trolls and dark forests, bigger than even kisses.

I love you. Those words could unravel the darkest hour of a human's life.

They undid me completely.

"Anders? I . . . I love you, too."

He smiled and kissed me again.

We stood there in the firefly light, breathing one another in, for a long time.

Anders broke away first. "We should get going. We have those movie tickets."

"Right. Tickets." It was hard to think of going to a movie with my head so full of him and those three glorious words.

We were heading back to our apartment building to get the camera stuff put away before the movie when my phone pinged with a message.

It was from Toni. "You haven't answered the interview questions from that writer's group in Texas, and you haven't responded to any of the comments on Instagram or Twitter. Also, I have an article set up for you to write about making goals for that online magazine *Seize the Day*. They really need the article tonight if they're going to publish it at all, so if you could take a moment."

I was on the clock.

I swallowed and put my phone away in my purse. I didn't bring up the fact that I was ditching our plans — at least not immediately. I didn't want Anders to correlate the phone ping to my sudden need to stay home. He already hated Toni.

Anders was talking. I only caught a few of the words, but it was something about the photography he'd just done and how much he liked doing stuff for writers.

259

"Maybe I can do a few covers for you sometime."

"What?"

"Covers. Pictures. For your books?"

"The publisher will be doing my book covers." The words came out almost absently, since I was trying to find a way to tell him that I had to bow out of the rest of the evening.

"Well yeah, but what if you decide to go the indie route for your fiction like some of your friends?"

I frowned. "Why would I do that?"

He let out a bewildered bark of a laugh. "Are you getting mad at me, Lettie? There's nothing wrong with indie publishing. This isn't an insult."

"I don't think it's an insult. But why would I do that? Do you not think a publisher will want my other books?"

I hadn't meant to get defensive. But so far, my agent hadn't sold the others. And it stung whenever I thought about it. Did Anders notice how the words had an unintended bite to them?

"Lettie, like I said, this *isn't* an insult." Yes. He'd noticed the bite. "I do freelance photography work so I can work on my own terms. I think independent publishing is a lot like that."

260

"Independent publishing would mean doing my own marketing, and there's no way I'm the sort of person equipped to pull off marketing with any kind of skill."

He snorted. "All you do is market. Isn't that the point of the shackles Toni has clapped on your wrists while you proudly display your British pride?"

Signing with a publisher had given me new hope for my fiction work. But each month that passed had dimmed my hope. "Leave Toni out of this. If I'd planned on publishing independently, why would I have put myself through all the emotional distress of being rejected for all those years?" I laughed, though I didn't feel the humor. Bite was in the laugh as well. The request for the interview coming on a night I had looked forward to made it impossible for some of the frustration to not come out in my voice. "Don't worry, Anders. You'll never be doing cover work for me."

"Ouch. Now who's being rejected?"

He fell silent, keeping his eyes on the road. Not sure how to gauge his silence, I stayed silent as well. Was he mad that I didn't need him to do photography for me?

As we neared our apartment building, I realized I had to speak up soon. Ditching him at the last minute would make me a monster. He deserved some lead time. "Hey, I . . . I'm not . . . feeling very well. Sitting through a late movie would probably be a bad idea for me right now. I'm so sorry, Anders, but can we call it a night?"

Surprise registered on his face, but he nodded. No verbal response followed. Just the nod. Parking, exiting the vehicle, and walking into the building all happened in silence, aside from a murmur of assent or acknowledgement. He walked me to my door. I no longer pretended to feel ill because my stomach twisted in unease. "Are we fighting?" I asked after opening my door to let myself in. Who fought after declaring their love for each other?

Did that sort of thing ever happen?

The idea mystified me. Anders and I didn't do silent fighting. We'd always practiced a verbal disagreement kind of friendship.

He licked his lips, but he didn't swallow down his words to replace them with untrue words. "No. I don't think so. Maybe. I don't know. I just thought it might be fun if we worked on something together. I guess it bugged me that you were so quick to shut that thought down. But don't let it worry you. I'm fine. You're the one who doesn't feel good here, so go inside. Get some sleep.

Feel better. If you need anything, let me know. I'll see you tomorrow."

"But —"

He finally did smile. "We're not fighting, Lettie."

"I'm sorry about wasting the movie tickets."

"They won't get wasted. I'll call one of my buddies to meet me. No worries."

"Okay."

It was what I said but not how I felt. Especially when he kissed me on the cheek before turning to the stairwell. A kiss on the cheek could have come from anyone. It wasn't the sort of farewell I'd come to expect from the man I was dating — not the sort of farewell I'd expect from a man who had said he loved me, especially since he didn't repeat the sentiment now.

"Anders?"

He turned. I caught up to him in a matter of a few steps. "I'm sorry," I said and meant it. I was sorry I'd hurt his feelings with the conversation about him doing photography work for me, but more than that . . . I was sorry I'd brought our evening to an end with a lie.

"Me too. I was up late last night. It makes me grumpy." He leaned in for a real kiss. As soon as his lips settled on mine, I felt better, which made the lie about not feeling well a little more of . . . well . . . a *lie*.

But his leaving without being angry or hurt or whatever it was that had made him go silent on me made it so I could go back to my apartment and work.

He went to the movie.

I stayed up until nearly three in the morning writing an article and answering questions in a witty, personable way. It was important to me to get every word right because the publisher had paid me a lot. I wanted the book to sell and earn out its advance.

Every minute of the process tortured me because of what it had cost me in terms of time with the man who said the magical words — words I believed and returned and felt in my bones. "It's just this one night," I promised myself. "They won't need much more from me after this until the book releases."

Except they did.

They needed me quite a lot.

After that, Toni didn't allow me to skip a day of responding to comments. She had a vigorous schedule of times I needed to tweet, times I needed to post images on Instagram, times I needed to write contemplative commentary on life on Facebook.

My life was filled with Toni's lists of requirements. Whenever my phone pinged, Anders said, "Tell her no."

Even Kat had grown tired of Toni's interruptions. "Your outfit looks great, and if Toni doesn't like it, you can tell her that I think her cats of Instagram are as unoriginal as vanilla ice cream." Kat had taken a particular dislike to Toni because Toni criticized every outfit Kat had put me in that made its way to a public profile. I finally stopped asking for Kat's advice.

Kat could say very little good about Toni.

Anders had nothing good to say at all.

He would watch as I disappeared back to my apartment with some excuse of a headache or a stomachache or a toe ache or the pleas of needing to get work done on a new writing project.

Which was the biggest lie of all — even bigger than the toe lie, since I actually *had* stubbed it while walking in sandals Toni had insisted I buy but that didn't fit right.

There was no new writing project.

I suffered from social media exhaustion. I responded to people's comments, wrote platitudes worthy of being framed on walls, answered interview questions, and wrote articles that would allow the book to hit the ground running when it released.

From the time my fingers had gripped the pen used to sign the contract to now, I'd scarcely written anything new for *me*.

And with every new day that no creation happened, I became more unsettled. When I wasn't creating, I felt like I was tangling instead. The last time I'd written anything unrelated to marketing my book had been when Lillian had direct messaged me and asked me to do a writer's sprint with her. She'd scolded me when I told her I couldn't find the time to write. "Oh, honey," she'd written. "Time is made, not found. You never find time for the important things. You make the time. That's how you're sure they're the important things. You wouldn't be scooting over to make room for them if they weren't." I cancelled my plans with Anders so I could do the writing sprint with Lillian.

When she found out I'd cancelled plans for a date, she called me so she could scold me again. "Not people!" she said when I answered her call.

"What?"

"You do not ditch humans for writing."

"You told me I had to make time for the important things."

The harrumph that blew through my

phone told me that if we were in person, she'd smack me upside the head. "People *are* important things, Lettie. People are the most important things. You do not ditch humans. You can ditch Instagram and Twitter and article writing — especially if the articles are strictly for marketing and not for pay, but you do not ditch humans."

She was right. Of course she was right. I promised her I would do better.

"You'd better do better because it's like my momma always said, 'If you can't get your priorities straight now, those hairpin turns are going to make up the mountain you careen down later.' So do better. If you can't balance your human connections with your creative connections then nothing will connect. Do you understand me?"

I assured her that I did understand. But understanding and accomplishing were not the same thing. Other also-important things kept coming up to take the place of writing and humans. A few sales internationally went through. It meant more money — enough that I was overwhelmed with the windfall of it all. But it also meant more work. More places that required my focus. Although Mirror Press was rushing to get the book released domestically, a few of the international publishers actually beat them to the punch. In August, the book released in Great Britain to shining reviews and accolades and brought a wave of new hype for the book domestically. I wore my Cora original with the British flag for that release. Anders didn't say anything about the shirt, but he did hum the tune to "God Save the Queen."

In the little time left over for me, I tried to take Lillian's advice and focus on the humans in my life. I spent time on the phone with Kat to try to talk her off the ledge that was running away from my mom to join the circus. I spent time helping Anders do a growing number of photo shoots for various authors.

But not enough time. I had to end calls far too quickly with my sister so I could answer other calls ringing in — other calls that were almost always Toni. I had to leave early from time spent with Anders so I could be on time for interviews with radio station and talk show hosts who'd been given ARCs and wanted to be a part of increasing the pre-release buzz. Saying no to those interviews at such a crucial time would be like book murder. So I never said no.

Lillian's words haunted me. My human connections and creative connections had no balance.

I'd been emptied, creatively speaking.

I felt it in my response to Kat when she called and told me she just couldn't take my mom anymore. "Seriously, Kat. You gotta learn to handle it. There are going to be people you don't get along with through your whole life. You won't like all your coworkers or your bosses or your college professors. It's just life. You need to learn to deal."

I'd sounded just like my mom talking.

I felt it in my response to Anders when he suggested we had potential for a long and happy life together. "Get serious, Anders. You don't want to be saddled with someone who can say she doesn't believe in marriage even when there's a possibility that a married couple falls down dead every time she says it."

That was my fear-of-turning-into-my-mom talking.

How many times had Lillian cautioned me to be careful to protect my relationships?

Not enough, I thought, as Kat started to take hours to answer my texts and as Anders invited his friends from work to go out to the movies with him — even before asking me.

I planned to do better. I *would* do better.

To prove it, I took Anders to a Red Sox game. I wanted the night to be special for Anders and so I got the best seats available. Anders brought his camera, insisting he wanted pictures to commemorate a day with just the two of us.

"And the thousands of other fans and the two or three fans over on the visitor side," I said. Anders laughed at my joke and hurried to take several successive shots of me. "Hey! I wasn't ready!"

"Which is why the pictures are beautiful."

We shut up because the game started.

Shortly into the second inning, my phone buzzed with a text.

Anders didn't seem to notice with all the noise of the crowd and the announcers. I slipped my phone out of my pocket, justifying to myself that the text might be Kat. It was Toni. I would have put the phone away immediately except that I saw part of the message: catastrophe. I had to keep reading — to know what had been a catastrophe.

It was the Dawson's Morning Show interview schedule. She needed it rearranged because the launch date and the interview had been set up on the same day, which would mean I'd be late to my own book launch.

I had to respond.

Several minutes later, Anders nudged me, "You're missing the game, Lettie."

I hit send and looked up.

My phone buzzed again. Anders tensed. I willed myself not to look.

And I didn't.

Not for that first message. Or the second one. Or the third.

"I just need to see," I said helplessly as I slid my phone out again on the fourth message buzzing in.

When I started texting again, Anders got up. "Where are you going?" I asked.

"The lost and found," he said.

"What did you lose?" I asked.

"Your attention, apparently." He stomped up the stairs.

CHAPTER THIRTEEN

"Pinocchio teaches us the hard truth about honesty. Be honest with others. Be honest with yourself. Even if you can afford a nose job later, you can't guarantee no one will take your picture before the surgery and post it online where the whole world will see."
— Charlotte Kingsley,
The Cinderella Fiction
(The "Honesty" Chapter)

I went to follow him up but dropped my phone as I stood. By the time I found my phone, picked up his camera bag so it wouldn't be left unattended, and jostled my way through the people, he'd disappeared. "He won't leave me," I muttered to myself. This assurance wasn't because I believed I didn't deserve to be left. It wasn't even because he'd left his camera bag and would have to come back for it. It was because

Anders wasn't that kind of guy.

I texted him an apology and went back to our seats. The first rule of being lost is to go back to the last place you saw the people you are currently missing. I could wander Fenway Park for the whole night and never find him.

Anders returned a short time later with two bags of cashews. "I'm sorry," I said as he put one of the bags in my hand.

"I know," he said. "Me too."

I turned off my phone while he was watching and put it away, hoping that he would accept my sacrifice. It took some time, but somewhere in the fifth inning, he had his arm around me and was cheering along with the crowd. We would be okay.

On the way home, Anders took his eyes off the road for a moment to look my direction. "Hey, what are your plans December 19th?"

I laughed. "Probably lying on my couch with a cold rag over my head because I'll be coming off the crazy book tour schedule."

He tossed a smile over my direction. "You'll have been home for over a month by then. Will you still need a cold rag?"

"As nervous as I am about all the public speaking they've set up for me, it will take months — maybe even years — to recover."

"If I give you a shoulder massage, would I be able to coax you out of the house?"

"Why? What's going on?" I hooked a finger around the slingshot handle hanging from the interior's roof. Sometimes Anders took turns too fast. It was good to hang on.

"There's the opening of a photography exhibit my friends and I are putting on called 'Many Faces.' "

"Well that sounds . . . ominous and creepy in the back-alley, selling-parts-to-Dr.-Frankenstein kind of way."

He made the left-hand turn before rolling his eyes at me. "Really? Selling parts to Dr. Frankenstein? You should be writing scary books with that kind of imagination. The point of the exhibit is to show the many faces a person has to wear during the day."

"Still sounds like Dr. Frankenstein."

"Lettie, you're killing me. You know what I mean." We arrived at our apartment building. Anders pulled into his parking space under the building, turned off the car, and turned to me to try to explain again. "It's to show how people have different sides of themselves. It's a display of the authentic and the false. Will you come?"

"Of course. But remember, my attendance is based on the promise of a shoulder massage while we watch *The 10th Kingdom*."

He got out of the car, leaned down, shook his head, and said, "Nice try," before he closed his door.

When I was safely tucked into my apartment, I turned on my phone. Toni had written.

And written.

And written.

And called.

Eighteen texts and three missed calls with lengthy voice mails scowled at me from my phone's screen. I considered throwing the thing against the wall but instead sat down on what Kat called the Flintstone couch because it felt like it was made out of rocks. From there, I read and listened.

And felt sick.

Her first text said, "I need to talk to you about your boyfriend."

Her second text said, "Seriously. I need to talk so call me."

Her third said, "Char, you're getting sloppy regarding important stuff. He's tagging you in his posts where there are many pictures of the two of you looking very much like a couple."

I had imagined hiring a PR firm would give my life an extreme makeover. What it had turned out to be was an extreme takeover.

Her voice mails were long and delivered in her cool, always reasonable, always unruffled tone. She talked about the thing we'd discussed to pieces: My book wasn't about Cinderella getting the guy; it was about Cinderella getting her head right. I needed to toe the line and do my part.

"I'm not trying to tell you what to do," she said in her last voice mail, "or how to live your life. I'm just trying to help keep your brand untarnished for the first little while of this release. You can keep your relationships, obviously. Just don't allow them to have advertising space in the online world."

There was no way I could tell Anders not to tag me in photos. I liked the photos he took and posted. I liked occupying space in his social media life. Those photos and his willingness to make them public made me feel cared about — cherished. It made me really think about how he felt regarding all the space that should have belonged to him in mine.

As soon as this initial push of sales and the launch was over, I'd make it up to him.

Anders and I had an afternoon date to go listen to a local high school youth symphony play at the Hatch Shell in the Common. He had the whole day off, but, since he'd worked nights the entire week prior, he'd be sleeping in until later, so the concert not starting until three in the afternoon worked out well for us.

I packed us some snack foods, zipped everything up into my backpack, and went to get Anders from his apartment.

He opened the door before my knuckles could rap against the wood. "I am ready for a day to relax!" he said. He took the backpack from my hand, slung it over his shoulders, took my hand, and gave me a kiss before we set off to the shell.

I'd brought a blanket, which Anders spread out on the ground under the trees heavy with foliage. He arranged our "table" on the ground. He set out all the food and made everything look properly presented. "You and your artist's eye," I said when he rearranged a few things because the display felt "out of balance."

"Is that a bad thing?" he asked, settling down next to me so we could actually eat.

I leaned into him as the first leaves of autumn fluttered down every now and again around us. "Mm, no. Never. Your artist's eye is one of the things I love most about you."

He grinned. "What other things do you

love about me?"

"All the things. If I had to list them all, we'd have to live here because it would take forever. But if you want to know another thing, I love that you are patient with people."

"I'm not always patient."

I pulled a few grapes off their stem. "You are too. You're even somehow always patient with that dragon Shannon — even after she accused me of sabotaging pipes." I'd nearly clubbed her with a pipe just to show her what kind of damage I could really do with one, but Anders had stepped in and explained why her theory was impossible.

As if reading my thoughts, he said, "The way she was getting you all worked up would have ended in violence. I wasn't being patient. I was keeping us out of jail."

"You're the only person who could have talked her out of charging me for the cleanup and damage fees." I raised my voice to something shrill and borderline malevolent, "Oh Anders, Anders, is there anything I can do for you? Would you like me to massage your feet while I feed you grapes and fan you with palm fronds and poison your girlfriend?"

"Shannon does not have a crush on me," he said, though he laughed at my impersonation of her. "You and Kat and your conspiracy theories. But if she offered me a foot massage and a grape feeding . . . I might take her up on it."

"What about the poisoning of the girlfriend?"

"Well . . . I mean . . . it's not like you've ever offered to feed me grapes."

"Let me remedy that for you." I flicked a grape at his forehead and hit my mark, not that such a thing was hard, since he was sitting right next to me.

He raised his hands in surrender. "I kid! I kid! And you have wicked good aim, Charlotte Kingsley."

"This would be a good thing for you to keep in mind."

"Noted. But seriously, if Shannon ever offered to poison you, I'd let you carry out your plan to club her with a water pipe, even though doing such a thing would make us bad people. We'd end up being dragged to the underworld for an eternity of torment along with people who don't string their string cheese and who talk in movie theaters during the movie."

"Not stringing your string cheese is worthy of endless torment?"

He nodded.

"Anders, I have something to confess —"

"Don't even think about finishing that statement. Besides, I know for a fact you do string your string cheese *and* that you're a good person, so there."

Anders scooped up some of the spinach artichoke dip with his pita chip, took a bite, and closed his eyes while he chewed. "And this . . . is one of the things I love best about you. You're an artist in the kitchen as well as on the page."

That man really knew how to make me feel good.

"I might have to enlist your help when my sister comes into town," he said. "You can help me figure out how to feed her. I swear, Magdalena's the pickiest eater I know. It's a serious character flaw. No one likes to feed picky eaters."

"I did hear a rumor once that picky eaters would be the first to die in the apocalypse."

"Serves 'em right."

I wiped my hands on one of the napkins I'd brought for us and took a long drink from my water bottle. "Why is she coming into town? Is it that cold already in Canada?"

Anders laughed. "It can never get too cold for a Swede. It'll be a while before she comes. She wants to discuss *Farfar's* declining health. We're trying to figure out how to best take care of him."

That was a sobering thought. Anders must have thought so too, because his laugh came to an abrupt stop and he frowned. His hero and best friend experiencing declining health had to create a huge hole in Anders's heart. All his family was in the United States or, in Magdalena's case, Canada, so no one remained in Sweden to be a guardian or caregiver.

"I'll absolutely help you feed your sister."

"I can always count on you."

I hated that he was saying such things when Toni was, at the same time, complaining about his presence in my life — when she wanted me to hide him away like he was something for me to be ashamed of. But I hadn't backed down. I hadn't agreed to get rid of him or even to hide him. Most of the time, he could count on me. Those times had to count *for* me as well, didn't they?

The youth symphony began. We settled in to enjoy the music.

By the time the symphony had finished and the food had all vanished into our stomachs, Anders and I reclined on the blanket to stare up into the tree branches. A leaf had twirled down and landed on Anders's chest. I picked it up and rested my head there instead, while twirling the leaf in my fingers.

I'd actually thought Anders had gone to sleep when he asked a question. "What's your favorite sound?"

"Sound?"

"Yeah. Sound."

I stared at my leaf as it spun slowly between my index finger and my thumb. "I don't know. I guess I've never thought about it before. But I guess . . . my favorite sound would have to be ocean waves. Not the crash as they come in exactly, though that's part of it, but the sound of the waves pulling out again, that foamy, slurry rush of the water pulling at the sand."

He smiled at me. "Only a real writer could come up with that kind of description that fast."

I turned my head and rested my chin on his chest so he could see me roll my eyes at him, but I felt all the pleasure of his compliment. He meant it. Anders really believed in me in a way no one else did. From the beginning, he had always been on my side. "What about you? What's your favorite sound?"

His smile softened into something nostalgic. "I love the hum of tires on the highway during a road trip, where there's that occasional Doppler swish as other cars pass."

"Hmm. Doppler swish. I like that. I don't think that's a sound I've ever thought about before."

He shrugged. "That sound, along with the sway of the car lulling you to sleep, means that when you wake up, you'll be somewhere else. It's the sound of progress, movement, adventure, something new."

I settled my head on his shoulder. "Now who's the writer?"

His phone pinged. He pulled it out to look and started to laugh hard enough that I had to move my head again or suffer a concussion. "Google maps just asked me if the place we're eating at is romantic or if it is all-you-can-eat." He tapped his phone a few times, then started laughing harder. "And now Google has thanked me for my answers because they will help others who have searched for all-you-can-eat romantic restaurants. I know I'm a pretty basic guy, Lettie, but is there any such thing as all-you-can-eat romantic restaurants?"

I smiled and kissed his ear because I couldn't quite reach his lips from our position. "Eating from a garbage can is romantic when you really love the other person."

His chest vibrated with another laugh until he fell still and silent again.

I stared up into the tree branches and

thought about how much I loved the moment surrounding me.

Our relationship was going pretty well. We were taking things slow — like I'd requested from him, but he didn't seem to mind that. He seemed to appreciate the friendship, the solidarity, the *genuineness* of who we were when we were together with no other strings attached.

I appreciated all the same things. I loved having him as my best friend and constant companion. I loved telling my sister about our relationship and hoped she would find something like that for herself someday. Something true.

True. Genuine. Real.

So why could I hear Toni's voice mail ringing in my ears? Why did I hear her voice telling me that I could keep my relationships, but I couldn't give them advertising space in the online world? I could see her texts telling me not to tarnish my brand.

"Anders?"

"Yeah?"

"Did you climb trees when you were little?"

"All the time." His voice slurred with the sleep he hadn't been able to get the night before because of work.

"Did you ever climb too high? So high

that the branches got smaller and smaller until finally there wasn't anything to hang onto except a few random leaves, and the branches under your feet bowed under your weight? Have you ever felt like you were hanging on by a leaf?"

He peeked open an eye and strained his neck to be able to view me better. "Are we still talking about climbing trees?"

I shook my head. "No. Yes. Never mind."

"Lettie? What's up?"

"Nothing. There's nothing. Just looking at the trees and thinking too much."

He murmured something noncommittal like he was fading from consciousness again, which meant he'd believed me when I said nothing was wrong.

But he couldn't *really* believe me. Hadn't he been the one to raise his eyebrows at my ever-shifting wardrobe, where a single T-shirt that looked casual and fun now cost more than my whole previous wardrobe, or, under Toni's instructions, at the way I now did my hair? Another leaf fell silently until it hit the ground, making a crunching sound — little leaf bones breaking on impact.

"You're climbing too high, Lettie," I murmured to myself. But there was no way to go back down, not when I only had to reach up a smidge higher to finally attain the prize. I only had to hang on for a bit longer.

The book launch was soon. I could go back to being the me Anders wouldn't raise his eyebrows at.

286

CHAPTER FOURTEEN

"Beauty and the Beast proves that being able to meet the deadline imposed by an old crone and a dying magic rose can really make a difference in your love life."
— Charlotte Kingsley,
The Cinderella Fiction
(The "Pace Yourself" Chapter)

I awoke the next morning to a knock on my door. I opened my eyes and stared at the ceiling, unsure if I'd actually heard the knock or if it had been part of the already fading dream where it seemed someone was on the rooftop of my apartment building throwing pinecones down at the guy on the street he'd accused of dancing like a pony. I'm pretty sure he meant it as an insult. Or maybe he didn't. I couldn't decide because the knock at my apartment door came again.

Why would someone be at the door? What day was it? And then it hit me: October first, the day of the book launch.

I sat up straight and gasped with the fear that I'd slept through my book launch. But my phone informed me that it wasn't even nine in the morning yet. I smirked to myself at that. *Not even nine in the morning, and I feel like it's okay to be in bed?* The days of Frankly Eyewear and being in the 7 a.m. commute really were over. I remembered someone was at the door when they knocked a third time, prompting me to get out of bed, slip on a robe, and answer.

Anders stood in my doorway. His arms were crossed over his chest, and he had on his scowl face. "You locked your door."

"You're always telling me to lock it."

"Yes, but you moved your key."

"That's because I'm pretty sure Shannon knows where it is."

"Well, you'd better let me know where you hid it this time, because not knowing ruined the surprise I found lurking by the front gate." He stepped to the side.

Lillian Christie poked her head from around the corner. "Is that my cue?"

"Lillian!" I pulled her into a big hug and felt a huge relief to see her there. "What are you doing here?"

"Moral support. Happy book birthday, Lettie!" She squeezed me tighter.

"Don't you mean Char?" Anders asked. If sarcasm could be given a name, it would have been called Anders. He hated that my online persona went by Char. He hated even more that some of my fan followers had made a flame for me as a logo.

Toni loved the logo and loved even more that people totally unconnected to me had made it because it meant that I had reached "the people," and they had declared me theirs.

"Don't you go sassing on the woman of the hour," Lillian said to Anders before she released me. "How are you feeling? Are you ready?"

"I thought I was, but honestly, I don't know." Out of all the people in the world, Lillian would know how to get me through this day. Terror threatened to consume me at the thought of getting up in front of all those people.

"You're going to be great, baby girl. You're going to show the world who you really are. But first, I've come to take you to breakfast."

"I'd love to go to breakfast with you!" I looked down at my pajamas and laughed. "Maybe I should get dressed first. I'll be right back."

I hurried to my room and shut the door.

The noise from outside my room proved they weren't having trouble making conversation. "So are you and Lettie dating? We talk all the time, and she hasn't mentioned you," Lillian said.

It hadn't occurred to me that they'd go into that type of conversation. I hadn't told Lillian about my relationship with Anders. I hadn't really told anyone because Toni had wanted to keep him under wraps.

Staggering to get dressed faster with the intent of getting back out there and limiting their chance for an in-depth discussion, I ended up tripping on my pant leg and falling face first onto the floor.

"Oomph! Ow!" I cried out.

"You okay in there?" Anders asked after tapping on my door.

"Great. Fine!" I called back.

Half-dressed, I stood just inside my bedroom door and found myself too paralyzed to move. I was not so stupid that I hadn't felt the beat of silence from Anders after Lillian had asked if we were dating. It meant he was internally translating what she'd told him.

Why had I kept him a secret from Lillian? She was my friend and certainly wouldn't have gone off tattling on me to Toni.

I could almost feel Anders taking a glance

at my bedroom door and then reassessing our entire relationship. I closed my eyes and held my breath.

"I'm just a neighbor from downstairs." He didn't go into our relationship or why he knew where my key used to be hidden. Lillian made a comment about me being so lucky to have such a nice view.

He must have been confused because it took him a moment to say, "View? All of her windows look out on alleys lined with dumpsters."

I opened my eyes as if I could somehow see the two of them through the door.

Lillian let out a booming laugh. "No, honey," she said. "I was talking about the neighborly view. You're a handsome man. Handsome neighbors are hard to come by. Nice, handsome neighbors are even more rare."

That made me smile. If I knew Anders at all, he was blushing right to his blond hairline. He turned it around the only way Anders knew how and that was to make the conversation about her. "Well, Lettie's pretty lucky in a lot of ways. I mean here you are. And she's one of your biggest fans. It must be a pretty big deal for her to have you here."

He must have been showing her my collection of her books because she gushed over how amazing it was to see her books so well-loved and how she couldn't be better complimented, since she was such a fan of my work as well.

"Really?" Anders asked. "You've read Lettie's book already?"

"We have the same agent. Jen gave me an ARC to read."

Anders hadn't been given an ARC to read even though I had one. It hadn't occurred to me to let him get a preview.

But wasn't he always promoting me?

His promotion of me reminded me that Lillian was there to see me and hiding behind my bedroom door wasn't exactly me being a good hostess *or* a rational adult. I hurriedly finished getting dressed and then opened my bedroom door. I found Anders and Lillian in the kitchen, where Anders had offered her a glass of water.

"Your neighbor was showing me around."

"He's more than just my neighbor. He's my boyfriend." I smiled and linked my arm through his. He deserved to be acknowledged.

A breath exhaled from him. Had he been holding it while wondering if I would introduce him properly?

"And here he's telling me he's just a

neighbor." Lillian laughed a booming and delighted laugh. "Why are you keeping your relationship a secret?" she asked him.

His smile tightened. "That's an excellent question."

She didn't notice the snick of a bite in his response. "I cannot believe you have all my books!" she said. "I'd accuse you of going out and buying them all just to make me feel good about myself except you didn't know I was coming. So really, I'm very complimented. I don't even think my mother has all my books!" She laughed. I laughed. Anders laughed.

My personal and writing worlds colliding made the idea of being an author real. I'd always been able to say I was a writer for my profession when people asked what I did for a living, but it occurred to me that I could now, as of today, say I was an author. While Lillian signed all of my books that were her titles, I texted Kat to tell her who was over. Kat's reply was nothing but exclamation points and question marks. "Will she sign my books?" was Kat's next reply.

"Bring them to the launch, and I'm sure she will."

"I'm packing them now! Oh. And, so you know, your mom is saying she might not be able to go tonight."

The disappointment smoldered in my throat and threatened to choke me until I swallowed it back down and texted, "But you're coming, right?"

"Anders said he'd pick me up."

I glanced his direction and felt love swell up and take the place of disappointment. Anders. He caught my look and his expression turned into a question. His head tilted and he squinted as if trying to see me better, probably wondering why I was looking at him like a crazy person. Could he see the shine of tears in my eyes for the gratitude I felt for him?

"What?" he mouthed.

"Thank you," I mouthed back.

He raised his hands in questions and mouthed, "For what?"

I simply shrugged. I'd thank him out loud and with real words later.

"So let me tell you why I'm here," Lillian said, interrupting the silent moment between Anders and me. "This is your book birthday. It's your first one. You'll probably have dozens more after this, but this is the one that sparks that chain of events, and as such, I think it needs to be a book birthday worth remembering. I've got a day planned!" She took a drink of the water

Anders had fetched for her and slid her gaze toward him. "Unless you have plans and I'm intruding?"

Anders waved her off. "We didn't have plans, so don't worry about me. Besides, she sees me every day, and she'll see me tonight at the launch."

"Why don't you come with us to breakfast at least?" Lillian's offer was generous, since I didn't want to part with Anders yet. I had planned on being with him for some part of this day. I had planned on the celebration being something we shared.

He agreed. Lillian took us to a new little crepe cafe and then revealed the rest of the day's plans by handing me an itinerary on cardstock covered in swirled designs.

11:00 a.m.: Massage — to work out the kinks from your social media marathon

12:30 p.m.: Pedicure — so your feet are relaxed and able to "stand" all the attention

1:15 p.m.: Manicure — to make sure your nails are worth biting off in case you get nervous

2:00 p.m.: Shopping — so you can enter your new author life in clothes that match the moment

4:00 p.m.: Hair stylist — for a do that

does as much work as you've done
   5:00 p.m.: Dinner
   6:00 p.m.: Bookstore — Melissa and Jen will kill me if I don't get you to the party on time

I loved the itinerary, but for Lillian to do so much for me? Sure, we were friends, but this was too much.

"I see that look you're giving me. Don't worry, Lettie. This is a gift from Melissa, Jen, and me. We all pitched in. When they heard what I wanted to do for you, they were thrilled to be part of it. I'm just the lucky woman who gets to do it with you."

"What's the gift?" Anders asked. I handed him the cardstock itinerary. He scanned through it and whistled. "Sounds like quite a day."

The idea that my agent, editor, and hero writer had gone in together to make this day so special meant everything to me. It meant they believed in me. It meant they were in this with me and would cheer for me. It meant that we were all friends.

Anders stayed through the remainder of the meal. Lillian had welcomed him to come along with us, but he had declined, claiming that he was tired from all the graveyard shifts he'd pulled. He kissed me goodbye and left. I was glad he'd be getting some sleep. He'd had several rough nights in a row, rough enough that sleep was desperately needed.

"What if no one shows up to the launch tonight?" I asked Lillian later that day.

She put her hands on my shoulders and said, "That's not even a possibility. Too many other authors have shared this event with their followers. I have several dozen of my own fans who are committed to coming. And Toni has done her job in regards to creating an aura of approachable leader about you. Besides, you already have a fan base in all those reviewers who seem to think no good life advice had ever existed before you showed up on the scene. What I'm trying to say is that people will be there."

The pep talk worked, allowing me to stamp down my paranoia for a bit. As we stood in the boutique, trying on clothes that would be appropriate for the night, I passed by the gowns and ran a whisper-light hand over the various fabrics, listening to the swish of them as I made my way past. Tonight was not a ball-gown night, but it felt like it should be. I smiled at Lillian as she looked over the sorts of clothes that made more sense for me to wear to a launch party. What would she say if I told her I wanted a ball gown and a tiara? Toni would put her foot down so firmly on such an idea that she'd likely break through to the earth's core. Lillian would go with it.

I had told her that I wanted to wear a pantsuit for the night.

But that had been what Toni wanted me to wear.

"You know, Lillian, I think I want some new jeans."

Lillian turned to me with a knowing grin. "Being *you* for your launch is a great idea. Let's get out of here then."

I ended up with an amazing pair of skinny jeans that featured a woven denim pattern that ran along the double set of pockets. "Pants with pockets that actually work!" I'd gushed to Lillian enough times she likely wanted to pull a pair of socks from the display and stuff them in my mouth to keep me quiet. But really, why did designers assume women didn't need or want pockets?

Finding a top had been more difficult. I imagined Kat's voice in my head with every piece of clothing I picked up until finally I heard her say in my mind, "Do it!"

It was cream colored and almost looked like a blousy pirate shirt. I tucked it into the jeans and rolled the pant legs up to just above my ankles so I could show off the ankle bracelet Kat had made me for my twenty-seventh birthday a few months prior. Over the shirt, I put on a black sleeveless jacket that hung down to my knees. I sighed at myself in the mirror. Toni probably would never have approved.

I exited the dressing room to see what Lillian thought.

"I love this outfit, with a caveat. Those flats make it too casual. You need some killer heels."

She picked me out a pair of black heels to match the black jacket. Before Toni, I'd never been able to walk in heels, but after much insistence on her part, I'd trained myself to not stumble like a toddler walking over rocky terrain. I was glad I'd learned to walk in heels without falling because Lillian was right: the shoes finished the outfit. "Classy, chic, and casual all at the same time," she said.

We arrived in front of the bookstore early enough that we should have been among the first ones arriving. But the store was already filling up.

"And you thought no one would show up," Lillian said as we entered the bookstore.

"My mistake," I whispered.

"Are you here for *The Cinderella Fiction* signing?" an employee with a name tag that read Theo asked.

"She *is* the signing," Lillian answered. "This is Charlotte Kingsley."

As if Lillian had handed me off like a baton to another runner in an urgent race, Theo bustled me over to the small dais where Jen and Melissa were talking with several other store employees about the reading, the question-and-answer session, and the crowd flow for the signing.

Jen hugged me when she saw me. "You look stunning! How was the day?"

"Amazing. Thank you. Both of you. It was unexpected and generous and meant so much to me."

They were both pleased with my report and explained the itinerary for the night.

"Lettie!" Kat wove through the crowd of people choosing seats for the reading part of the evening and nearly knocked me over.

"You look great! I couldn't have dressed you better myself!" She was wrong though. Her own clothing choices proved she knew her business. She wore a tangerine button-up that was blousy and casual while looking incredibly whimsical and vogue. She wore it over black jeggings that tucked into low-heeled black ankle boots with what looked like small silver button embellishments done in a circular pattern. The day bag slung over her shoulders with embellishments that matched the boots made me think they must be her own design.

They were fantastic.

Maybe I'd ask her to make me a set for Christmas.

She circled me. "And those shoes. The next book you write could be a murder mystery. You could call it *Stabbed by Stilettos.*"

"I call dibs on that title!" Lillian said.

"Kat, I'd like to introduce you to my friend, L. M. Christie."

My sister's mouth dropped open, and for the first time since I'd met my sister, she had no words.

"Did that sound like I was name dropping? Because I totally was, but I kinda hoped it appeared like I wasn't."

"It totally sounded like you were name dropping," Lillian said. "I'd make a joke that I didn't think we could be friends if you were just going to use me like that, but, since we've already stunned your sister, I don't think she'd know I was kidding."

"I brought all your books!" Kat blurted out. "Lettie said you'd sign them for me." Kat pointed at me as if I'd done something bad and she wanted to make sure I got the blame. Lillian laughed and said she'd be delighted. She followed Kat over to where Kat had procured a chair in the front. Just one chair with her box of books on it. No one occupied the chairs near hers. Not my mom. Not Edward. Not Anders.

And then I saw him.

Not Anders.

But my father.

And he wasn't alone. Oddly, my mom stood behind him.

"Daddy!" I yelled loud enough that many people stopped chatting in their little groups and turned to see who was screaming. Then they all turned to see where I was staring. I leapt from the dais and maneuvered toward him until I could let him wrap me up in one of his bear hugs. "I never thought you'd be able to make it!" I said into his leather jacket.

"As if I'd miss my little storyteller's first book signing!"

Tears stung my eyes.

Don't cry! I scolded myself and hoped it would work. How stupid would it be for me to be bawling before the whole thing even began? "It's just so far."

"It's not too far when you consider I haven't visited in a long time. We were due."

He looked around the store. "Even if our time is shared with a crowd of strangers."

"And Mom?" I only said it because her presence actually startled me more than his did. Kat had already said she wasn't coming because she didn't feel well. "What are you doing here?" I asked. She had an iron grip on Edward's hand but an exuberant, borderline-manic smile on her face. "I wouldn't miss this for the world!" she insisted, even though earlier that day, she'd told Kat she'd been willing to miss it for a headache.

Whatever had happened that prompted her attendance, I was glad she was here, glad she'd be able to see this crowd and partake in the excitement. She would be able to see I hadn't failed.

My parents exchanged civil, if not exactly warm, greetings. My dad and Edward did better by behaving as they shook hands and asked after each other's lives. My whole family had come together to celebrate with me. Maybe it was the stress, or the nervousness, but seeing them all in the same room made the back of my throat burn and my eyes sting.

But where was Anders? Why wasn't he here? I checked my phone for any missed calls or messages, but nothing indicated he'd tried to contact me. Kat was still with Lillian, so I couldn't shake her down for information.

My hands and feet were numb, as if my circulatory system had decided those extremities didn't actually need blood. My tongue felt fat in my mouth. How was I supposed to speak to all these people when my tongue had decided to hit a growth spurt in the last ten minutes?

Melissa touched my elbow and smiled at me.

It was time.

Time for my book to debut into the world for real, with sales that would be counted. And sure, it had already released in England, but I hadn't been a witness to that release. This was here, now, tangible, and taste-able.

Fat tongue and numb feet aside, this was happening.

I shot a desperate last glance around the crowd to look for Anders smiling at me from among all the people.

There were friends. People from work. Nate and Ali were seated several rows back. Even Nicole, who hated me while working for Frankly Eyewear and hated me even more for quitting, was standing in the crowd behind the chairs. People from various writing conferences and critique groups beamed at me from where they'd managed to snag seats.

The world had come to see this moment, to share it with me, but Anders had not.

"It's time," Melissa said, prompting me again towards the dais. Melissa took the microphone and thanked everyone for coming. Applause. Cheering. Whistles.

For me.

Though my eyes were on Melissa, my ears were on the noise of celebration. Melissa gave a short introduction, sticking to the bio that Toni had placed online and that had made it to the inside cover of the book. Then Melissa stepped aside, and I had to step forward to take her place at the center of attention.

I gave the crowd a shaky smile as I heard Toni's voice chastising me, reminding me that I needed to be confident, to be someone people wanted to follow. I heard her saying that no one wanted to follow timid Charlotte Kingsley. They wanted to follow Char, the girl who has it all and can tell the world how to have it all as well.

I cleared my throat and wrapped my trembling fingers around the microphone. "Hello! Thanks for coming tonight!"

More applause, more cheering, but I

305

heard only the static fuzz of the roaring blood in my veins shoving past my ears. I bent down and picked up a book out of the stack of boxes to my right and began turning the pages — past the publisher information and the dedication page to the page that marked chapter one. A survey of the room told me there was still no Anders, but even so, and even though Toni would have shrieked at me for being sentimental at a time when I needed to remain aloof and available, I turned back to the dedication page.

"To my Asgard hero," I read. "You are the prince, the frog, the knight, the dragon, the best friend . . . and I won't call you the fairy godmother, since you'd only be insulted, but you do make it so I don't need one. Thank you for all of it."

Toni had been against the dedication, but after I'd removed the name and changed it to Asgard hero, she'd decided that it added mystique to my situation. After all, the Asgard hero didn't have to be a boyfriend; it could be a father or uncle or grandfather or brother. "Besides," she'd told me, "no one reads the dedication anyway."

She was wrong. *I* had read the dedication, but the person it would matter to hadn't been there to hear it. I swallowed my disappointment. What if he didn't have a good reason? No. He'd have a good reason. Maybe he'd been kidnapped. Maybe he was being held at knifepoint while the kidnapper wrote a ransom note. Or maybe he was sick and passed out and was now in a coma in the hospital. Or maybe he was lying dead in the gutter somewhere after having been mugged and shot. I briefly considered that maybe he'd been called into work, but he wasn't on call. Whatever his reasons, Anders wouldn't have missed this night if it hadn't been important. I shook off my concerns and my fears that something bad had happened to him and did what everyone expected me to do. Perform.

The reading of the first chapter mesmerized the audience. People laughed. People nodded. People cheered. My words evoked real responses from the crowd. I ended my reading of the first chapter by calling out the last lines — the ones that had been repeated several times before in the chapter.

"Because what do I not believe in?"

"The Cinderella Fiction!" They all called back at the same time I read the words. I hadn't expected them to say it with me, and their response startled me enough that I fell silent halfway through and let them finish.

How many people were there? Several

hundred at least. The store had become hot and humid with all those bodies pressed tightly together, in spite of it being a chilly night. All those people chanting my words.

The signing met and exceeded all expectations. My father hovered near as if the line to get books signed was a reception line at a wedding. He talked to people still waiting, though he shut up and let them talk to me when it was their turn to get a book signed. His pride in my accomplishment shone around me and radiated through me.

My mom gave no indication that she might have had a headache. She and Edward had ended up running into a group of friends who had come to the signing at the recommendation of others. Their friends hadn't even put together that I might have been my mom's Charlotte because of the last name difference.

People had their picture taken with me as if I was some sort of celebrity. They also had pictures taken with Lillian. Several of her fans had been in the crowd. They made themselves obvious by the shirts they must have had privately made. One of the shirts said, "L. M. Christie I love you!" Several shirts had crying emojis on them and the words "Why did you kill Carmichael?" It made me wonder why Lillian ever posted publicly where she might be. The passion of her fans was slightly terrifying.

My hand felt abused by all the personal notes of good will and best wishes written into the fronts of books over the night. My parents left when they realized the line didn't seem to be shrinking and they would never get a chance to have a private moment with me. They promised to be in touch. Kat went with Mom and Edward. I wanted to ask if she knew what had happened to Anders, but the line demanded my attention, so I had to let her walk away.

When it was over, and the last patron left with my book in a store bag, Jen, Melissa, and Lillian took me out for a late-night snack to allow me to regain some of the energy I'd spent in the night.

"It's hard to be 'on' at events," Lillian said. "It takes more out of you than you can know. Make sure while you're on tour and doing your speaking circuit to stay hydrated, eat often, and exercise appropriately. You need the physical exertion to help balance the mental and emotional exertion."

I felt like I should have brought a pen and paper to take notes with all the advice the three women had for me.

While we finished our beignets, Melissa tilted her head to one side. "So if you don't mind me asking, who is your Asgard hero? Was he there tonight? Jen and I made guesses on who he might be. These are mine." She pulled out her phone and showed me a dozen pictures of various men.

I laughed. "You stalked the audience? Wow. I'm torn between being impressed and being creeped out."

She flicked her hand to shoo away my comment. "Be impressed because some of these pictures were really hard to get without getting caught. So? Were any of them right?"

I lifted my shoulders. "Nope. Sorry."

"Ha! That means I win," Jen said.

Melissa narrowed her eyes. "You don't win by default. You could be wrong too. You have to at least show Lettie."

I appreciated that none of these women called me Char.

Jen scooted her chair close to me so she could show me the pictures on her phone. Part of me had held out hope that maybe they had seen what I hadn't. Maybe I'd just missed him in the crowd, but none of the pictures were of Anders. "Sorry, Jen," I said.

"Was he even there tonight?" Lillian asked, a small wrinkle above her brow. She'd met him. She knew he wasn't the type of man to abandon me on the most impor-

310

tant night of my life.

Yet, he had done exactly that.

"No. I guess he wasn't."

CHAPTER FIFTEEN

"When the dance is done, and the gown
and glitter are gone, what is left of you?
Who are you when the clock strikes
midnight?"
— Charlotte Kingsley,
The Cinderella Fiction
(The "Reality Check" Chapter)

When I was finally alone in my apartment, I paced. The evening had been wonderful and magical and *lonely.*

Even with my dad, who hardly ever made his way to New England, even with my mom who'd never before worked to show me actual support in my endeavors, even with my sister and my friends and the crowd of supportive and excited strangers, I had never felt more alone.

And the downstairs neighbor, who would be bothered by my pacing, was the reason for the pacing. I'd texted him three words:

Where are you? but received no response. I called his phone, but it went to voice mail. I considered calling the police, but he was a grown man. A grown man not answering his phone didn't constitute an emergency to anyone except me.

What if something had happened to him?

I stomped down the stairs and to his apartment door, where I thumped on the wood hard enough that Ms. Schofield opened her door as wide as her chain-lock would allow so she could glare at me. He didn't answer. I tried the knob, but, unlike me, Anders always locked his door.

I called the station. He wasn't scheduled and wasn't on call. He'd arranged for this night to be free months earlier, but I still made the call. "Hey, Jazzy," I said as soon as Jasmine answered the phone. "By any chance, did Anders go into the station tonight?" I held my breath. This was the moment between me putting in a call to the police and me spray-painting unkind graffiti on his door.

"Oh, hey, Lettie. Yeah, he's in. He's upstairs. Want to talk to him?"

My heart took a freefall from my chest to my feet, where it shattered. Of course it shattered. What heart could survive a fall of that magnitude? "No. Thanks, Jazzy. I'll talk to him later I'm sure."

I ended the call and considered making a new dent in my wall with the phone, except I was supposed to leave for my book tour in just a few days which meant I didn't have enough time to order a new one. I needed my phone for directions, emails, reservations, and schedules.

I yanked off my heels and threw those at the wall instead.

He hadn't even called? He hadn't even texted?

He hadn't even shown up.

My phone rang in my hand, startling me enough that I let out a scream. I looked down. It was his number. "Too late." I dismissed his call.

He called again. I turned my phone off. Now that he wasn't dead in the gutter, talking to him was the last thing I wanted.

He could talk to my voice mail all night because I was exhausted and needed to sleep.

Except I didn't sleep.

There might have been tears.

There might have been cursing.

There definitely was ice cream.

But no sleep.

I awoke the next morning to the worst headache I'd had in my life.

I rolled over in bed and pulled my phone off the nightstand to check the time. It took several moments to process that my screen was blank even though the phone had been plugged in all night. It wasn't out of battery.

The memory hit me hard in the stomach, an ache that made me curl into myself for protection.

Staying curled into a ball of self-pity wasn't an option. Packing had to be done to prepare for the book tour. I had to pack in a way that prepared me for all events. There would be interviews on TV, on the radio, and in front of groups of people. There would be the actual signings themselves. There would be the dinners and events with a whole list of people, and I wasn't sure what half of them actually did. And then there was the casual time, when I'd be alone and want yoga pants and a sweatshirt.

I'd come a long way from being the woman who had been terrified of going to a work costume party with Anders the year before. Though the thought of all of the social engagements that would be required of me terrified me, I knew that I could get through them. The Char persona so carefully created by Toni had shown me a level of bravery and confidence that hadn't existed in me before.

I stared at my luggage. The packing was important, but not most important. I needed to talk to Anders. I needed to know what went down before I decided to hate him or feel sorry for myself.

What if there was a reasonable explanation?

I unfurled my body but couldn't seem to unfurl the ache. How could there be a reasonable explanation? He hadn't been dead in a gutter, and he'd already taken the day off work. So why was he in the station when I called? No email. No text. No phone call. No actually *being* there.

Stop it! Let him explain!

But . . .

With a grunt of disgust with myself for having such thorough and fully realized two-sided arguments with myself, I stormed downstairs to his apartment.

I thumped his door hard enough to require me to apologize again to Ms. Schofield when she peeked out to see who was making all the noise. She grunted at me, mumbled something about liking us better before we were dating, and closed her door at the same time a bleary-eyed Anders opened his.

"Lettie!" He looked surprised to see me.

316

He then looked down at my clothes and frowned. "When was the last time you left your apartment like that? I almost didn't recognize you without your full wardrobe, hair, and makeup."

I shoved the door so I could enter his apartment and didn't feel bad when the door connected with his bare toes. "So you're not dead, but you're clearly trying to get yourself murdered."

"Are you planning on murdering me or just my toes?" he asked.

His attempt at a joke irritated me. "I just figured that with all the promises you made to be there for me last night, maybe you'd died. It was the only logical explanation, seeing as how you *weren't* there for me. And I needed you, Anders. I really needed you." My voice cracked like ice too thin to hold the weight of my ache.

"I can explain," he said. His hands were up in that placating gesture he did whenever he worried I might throw something at him — which I hardly ever did, so his need for such a gesture was idiotic.

What was I even doing in his apartment demanding an explanation? Shouldn't he have been the one to come to my apartment to give that of his own free will without it needing to be extracted from him?

317

I turned back to his door, rethinking this absurdity of mine when there was packing to be done and running away to be doing. Anders grabbed me around the waist and swung me back to face the inside of his apartment. "I tried to call," he started.

"You did not!" I squirmed out of his grasp and spun to face him. He now held the advantage of standing in front of the door to keep me from leaving. "You didn't call until I called the station."

He closed his eyes briefly. Only in that instant did I realize how tired he looked. Of course, he'd worked a graveyard shift and this was basically his middle of the night, but the way he closed his eyes and dragged a hand over his face made him look tired in his soul.

His demeanor shifted my anger into concern. "Okay, I'm listening. What happened?"

He led me to his couch.

"Doug asked me a long time ago if I would be willing to take his shift when his wife went into labor. I agreed. He's my friend, and it's not like the favor seemed to be that big of a deal. It was a long time ago, before I knew the launch date, but she isn't due for another two weeks, so it wasn't supposed to make a difference regardless."

I didn't interrupt him when he paused.

Listening meant *listening.* If I felt like my heart had been bruised by his absence the night before, he looked like his had been ripped out and flayed open.

"But she went into labor last night. I was texting Kat to explain why I was at work when a call came. I was going to text you right after I texted Kat. But there wasn't time. I figured I could still go to your launch party during my lunch break, but . . ."

I tucked my hand into his.

"She was only thirty-nine." Tears leaked out of his eyes. "What kind of thirty-nine-year-old has a heart attack?"

She *was.* Was.

That meant she hadn't made it.

Anders stared at where our hands connected. "I couldn't . . . I tried. Everything. Her kids were there watching from behind where their dad stood begging for us to fix his wife like I was some miracle man with more than CPR on my side. She was dead when we arrived. We couldn't revive her. I'd just come back when you called. I was trying to decompress for a minute. I'm sorry that in all of that I forgot about the launch, but I did forget. I'm so sorry."

I wrapped my arms around him, feeling the scratchy bristles of new-beard growth against my cheek.

319

He sagged against me and let me hold him for a long time.

His reasons for ditching me were worthy. He murmured a few things in Swedish — always reverting to his childhood language when he hurt. I tightened my grip on him, letting him know that we were okay. Whatever else he had going on inside him, on the outside, I was here for him.

Grief is a poltergeist. It seemed to haunt Anders for the rest of the day and into the next. I knew he was putting on a brave face because I was leaving and would be gone for several weeks, so he tried to keep that poltergeist in his back pocket where I couldn't see it. But Anders wasn't good at hiding things.

Anders needed a pick-me-up to get his mind off the things he couldn't change. And, since I couldn't be with him while he worked, I decided to give what little bit of relief and help that was in my power.

While he was gone, I broke into his apartment via the fire escape between our apartments.

Once inside, I did the kind of deep cleaning for him that I had done for myself when Toni decided to send a camera crew into my apartment. Though Anders was a tidy guy, I'd noticed he'd been letting some

320

things slip as far as organization went lately. Maybe it was because we were dating and his time outside of work was tied up in us, but I didn't think that was it, because we each had down time from one another thanks to all the work I'd had to do for the book. Toni's militant whip-cracking gave him plenty of time off from me. Yet, his apartment was becoming its own ecosystem. And, since his couch was more comfortable than mine, we spent enough time in his apartment to make it a benefit to both of us for me to clean it.

On the wall to the right of his television he'd hung a bunch of pictures he'd taken. Some were of me. Some were of nature. Some were of us. The big one in the middle was a selfie he'd done of us with his nice big camera, which meant our faces took up the whole frame. I stood staring at those photos of us for a while and smiled.

He'd never put up photos of any of his other girlfriends. Not once in all the time I'd been his neighbor had I ever seen a picture of a female in his apartment aside from a few that were his mom and his sister.

What a privilege it was to take up such space on his wall and in his life.

I invaded his laptop and paid for and downloaded a few new albums he'd been wanting but not getting because he was trying to save money. He loved the band Sleepless. They had a good vibe and seemed to make him happy in general. What he could be saving money for that would eclipse his music-purchasing habits eluded me.

Sneaking into his laptop made me glad I kept mine locked. If he'd ever tried to do the same thing, he might see conversations with Toni telling me to hide him away like he was a terrible, shameful secret.

Toni had turned my life into a never-ending game of hide-and-seek. Her emails demanding that I hide this from the world and seek after that so the world would think of me as a leader were becoming exhausting. Anders continuing to tag me in posts had actually led to the outcome Toni predicted. People wanted to know: who was this guy I spent so much time with? They wanted to know if he was my Asgard hero. They wanted to know why my status was declared as single when my face showed up in this random guy's photos. The internet had a way of turning information into the undead. That information made life immortal. People saved screenshots and forwarded those things on and on and on.

The internet was a very untrustworthy friend.

Frowning at those thoughts, I tucked the series of desserts I'd made into his fridge and then made my way to his bathroom, where I turned on the shower and let it run hot enough to steam up his mirror. I wrote the words, "I love you" in the steamy mirror, turned off the shower, and went back to the living room area.

I kissed my finger and placed it over the image of his mouth on the framed selfie of us and then sneaked back out through his window. I laughed to myself as I made my way up the fire escape. And he thought Steve was creepy? I bet Steve never broke into apartments via the fire escape.

At least I hoped not.

I locked my window just in case.

My dad texted to ask if he could take Kat and me out before I left for the book tour. Since time with my father was rare, I agreed immediately, knowing that Anders wouldn't be upset even though it was the night before I left town.

The next morning, my phone had a text that said, "Fire escape?"

I smiled in relief. "If I shouldn't leave my door unlocked, you probably shouldn't leave your window unlocked."

"Sorry I didn't text sooner. I got home late and didn't even bother turning on a light. I fell straight into bed and crashed hard. When I woke up though . . . nice!"

I settled back onto my bed as we texted back and forth, curling into the coziness of my covers and his words. "I promised I'd do it sometime," I texted.

"Sure, but I thought you were kidding."

"Promises are like wishes. Don't make them unless you mean them."

"Do you know what I loved best?"

"The meringue cookies on your counter?" I guessed.

"Those are awesome, but no. My apartment looks great, and the desserts are bestowed upon a grateful belly, but my favorite was finding a secret message on my mirror. Well-played."

"I don't know anything about any message. Maybe you have a ghost in your bathroom."

"How do you know it was the bathroom mirror if you didn't do it?"

"Rats! Caught!"

"Haha. I love you, Lettie. I wish you weren't leaving."

"I love you, too. I wish you were coming with me." I almost typed that I wished I didn't have to go, but that would have been a bald-faced lie. I'd always wanted to go on a book tour. It was the thing people talked about but that most authors didn't get to do because digital tours were more convenient and less expensive for everyone.

Going on a physical book tour, actually having a speaking circuit, filled me with joy.

And terror.

I'd spent weeks preparing my notes and funny anecdotes to share. I'd wanted to try them out on Anders to see what he thought, but with everything going on, we'd had no time. So much of what I'd put into that book had been stolen from parts of him — parts of us. Would a muse recognize the creation he'd inspired? If he heard me talking about the book, would he see the pieces of him layered through each sentence, tucked between each word?

I really hated that he hadn't been with me the night of my launch. I'd wanted him there to hold my hand and celebrate with me. I didn't care that Toni said I should never divulge his existence; I would have announced to everyone at that launch that Anders Nilsson belonged to me.

I understood his reasons for not being there, but I still hated his absence. And I hated that he would be absent from my life for the next several weeks. I wasn't even gone and missed him already. The idea of being without him felt like I'd reached one of those levels of hell Dante talked about. "Let the first of the nine circles of torment begin," I whispered.

With Anders out of sorts, I told him to go to bed early, and I drove to my mom's house to help Kat with her homework.

There's no downside to the opportunity to be a good girlfriend *and* a good sister.

Fortune smiled on me because my mom and Edward were out for the evening. Kat answered the door and yanked me into a hug. "Please say you've come to get me forever."

"Did FedEx deliver a set of new knives today?" I asked when she released me and gave me the most sorrowful gaze any teenager had ever managed.

"Can words be considered knives?"

She followed me into the living room, where I spied her closed laptop, which meant she likely hadn't started writing her book report. "Can FedEx deliver them?"

"Felicity sure can."

So it was Felicity today. "What did she say?"

"Felicity hates my culture." Kat flopped herself down on the couch and groaned.

I sat next to her and pulled her to me. "What happened?"

"I was making *kleicha,* my grandma's

326

recipe, and I'd messed up the kitchen because the almond flour bag failed. I had to use all the almond flour that was left because of all that got spilled, you know?" She sat up, too irritated in telling the story to calmly lean against me. "So Felicity comes in and freaks 'cause the kitchen's a mess and then she freaks again when she sees I used all the almond flour because she was gonna use that for the dinner she was making tonight, and now I ruined all of dinner for the entire world, and blah blah blah why can't I learn to make cupcakes from a box like other kids?"

"Does she even keep boxed cake mixes in the house?"

"No. But she sure got mad when I pointed that out to her."

"Is that all that happened?" I asked.

"They went to dinner because I ruined her meal plans."

"Did you actually make the *kleicha*?"

"Yeah. I mean, why not, right? I already made the mess and was already in trouble."

"Mind sharing?"

She gave me the first real smile of the evening. Without more words, we were up and on the way to the kitchen. While she plated my serving, I took inventory of the mess. It was tough to be torn between wanting to take Kat's side and understanding why my mom blew up. Kat wasn't kidding when she'd said she'd experienced flour-bag malfunctions. A fine powder coated pretty much everything in the kitchen.

I took my date-filled pastry from the plate she handed me and ate with appreciation. I was a sucker for cardamom and cinnamon together.

Then I helped myself to seconds.

She sighed. "I did promise my dad I'd clean the kitchen before anything else." She looked to me as if I'd approve her breaking that promise.

I didn't.

Instead, I helped her clean the kitchen. Kat was great with fashion, and I prayed she'd find success enough to afford a maid, because she hated housecleaning. Together, we made short work of sanitation duty and moved the party back into the living room, where we could work on her book report.

We were almost done when Edward and Mom returned home. Mom went to the kitchen, and I heard an audible sigh of approval. When a text came in on my phone from my mother, I was surprised. Mom didn't send me messages.

"Tell me honestly. Did you clean or did Kat?"

"We both did," I texted.

"Good. As long as she helped."

I stared at my phone in wonder. This was normally a conversation she would insist on having in person so we could bring the contention out into the middle of the room where we would all have to feel it.

"What? Surprised to see me taking lessons on discretion?" she texted.

My head shot up to see that she was watching me watching my screen.

She smirked, nodded once, and went upstairs.

Her last text to me was, "Thank you, Charlotte."

The brief interaction had been enough to later make me feel like I was standing on solid ground when I said "not yet" to Kat asking to move in with me.

Kat harrumphed at me but hugged me good night anyway.

It seemed goodbye was the only thing on the menu of life now that I was counting down to the moment I had to leave for the book tour. I had to say goodbye to my mom and Edward. I had to say goodbye to Kat. I had to say goodbye to my dad, and I had to say goodbye to Anders.

The next evening, when I opened my door, he stood waiting to take me to the station where he worked. They were having a farewell party for one of the guys.

The party was held at the station, where those who were working had already been on several calls: one overdose, one elderly woman not breathing, and two car accidents — one fender bender where the passenger hadn't been wearing a seatbelt and ended up with serious head injuries and one where a guy had been drinking and then walked into oncoming traffic. He was a mess but would probably be okay long-term.

Anders loved the people he worked with. They were his family. But as the night wore on, I noticed he had pulled back from them. He laughed and joined in the conversations, but something was different.

"What's up?" I asked when we had a minute alone.

"Ask me on the way home," he said.

Which made the rest of the evening torture to get through. Was it me? Was it work?

I asked as soon as we were in the car and pulling out of the station.

He licked his lips — a sign I now recognized as Anders making life changes. "I think it's time I change career paths," he said.

Did not see that coming. Even with the lip signal.

"But you love the station and the work you do." He had me all confused. Was it watching one of his coworkers moving on that made him rethink his career?

"True, but the pay isn't great as compensation for the things I have to see in society, and I'm burned out. My ghost card is . . . full."

Anders wasn't talking about a real ghost card, not anything tangible and full of punch holes. It was a tally system he kept in his head of some of the worst things he'd seen as a paramedic. He'd been there a long time, outlasting most of the people he'd worked with.

"So . . . are you going to be a full-time photographer?" I asked.

He smiled. "I'd like that. I'd like it a lot. Maybe. Maybe I'll go back to school and go into a medical field of some type or another — one that doesn't require lifting gurneys with three-hundred-pound men on them. I love the work but not necessarily the *work*."

I nodded. "Whatever you decide to do, Anders, you know you've got my support all the time in every way. You're one of the smartest people I know. Whatever you choose, you'll be great at it."

He checked his mirror and changed lanes. "Thanks, Lettie. That really means a lot, especially since I think I'm going to be pulling a ton of overtime for the next few months so I can save up enough to get me by for several months until I get things settled."

"Overtime?"

"I know. It's not ideal, but it'll be better long-term."

"Sure. Of course. Better." I nodded and tried to sound supportive and enthusiastic, but really, the idea of him doing a ton of overtime just meant I would be doing overtime spending time alone once I returned from the book tour.

Even the thought that I might get some writing done didn't make me feel any better about the time spent together that we'd miss.

Funny how when I had a job, I managed to fit in things like a social life and writing without any issue. Now that I didn't have a job, there didn't seem to be enough time for either — and certainly not both at the same time.

"It'll be good," Anders continued. "To have me away more."

"How could you being away more ever be good? Not that I'm saying you need to not take overtime or anything. It's not your job to entertain me, but I don't want you thinking I want time away from you."

"I don't want time away from you, either. But you've got the tour, and we both know you need to write."

"I'm writing." The defensive words tattled on my lie. How strange that he should echo thoughts that had already crossed my mind.

Or maybe not that strange considering how well Anders knew me.

"You are not," Anders said with a smirk. "And every day you're not writing, a bit more of the woman I love fades. You definitely need some time. Time to create. Time to be who you are with no apologies given — not to Toni, not to your online fan club."

Truth shuddered through me. To create. To be who I am with no apologies given. My head was nodding before I'd fully registered the words in my mind.

I almost asked him about his need to create. If he was doing the amount of heavy overtime he mentioned, when would *he* have time to create? To be who he was with no apologies given?

When we arrived back at our apartment building, he walked me to my front door, where he kissed me good night. Something felt missing in that kiss. Something felt wrong. I brushed off my misgivings as nothing more than my paranoia. Anders said I was fading under the burden of my creative abstinence. He wasn't wrong.

But when he said to be who I was with no apologies given, did he also mean no apologies to him as well? Because, though I didn't love my couch, I loved the coffee table. I didn't love some of the kitschy knickknack-y things on the coffee table that Toni thought made me look interesting and relatable while also being eccentric and mysterious, but the white curtains made my apartment feel breezy and clean. Anders hated everything that had come due to my arrangement with Toni.

Who was I when I was being me with no apology? Was I the heels or the flats? Was I the modern truth writer or the nineteenth-century fairy-tale storyteller?

I didn't know.

Life stayed too busy for me to analyze my feelings enough to find out. The next evening, Dad picked me up first. Before we left my apartment to retrieve Kat, he handed me a string.

"What is this?" I wrinkled my nose in confusion.

"I have a present for you. Follow the string and find the present."

"Dad . . . You don't need to get me a present. You being here is the best gift I could ever get."

"Consider it an early Christmas, since I won't be here for that." He nudged my elbow and nodded his head.

I followed the string, winding it around my elbow and hand the same way I did electrical cords. Anders continually got after me for wrapping cords that way because it wasn't the "right way." It likely bugged him that I didn't change my methods, which was fine, since it bothered me that he failed to accept my methods.

The string went down into the stairwell. "Since I couldn't figure out how to make it work through the elevator," Dad explained. It twined all the way down to the ground floor and down still farther to the underground parking.

It ended at the metal beam above his rental car. From it, hung a key.

I tugged hard enough to pull the key down from the string, then held the key out in my open palm.

"Should I assume this goes to your car?"

He nodded. "Check the trunk."

I slid the key in and opened the trunk with a click, which turned the trunk light on as well. I gasped. "How?" Inside was a signed, numbered Vladimir Kush *Atlas of Wander*. "This had to cost you a fortune!"

The painting had been on my to-buy list as soon as Toni stopped controlling what went on my walls. How many times had she told me that surrealism wasn't relatable to everyday people?

"Do you like it, my little storyteller?"

"Dad . . ." My eyes were leaking. "I love it."

"I thought of you as soon as I saw it."

I hugged him tight. "It's been something I've wanted for a long time. And I thought of you the first time I saw it."

"I guess it was meant to be then." He gave me a teary, sentimental smile.

He helped me take it upstairs and secure it in my apartment before heading back to the car to get on with our night. I almost didn't want to go out anymore — not when I had such a piece of art to inspire me.

Once we pulled up in front of Mom and Edward's house, my dad stayed in the car while I went to the door to fetch Kat. Mom tugged me inside and shut the door at the sight of Dad's running rental at her curbside. She whispered to make sure Kat didn't hear. "Why is he taking your sister, too?" she said.

"Maybe he just wants his daughter and her sister to have a nice time together," I said.

She opened her mouth to respond, but Kat joined us, which flustered my mom and made her drop the argument.

Part of me had wanted the argument to continue because I wanted to know why she hadn't wanted to come to my book launch. I also wanted to know why she had ultimately chosen to show up. I wanted to know why she was being so weird lately. Cross-and-irritating Mom was someone I understood, but this up-and-down woman? I glanced back at the door, wishing there was some way for me to understand her.

"It smells like Halloween out here," Kat said, calling me back to the present.

I smiled and took another deep breath that held the faint smell of a fire burning in a distant fireplace, along with freshly dried leaves that had flown along in the crisp wind that made my breath catch and forced a shiver through me. I even caught the scent of freshly cut pumpkins because Mom's neighbors must have hosted a jack-o'-lantern carving contest, if the variety of orange grins in front of their house was any indicator. We were still early in the season, but there were no rules against carving pumpkins before Halloween. "Yes. It absolutely does."

Anders had asked me about a favorite

sound, but if he had asked about a favorite smell, this would be it. I decided to ask him about his favorite smell when I saw him again.

The evening had been fun, with my sister explaining to my dad all the various ways an oblong strip of cloth could be used to accessorize — or even become — an outfit and with my dad raving about his "famous" daughter and spooning praise and attention over me. I was sad we'd chosen to do a movie rather than hang out and just talk and was even sadder to see the evening come to an end.

The one bright spot in saying goodbye to my father was the realization that money wasn't the obstacle it once had been. Visiting him would not be as difficult.

The one dark spot in saying goodbye to my dad was that I didn't have Anders to mourn his leaving with me.

Because of the way the timing worked, Anders and I wouldn't have any more time together before I returned from the book tour. I knew we wouldn't see each other before my departure, but I thought when he came home from his shift, he would say something — a text, a tap on the ceiling from a broom handle, a *something*. I went to sleep feeling heavy. He'd come home and said nothing?

I stared at my new painting and felt the pull of the boat on the water. Like that boat, I felt like I was sailing off of the dusty pages and into an unknown adventure.

I hated that sometimes I felt like I was sailing alone.

CHAPTER SIXTEEN

"Happily ever after sets up false
expectations. Were they really happy
every minute of every day forever after?
The minute Prince Charming put the toilet
paper roll on backwards or the fair
damsel missed a dinner date, I'm betting
there were shots fired."
— Charlotte Kingsley,
The Cinderella Fiction
(The "Be Present" Chapter)

Book tours, it turns out, are glamorous only
in the imagination. In reality, they were a
lot of nervous energy spent all at once, followed by incredible amounts of exhaustion.
They were a lot of hotel rooms and airports
and rental cars. They were extreme highs of
applause and extreme lows of eating alone
in a hotel restaurant. They were enough to
make me feel off-balance mentally.

It didn't help that Toni played critic to my

every move. She monitored the internet to see how people complained about me and then made certain to point out those complaints so I could "do better next time."

My texts and calls with Anders didn't offer the relief and comfort I had hoped for. While Toni criticized every move I tried to make *without* her guidance, Anders criticized every move I made *with* her guidance. For every "Why didn't you wear what I told you to?" from Toni, there was a "Why are you always wearing what she tells you to?" from Anders. It didn't help matters that Anders had made his social media accounts public again. Toni all but demanded I have him change them back to private. It was difficult to explain that dating someone did not give me license to dictate his life to him.

Going home was a greater relief than I had ever imagined. It meant I could smooth things over with Anders and fix the few pseudo-fights we'd had via text. I hoped it meant I would get a break from my phone pinging and buzzing every time Toni found another string to pull.

My red-eye flight got me home at 5 a.m., so I'd gone straight to bed, happy to pay a sleep tribute to the sandman after the exhausting tour and jet lag.

Waking up at nearly noon to find that

Anders hadn't written me or called me was . . . well, *weird*.

I texted him.

And called him.

And checked the calendar to see what shift he was working, only to find that he was, in fact, home. Or at least he should have been home.

So I thumped down the stairs and knocked on his door. Maybe he'd slept in late as well.

He didn't answer.

I knocked again and checked the door-knob. Locked. "Anders?" I whisper-yelled, which was the same thing as yelling really.

I knocked some more, but he didn't answer. Ms. Schofield opened her door a crack. "Don't the two of you have phones?"

I went home and texted again. He didn't respond the entire day.

I didn't want to do what I'd done before and call around to places where he might be to see if anyone had seen him. That had caused me enough trouble to last a lifetime.

As the evening and the path on my floor wore on, I gave up and used the fire escape to enter his apartment and search for any clues of foul play. It was dark out, making the fire escape a bad choice for my point of entry.

Once inside his apartment, I flipped on

342

the light. No signs of a struggle seemed readily apparent. Everything was perfectly clean, even though it had been a few weeks since I'd done maid service for him. He'd done a good job of maintaining my hard work. And everything was in its place.

Everything . . . except the pictures of us and the pictures of me that had hung on the wall. The only evidence of pictures having once hung on the walls were the little brass nails.

Anders had taken my pictures down? Our pictures down?

I tried not to let that panic me. Sure, he'd been judgy of the things I'd worn lately. Sure, he'd made fun of my couch from the first moment he'd sat on it. Sure, he'd scoffed at the eyelash extensions that had happened on the third day of my tour and the hair tinting that had taken my hair from its natural red to a more subtle auburn on the fifth day.

But none of that merited removing my pictures from his wall.

Did it?

"Anders? What is your deal? Where are you?" I said to the empty apartment.

Imagine my surprise when the empty apartment answered me.

"He's at work."

I whirled on the voice in the doorway. Sadly, my arms and hands had a habit of going out in front of me karate-chop style whenever I was caught unawares. When I saw the thin blonde standing still and staring at me with something that could be called less than enthusiasm, I tried to nonchalantly lower my hands in the hopes she hadn't noticed how my fight-or-flight response had gone all Mortal Kombat. I swallowed down my alarm enough to say, "Who are you?"

She raised her left eyebrow in a delicate arch over her eye. Her features were all like that: delicate and perfectly positioned. She looked like a female version of —

I blinked.

And stared harder at her — if such a thing was possible. She looked like Anders, which had to mean . . . "You must be Magdalena," I said, since she hadn't answered my question.

She didn't relax, even though I'd managed to reveal her name, which should have put her at ease that I wasn't doing anything wrong by being in his apartment — because if I knew him well enough to know her identity, didn't that put me on the safe list?

"I'm Let —"

"I know who you are." She straightened

344

from where she'd stood in the doorway —
clearly a family-favorite position. Anders
seemed to always be standing exactly like
that.

With introductions off the table, and
because I didn't know what else to do with
myself, I said, "Anders didn't mention having to work tonight." It hurt that he had
gone to work when he'd known my flight
brought me home today, but I tried not to
let the hurt seep into my words.

"One of his coworkers needed someone to
cover for them."

"Oh."

Well, that topic ran out of conversational
steam fast. She said nothing else for several
long moments. I considered asking her
where she'd come from, since the open door
indicated she was just entering the apartment, but decided it wasn't my place to ask.

She stared at me while I nervously worked
to look at anything but her. A roll-away bed
was made up and settled over by the window. I should have noted that detail right
off upon entering.

"Anders told me you were coming," I
started again.

"Yes."

"How long have you been in town?" I
asked.

"I got in this morning. I'll be leaving in a week or so to go to Sweden to take over for my parents. They're there now, caring for my grandfather."

"Right. Anders told me."

"I know. It seems he's got you in the middle of everything."

What did that mean?

"Sorry," she said, finally taking note of my discomfort and confusion. "I'm tired and not feeling well. I don't mean to be hostile."

Wanting his sister to like me, and feeling emboldened by her apology, I asked, "Have you eaten dinner yet? Because I haven't. If Anders has already gone to work, and if you have nowhere to be, you're welcome to come upstairs and join me for dinner."

She hesitated, which meant she hadn't eaten and was, in fact, hungry. The hesitation also meant she wasn't all too sure about going upstairs to my apartment.

"I'm a good cook," I said.

"So Anders tells me." She considered a long time more before she said, "Thank you. I'd be happy to join you, if you're sure you don't mind. Anders told me to order takeout, but I'm not really an eat-out kind of person. I'd just gone outside to see if there was anything close by, but . . ."

Right. Picky eater. Anders had told me

about that. Maybe inviting her over for food wasn't a good idea. But the offer was already out there. Plus, I'd already promised Anders I'd help him keep her fed.

So I left his apartment, and waited a moment while she turned off the lights. In a last-moment decision, I went back into the apartment and locked his living room window. I don't know why the idea of her sleeping by that window made me worry about leaving it unlocked, especially when I was the only one who ever used that particular entrance and his sister could clearly take care of herself, but locking it gave me some measure of relief.

"Thanks," she said. "Anders must have told you that it makes me nervous to be alone at night."

I shook my head and led her to the stairwell. "Actually, he never mentioned it. I just thought you might not like having that unlocked when you're in a new neighborhood — not that the neighborhood isn't safe; it's totally safe." My dad had actually checked on that when I was looking for a place to live. He'd given me a list of neighborhoods I was allowed to live in with his blessing, due to their low crime rates. He'd also given me a list of neighborhoods that I was never, under any circumstances, allowed to move to no matter how desperate I was to be out on my own.

Dad didn't communicate much, but when he did, that communication was full to the brim with love.

Up in my apartment, I decided to get honest about food. If she was picky, then knowing what she liked and didn't like would be half the battle in winning her over with flavor.

When she let me know she was vegetarian, I did an inward eye roll at Anders. Vegetarian didn't make her picky; it just meant she had dietary restrictions. Easy enough. I had good ingredients, thanks to a shopping trip I'd made earlier that day, and so I made the honeydew melon shrimp dish that I made for Anders on occasion, only for her I left out the shrimp. I also sautéed peppers, carrots, snow peas, and onions for a quick stir-fry to put over jasmine rice.

With the warming of my stove top, Magdalena had warmed to me. The prickly beginning had become a distant memory. It amazed me how food brought people together, how a cozy table and steaming plates forced communication — at least when electronics didn't get in the way.

I learned a lot about my guest in the course of eating. She loved living in Canada because the weather was so similar to her growing-up years in Sweden. She liked her job as a veterinarian . . . at least most of the time. She loved the pets but didn't always love the owners. She missed her parents and had no idea how they ever ended up in Texas, of all places, where it was hot and humid and nothing like home at all. She loved her grandfather as much as Anders did. And she loved Anders.

After only an hour and a half with the woman, the most important thing I had discovered about her was that she would do anything for her brother.

With the meal all eaten, Magdalena sighed. "I guess I should help you clean up and then get out of your hair. It was really generous of you to invite me over. I can see why my brother cares about you."

She had a slight accent — enough of one to tell that she wasn't from the United States, but not enough of one to reveal her origins. Anders had no accent at all, at least not when he was speaking English.

When he spoke Swedish — which I loved, but he didn't do very often — the accent became evident.

"How long are you in town for, again?" I asked as we worked on setting the kitchen back in order.

"A week. My husband had to work out of town for a while, so I came here. I hate being left home alone, and my clinic is doing well enough to hire a new doctor, so it worked out. My husband will join me when I leave for Sweden to help *Farfar*. It's a good time to visit, and I really miss him. It's been too long. I don't get back as often as Anders does. Things always seem to get in the way."

"Life is like that. We're all like that."

"Not Anders." She gave an indulgent smile, as if he were there to see it. Then she sighed and looked toward my door as if it had done something to personally offend her. "I should get going. It's late, and I keep trespassing on your hospitality."

"You know," I said, "Anders doesn't usually get in until early in the morning, which means when he comes in, he'll likely wake you up. And then when you *want* to be awake a few hours later, he'll need to be sleeping still, so you'll have to be totally silent or risk waking him up. Why don't you just spend the night here? That way, you don't have to worry about him, and he won't have to worry about you."

"Is it that obvious?"

"What?" I knew what she meant but pretended I didn't.

"You're just trying to make me feel better

350

about being afraid to be alone at night."

"There's nothing wrong with not wanting to be alone at night."

She pointed a dishcloth at me. "You say that, but you live alone. This is not something that bothers you."

"Just because it doesn't bother me doesn't mean it shouldn't bother you. We all have our vulnerable places. Mine are just different from yours."

Magdalena let out a laugh. "It's kind of ridiculous, though, isn't it? That I should worry, I mean. I'm thirty-three and still afraid of the dark."

I laughed too, glad that she was warming up to me. If people can share their fears, then they can be friends. It mattered to me that Magdalena and I became friends. "Being afraid of the dark isn't an age issue. It's a dark issue."

She laughed again while wiping out the sink. "How so?"

"Things can hide in the dark no matter how old you are. It's not like we get better night vision as we age, right? If anything, our vision gets worse and more things can hide. We're always afraid of what we don't know."

"You make a good case for me." She rinsed and folded the dishcloth, then left it

351

on the sink's edge and turned to face me directly. "Thank you. I would like to stay here. I will sleep much better."

"Good. I'll send Anders a text letting him know, so he doesn't panic when he gets home. Let's go get your stuff."

She ended up sleeping on the couch, even though I offered her my room. She said if I got stubborn about it, she'd just go sleep downstairs. I let her win because I believed she meant it. We didn't stay up late into the night talking like old pals or anything, but our rather chilly first meeting had warmed considerably.

Anders had returned my text with gratitude and promises to make it up to me, although there was nothing to make up. I enjoyed my time with his sister.

I enjoyed more the fact that Anders returned my text.

I didn't goad him about responding only after basically being told that I'd kidnapped his sister. He probably had good reasons for not texting earlier — like being out on a call — that he'd explain later. For me to get all paranoid and weird on him would be . . . well, paranoid and weird. Even Chloe the ex-not-really-fiancée hadn't ever been paranoid — otherwise she would have put her foot down about his having me for a best friend. The fact that she didn't mind our unique friendship had been a likable trait in her.

Or maybe she did mind and just never said anything.

Magdalena woke up later than I did and stayed at my apartment until Anders called her to find out if I really had kidnapped her. Hanging out likely entertained me more than her. Since she knew I enjoyed cooking, she gave me a few Swedish recipes to try. She also told me fun stories about Anders growing up: how quickly he trusted and how easy it was for her to trick him and how she felt only slightly guilty about that now.

Anders finally had to come up to get his sister, since she didn't go down immediately when he called. The way she acted when he did show up — like she was trying to prove to him that she and I were friends — made it seem that she'd made him come get her on purpose. She wanted to force us into the same space together at the same time.

She even forced physical contact between us by chiding her brother, saying, "Seriously, Anders? You're not even going to give your girlfriend a farewell hug or kiss or anything? I promise not to be scandalized if you do."

"Mags," he said, with what seemed like an edge of warning.

"Don't be so boring, Anders. Kiss your girlfriend goodbye, or I'm not leaving."

He did kiss me then and hugged me, too. Though it started out stiff and almost grudging, he softened into the embrace almost immediately.

"He's like that," Magdalena said with a laugh as she stood outside my door waiting for him. "He would get so irritated with me that he'd refuse to talk to me, but then Mom would make us hug. Turns out Anders is incapable of being irritated for very long. As long as you can make him pretend to play nice, he's all in after that."

I tried to look him in the eye to see if he could clue me in as to what she was talking about, but he turned away too quickly. Irritated over what?

They left. But not long after, an unknown number texted me telling me to save the number in my phone and claiming to be Magdalena. She then invited me to go sightseeing with them.

Part of me wanted to decline. After all . . . Anders hadn't been the one to extend the invitation. But I also didn't want to decline, because I liked Magdalena and because I wanted to see Anders.

I accepted. The things I wanted outweighed the things I feared. Wasn't overcoming your fears, to get what you wanted most, what I tried to teach in my book?

We wandered the city of Boston, through the Common and to several of the sites on the Freedom Trail. Anders and Mags — which I learned she preferred to be called — loved mentioning that Leif Erikson was actually the first European to walk on American soil.

That evening, I fixed us a dinner that catered to all taste buds involved, and Mags declared me the best find in all of Boston. They left right after cleaning up, because they had family things to discuss.

Pretty much every day for the next few days followed a similar pattern. If Anders worked at night, Mags spent the night on my couch. She didn't even complain that the couch was the most uncomfortable thing ever created. When Anders woke up, we all went out to explore the city — which was fun because . . . my city. I loved my city. Taking Mags around to see the historical sites and the Freedom Trail reminded me of all the reasons I loved my city *and* my country.

Anders teased me for getting choked up and actually shedding tears at a few of the places. He would whisper in my ear, "These may be your Founding Fathers, but Leif Erikson was the true discoverer."

I'd shove him away when he said such things, and Mags would laugh.

Her time with us, or my time with them, depending on how I looked at it, had become something I looked forward to each day.

Close to the end of her stay, Mags thanked me for feeding her so often, since she'd likely have starved under what she called Anders's limited take-out abilities. I defended him, because his ordering takeout had saved my own life on so many occasions.

"Can I ask you something? You don't have to answer if you don't want to, but . . . why did you not like me when we first met?"

Mags opened her mouth in what was sure to be a denial, but then she shrugged. "Anders had been showing me your posts online that morning. A lot of the comments on them had questions regarding him and the pictures you're in with him. We read them. You evaded most of the questions, but in one of them, you flat-out denied dating anyone. You called him an acquaintance — said he was nothing all that important to you. It hurt him. What hurts him hurts me."

I swallowed the guilt and hated the acrid aftertaste it left in my mouth. I remembered that particular response. I'd written it late one night, when my brain could barely focus on my screen. I remembered wanting everyone and their questions to just go away so I could sleep, but I knew that Toni expected me to be engaged with my fans.

Anders had seen it.

It had never occurred to me that he might read through the comments — especially when there were dozens and sometimes hundreds of them.

Magdalena didn't seem to be censuring me. I'd asked an honest question, and she'd given the honest answer.

"I don't have an excuse," I started to say.

She put her hand out and shook her head. "And I don't need to hear an excuse. This isn't about me — as much as I like everything to be about me. This is about the two of you and should be discussed between the two of you."

"What changed your mind about me?"

"You offered to make me dinner." She laughed and shook her head. "Okay, no. That isn't what changed my mind. You just seemed like you cared too much about him to mean what you'd said online. Anyway, I know you have things to talk about with him, but I need to steal Anders completely for the next day and a half. We still have schedule stuff we need to work out. Is that okay with you?"

"Totally okay," I said, and found that it really was. I needed some time to work through what to say to Anders, and the need to write gnawed at my insides like a dog with a bone. I hadn't made the time, the priority, or the effort to put new words to the page. With the book launched and the tour complete, it was time to get writing.

I sat on the couch, opened the laptop, stretched my fingers in preparation, and . . . went online to read reviews of my book instead.

Seriously. I hated my lack of self-control.

The praise for the book was overwhelming. I read the words that others used to describe *my* words. Life-changing. Game changer. Empowering. Charming. Hilarious. Healing. Honest.

I felt guilty because of the honest part.

Honest.

Anders couldn't think of me as honest, since I'd lied about my relationship with him. The guilt drove me away from the review sites and to my online writing groups, with the hope that someone there would be able to inspire me to stop dwelling on the book that was out and start focusing on something new — something my agent could sell.

I opened Facebook and found one of my favorite sprint partners. I private-messaged her. "Hey Jade. Working on anything new lately?" I typed.

"Lettie! Girl, where have you been?!?! Heidi and I were just talking about how you're never online anymore! Well, you're online but not available to chat like you used to be."

"Things have been busy lately, with everything. What's new with you?"

I'd avoided them because it had felt awkward after my career took such a huge leap forward. They'd made some comments that felt like veiled insults.

"I finished a new manuscript and am getting it ready to submit. Hey! Would you mind if I used you as a reference with your agent?"

"Not at all. Use me in whatever way you can. I was wondering . . . want to do a sprint? I really need to exercise my writing muscles."

"I'd love to! And what's up? Why has it been so long since you took your writer brain out for a walk?"

I lightly tapped on the keys but not hard

enough to actually press any of them.

How to explain why I'd gone MIA.

"Long story short — just having trouble figuring out what to write next. Kind of in a weird place."

I'd opened a blank Word document, ready to get to the sprint, when Jade's next message popped up.

"Really? Aren't you the poster child for motivation nowadays? How would it look to your public if they knew you were having trouble doing the one thing you profess to love so much?"

My fingers froze on the keys. Admitting that I lacked in any way, on a digital platform that could be captured with a screenshot and sent out to the world, was not anywhere on any of Toni's lists.

But Jade's words had been sarcastic, right? It was hard to tell. The little dots indicated she was typing. I always found it maddening to know someone was typing when I couldn't see their words. I hoped there would be something friendlier in her next message. Finally, the response popped up. "Or maybe the weird place is trying to figure out what to do with your dragon's horde of advance money, since you got lucky and are now too famous for the rest of us."

The smile that had found its way to my face at the beginning of our conversation sank. What she said was fine. But the bite to it was hard to ignore.

"So sprint?" The chime announcing that a new message had popped up startled me.

"Sure," I wrote back.

"Go . . . now!" she wrote.

But I didn't go.

No words. Only worries filled the time between Jade saying go and, twenty minutes later, when she wrote, "Stop!"

"How many for you?" she asked.

I made up a number, one that would seem like I had tried but that would guarantee I lost the sprint race. Knowing how fast Jade typed and what her averages were helped me make a good guess.

"Thanks!" she wrote. "I needed that! So what book are you working on?"

I made up something. That was my job, wasn't it? We chatted for a while longer about her newest work in progress before we finally signed off.

She ended with, "Be sure to tell your agent about me!"

"Right. Sure thing."

I shut my laptop lid.

When I saw Anders next, his shoulders

slumped in rounded mounds I didn't understand. His voice carried a hint of despondency and resignation. He'd taken a small break from overtime while his sister was in town, but with her gone, he was now buckling down and getting to work.

When he'd told me he was taking all the extra overtime, I hadn't realized how much extra he would be taking. He would basically be living at the station.

But it would only be for another month, and then he would quit so he could get his life together and regroup. And sure, regrouping would take time, but not anywhere near the same amount of time as this new work schedule.

"My sister's having a baby," he announced when we'd settled at the table to eat.

"Wow!" I just about dropped my fork with that news. "That's amazing! I wish I'd known so I could have told her congratulations."

He lightened with this bit of news-sharing. "She's going to be a great mom."

"She really will. Some people are meant for that sort of thing. And then there's . . ." I didn't finish the sentence in a way I normally would have. I normally would have made a declaration about not seeing myself in his sister's situation. I would have made a comment about it being impossible to imagine being a mother when I'd never had an example of what being a good mother looked like.

Anders had heard it all before: all the reasons why getting married and having a family were for other people but not for me. My time with him in a dating relationship had me imagining something else.

Anders likely wouldn't have thought anything about me tallying all the reasons regular family life would not be mine, but he noticed the trailing off. He noticed the absence of my no-family-life-for-me rant.

He made it obvious that he'd noticed by the way he smirked at me. "And then there's . . . ?"

I looked down at my food and busied myself with stabbing vegetables and placing them into my tortilla. "Then there's people like my mom." I groaned. "Do you want to know what's weird though?"

"I would love to hear what's weird."

I put my fork down again. "My relationship with my mom is the definition of toxic. She never approves of me. She hates the whimsical, light-hearted, and fun —"

"And therefore hates everything you love," he said.

"Right. But she raised me. And I don't

363

think I turned out that bad."

"I don't think you turned out that bad, either, but we're not really talking about that, are we?"

"Kat called again. She wants to move in with me." She'd actually called twice more regarding it. I'd kept making the joke about them investing in cutlery and guns, but the joke had worn thin. Kat wanted a real answer. My mother was getting more invasive in Kat's life. She kept laying down rules Kat didn't like. I would have said yes. I meant to say yes every time. But I never actually got the word to pass over my lips.

"And you're worried that if you do things differently from the way your mother raised you, you might mess her up."

"I'd accuse you of reading my journal when you come up with responses that seem like you're mind reading, except I don't keep a journal."

Anders did his slow smile — the one that said he knew he was clever. "That settles it, then. I must be a mind reader."

When I didn't laugh, he put his hand over mine.

"Lettie, you would not destroy Kat's prospects for a bright future."

"Mom's changing though." I sucked in a sharp breath. Had the day come when I actually defended my mother? "I think Kat's okay there. I think she's helping Mom to change. And Mom's rules aren't necessarily bad. Not liking rules isn't the same thing as the rules being unreasonable, right?"

"That's an interesting viewpoint," he said. "A little change and a little rule-keeping is good for all of us. As long as the change doesn't make us lose sight of who we are."

We weren't talking about my mom any longer.

Later, as he was leaving, he said, "Write something for you, Lettie. Something with a dark forest and a fierce main character. Write the *you* I know you are."

"Don't I always?"

He didn't answer but kissed me instead. There was something missing in that kiss as well. But there was also something added. The kiss held hope.

"Is something wrong?" I asked when he broke away.

"I don't think so. I think things will get better."

When I scowled at him, he smirked back at me. "Everything's okay, Lettie."

But he was wrong.

I tried doing what he told me, but the next morning, as I sat at my computer to write, an email popped up from Jen. I clicked the email open and began reading.

It was a rejection letter from a publisher. In the email, Jen apologized. She'd been holding out hope that *this one* would be an acceptance.

This one.

Meaning she'd received other rejections. Further down in the email, she confirmed that the manuscript had now been rejected by all the publishers she'd sent it to, and she'd sent the manuscript to all the first-tier publishers. All of them. And they had all turned it down. "I didn't want to distract you with the rejections," she'd written.

"That said," she wrote, "Melissa said they would love a sequel to *The Cinderella Fiction*. I think that would be a good opportunity for you to get some more writing experience in. After that, let's discuss something new for you to work on — something we can use to wow and woo publishers. I fear your other manuscripts that I've seen are too similar to the one on submission. Let's go in a different direction. Call me if you have any questions. Melissa would love an answer on the new book as soon as you can."

Ache.

They wanted another book.

Pain.

They just didn't want the "another book" that I wanted to write.

After the success I'd received, was it possible to get another rejection?

I didn't call Jen. I called Lillian. She answered on the second ring and listened while I wailed out the entire story to her.

"So what are you going to do?" she asked once I'd emptied myself of all my complaints.

I didn't answer right away. "I'm going to write the second book. I mean what choice do I have?"

"You could tell them no."

I grabbed a fistful of my hair and groaned. "I can't though, can I? The public loves it. The reviews have been nothing short of miraculous. I mean . . . I know you're used to that sort of thing, but it's all new to me and —"

"You've decided to stick with the safe bet," she interrupted.

"Should I tell them no?" I asked.

She didn't answer right away. "Lettie, I want you to tell them whatever it is that you want. If another nonfiction is the direction you want to go, then go. If you want to write something else, do that. You are financially independent now. You can choose the direction you go without anyone else pointing the way. And whatever you choose — if it's what you want — then it won't be wrong."

She moved the discussion to safer paths, discussing possible plans for the holidays, and her children and how grateful she was that they were holding down the fort while she was away on her own tour. She planned on going to her mother's house in New Hampshire for both Thanksgiving and Christmas. Her mom and sister would be doing all the food, since Lillian had been on book tour and they didn't want to burden her with more work. When she asked what I was doing, I stammered over a noncommittal answer that hopefully sounded more committed than it did pathetic.

We hung up.

I didn't write.

Not anything new for my own pleasure, and not a sequel that the publisher wanted either.

I scrolled through social media posts instead. I answered questions, made bright and witty comments, and updated my personal pages with new photos from the tour and snippets of reviews that had come in while I'd been away.

I scrolled down my own page and considered the girl in the photos, who had been so carefully manicured to be flawed in a way that the public could accept and love and admire but who wasn't accurate.

I scrolled and wished Anders was home. And wondered what I would say to him if he were.

Chapter Seventeen

"Shoes are not the answer. Remember
that Cinderella's sisters cut off toes and
heels for a shoe, and Cinderella likely
had to go to physical therapy for the back
damage caused from dancing on
high-heeled glass for a night. Shoes are
not the answer when you own a perfectly
comfortable pair of socks."
— Charlotte Kingsley,
The Cinderella Fiction
(The "Live in Your Own Skin" Chapter)

Anders worked all the time. When we were
together, there never seemed to be the right
moment to bring up the comments he'd
read with his sister, when I'd declared him
to be nothing all that important in my life.
Since he hadn't yet brought it up, I didn't
really want to. Maybe he'd forgotten already,
and bringing it up would just make things
harder for both of us. After a week of being

continually pathetic, I did what Anders would want me to do, and what I needed to do, and sat down to start writing.

The sequel Melissa had requested won out. Because what if they didn't want it later? What if right now was all I had? Though the writing this time went more slowly and felt more painful, the first chapter was pretty well hammered out by Thanksgiving.

Anders had signed on for working the Thanksgiving holiday, since the pay was double rather than just time and a half. I went to my mom's house for dinner. Not because my mom called and asked. Not because Edward called and tried to guilt me into it. But because Kat texted one word: please.

The problem with holiday dinners was that they included all the family: my mother's hypercompetitive sister showed up with her new plastic-surgeon husband, and Mom's hypersensitive brother showed up with his dog.

My mom hated dogs.

On Edward's side, his mother and her friend — that Kat referred to as a geriatric male escort — came late, which ticked my mom off, since we all had to wait on dinner until they arrived. And nothing ruined

Thanksgiving for my mom faster than the food not being served at exactly the right temperature.

The mixed company made for an eventful evening of barking, glaring, and one-upping.

I didn't mind. Not really. It was nice to have the dog, the new husband, and the geriatric male escort serve as distractions for the other guests so they didn't ask me questions about my life.

At least it was all fine until they *did* start asking me questions about my life.

It happened all at once. One minute, I was eating a second helping of candied yams because, really, my mom might've had her flaws, but her cooking wasn't one of them, and the next minute, a seemingly choreographed mass-ganging-up-on-Lettie-and-her-newfound-if-underserved-fame rose up from the crowd.

Mom loved my newfound fame; it helped her one-up her sister, whose only child was currently serving time for grand theft auto, and it gave her something to recommend to her hypersensitive brother, who needed a good self-help book. Even the geriatric male escort couldn't look down his crooked nose at me.

It fascinated me how some people wanted to hear all about my writing and others

372

wanted to know nothing. I'd discovered that a lot of it had to do with other people's insecurities. The less secure they were, the less they wanted to hear about success belonging to anyone else.

They did want to know about my romantic life, which I refused to discuss. Kat and Mom, taking the cue from my lead, also remained quiet on that subject, which led the others to decide that our silence meant there was no romantic life to speak of. More tongue-clucking and head-shaking.

"Do you know what you really need?" my mom's hypercompetitive sister asked.

"A muzzle for all of you," Kat whispered so only I could hear.

Instead of laughing, I let out a strangled snort. "And what's that, Aunt Gwen?"

"You need to settle down with a nice boy and forget all this competing-in-a-man's-world nonsense."

This comment was the perfect opening for my feminist mom and my Stone Age aunt to go to war.

I escaped to the kitchen to start dishes. Kat joined me. "When I see your mother's family, I feel sorry for her," Kat said.

"Yeah. Me too."

I drove home feeling displaced and uncertain as to why.

I called my dad to wish him a happy Thanksgiving and to hear him say, "With a name like Charlotte Kingsley, you must be royalty."

When I told him about the book situation, he said, "My dear Lettie, I'm sorry they don't see you for who you are."

A tear rolled silently down my cheek, and I was grateful to be inside where it couldn't freeze there. "And who am I, Dad?"

"You're the storyteller, Lettie. You're the little girl who saw whole universes in a single canvas. Don't let these people tell you who you are. You show them who you are."

It was enough to get me through the night and then the weekend.

I had a single night with Anders the following week that filled my emotional well for a while longer. He was tired from all the work he'd done, and he'd been witness to enough sad tales of holidays gone wrong from the paramedic point of view that I didn't bother him about my family craziness or even the book situation. My troubles looked pretty silly through the lens of someone who'd seen people die. Instead, I gave him a foot massage and a bag of grapes wrapped in palm fronds as a joke. He laughed and gratefully accepted the foot massage and then gave me one in return. Had he ever looked so haggard? Had his shoulders ever been so slack with exhaustion?

I knew it was more than just work. Other thoughts seemed to weigh him down from the inside. I thought about ways to cheer him up. The past couple of years, we'd picked out our Christmas trees together and then helped each other decorate, but when I brought up the idea of continuing the tradition, he said, "I'm so tired, Lettie. When I come home next, we can, okay?"

"Sure. Of course."

Jen called me the following Monday. "Congratulations!" she said.

"On what?" I asked.

"Well, it was announced that *The Cinderella Fiction* will be given the Literature for Society award due to its 'calling society to action for self-improvement.' "

The words all sounded nice, but I hadn't ever heard of such an award. "I don't know what that means," I admitted.

"It means that on December 27th, there will be an awards gala where we get all beautiful in fancy dresses and the press will be there and the dinner will be subpar, like those sorts of dinners usually are, but the sales of your book will be guaranteed to double."

"Double?" That was a sobering thought, since sales had already surpassed projections. *Double.* Double meant a lot of money for me, for her, for every one of us involved.

But it also meant more readers. It meant my words mattered. Since I was still licking my wounds from hearing that publishers had passed on my fairy tales, I needed that validation.

"Double," she confirmed. "Honey, you knocked this one right out of the park."

"Wow!" I said. "What will you wear to the gala?"

She laughed. "You mean what will *we* wear."

"I get to go?" My heart stuttered in my chest. Another author bucket list item. Check.

"Of course you're going!"

I hung up the phone and let my fingers hover over Anders's name. Every time something wonderful happened, he was the first person on my list to tell.

"I love you, Anders," I texted him. In between those words were all the other ones, the ones of me missing him and wishing we could go back to the days when he didn't look like he carried a mountain on his shoulders.

"I love you, too, Lettie." His immediate

text back startled me.

"When is the last day of extreme overtime sports?"

"Soon. And . . ."

Nothing followed that, so I typed, "And?"

"And I need to talk to you about things."

"If you're dumping me, I don't accept."

"Haha. Not anything like that."

I leaned back into my couch and tucked my legs underneath me. "Oh good. When do you want to get together?"

"Tomorrow night. I'll have the evening off. I'll come to you."

"Sweet. I'll see you tomorrow then."

An award and a night with the one person I wanted to celebrate with.

The next morning, I went shopping for my dress to the gala. Yes, there was time until the event, but what was the point in waiting? I'd never experienced great luck in finding clothing that worked well with my fire-red hair and pale skin, so it made sense that I could spend every day until the night of the gala searching and still not be able to find anything suitable for the event.

The Christmas season had come to Boston while I hadn't been paying attention. The world was decked out in evergreen and red bows. The smell of spiced cinnamon escaped from the doorways of expensive boutique stores, and holiday shopping was in full swing.

Where had I been when all this holiday cheer kicked off?

My bad luck in matching clothing to my hair meant it legitimately shocked me when, at the third store, I found a gown that I loved.

The cold-shoulder cutouts in the sleeves of the silver gown and the way it draped, cascaded, and shimmered as the fabric moved over my fingers compelled me to the dressing room. When the zipper was at the top and I turned to face myself in the mirror, my mouth fell open.

I looked like, well . . . like someone worth knowing.

I couldn't say for sure how long I stared at myself in that mirror, but it felt like I'd given Narcissus some stiff competition. Shopping without looking at price tags was not something my muscle memory allowed, so I almost swallowed my tongue when I saw the numbers on the price tag, but I removed the guilt by repeating "double the sales" over and over in my head as I laid my credit card on the counter. I think Toni would have handed me a diploma and shed a tear for me finally graduating into the sort of person she'd been trying to create online.

An hour later, I had a dress in a fancy dress bag that could only come from a store that charged too much for their gowns, and a pair of silver heels that Cinderella would have called magical. When I made it into my apartment building with my packages, Shannon glared at me, and I glared back, as was our typical greeting of one another.

It bothered me that Shannon had Christmas carols playing in her office, their tones trailing out into the hall. She wasn't ignoring the holiday that celebrated peace on earth and good will toward man. What did that mean about which one of us was the monster in our relationship?

In my apartment, I called up The Thai Guy to order food. It had been a long time since we'd eaten takeout, and Anders was sure to be hungry and very likely to be too tired to go out. Pravat himself answered. When I said hello and started to make an order, he said, "Look who finally calls? I about thought you'd broken another phone and a laptop, too, because I never hear from you anymore."

"Hi, Pravat. Sorry. I've had a lot of free time so I've been indulging in doing my own cooking."

"I don't approve of such indulgences."

I laughed. Pravat was a good guy. "How's

379

the head injury?" I asked.

He laughed, too. "Your boyfriend does good work. I didn't even look like Frankenstein's monster after all those stitches."

We joked around some more before I gave my order and hung up.

Still thinking about Shannon and her carols, I decided my apartment could use some kind of Christmas cheer. Anders likely had decorations at the station, and so he wasn't thinking about his own personal space. It was weird that the holiday had so far escaped me without him there to keep the celebration in it.

I tugged a box off the top nearly impossible-to-reach shelf of my bathroom closet and opened it, trying to not breathe in the dust that flipped up off the cardboard closures. A small, pre-decorated tabletop tree from my college days took up the bulk of the room in the box. It had been a gift from my dad. The ornaments were miniature fable and fairy-tale creatures along with tiny crowns, glass slippers, wands, and red apples.

I streamed some Christmas carols and sang along with them while I straightened all the branches, placed the tree on the end table next to the couch, and then crawled behind the couch to plug it in. The miniature white fairy lights still worked. The first Christmas miracle of the season!

Or maybe the second if I counted finding the dress on the first day of searching, which I did.

Not too long after that, Anders showed up. He had the Thai Guy delivery bags in hand. "You'll never guess who I ran into on my way into the building."

"Shannon?" I asked.

"Well, her too." He grinned at the bags in his hand. "I guess this means you had a good writing day?"

My mind drew a blank before I said, "Oh. Yes. Writing day. It was a good day for this writer; that is for certain."

He put the bags down and folded me up in his arms. "I am so glad, Lettie. I've been so worried about you."

I breathed him in and melted against him. "Worried? Why?"

He laughed. "I don't know. You're just so much happier when you're writing. Lately, you . . . well, you don't act happy."

"Huh. Are you trying to tell me I've been moody?"

"How about unpredictable?" he asked.

I snorted at that and wriggled out of his arms.

"Okay, you don't like that one? How

about . . . I can smell the Jekyll and Hyde on you."

I gave him my best flat-eyed stare. "I'm about to donate your dinner to Shannon."

He put his hands up. "I kid! I kid!"

I almost kidded him back about his own moodiness but decided not to go there. His moodiness felt more like that of a sleeping bear. Poking that bear could end up with me losing a limb.

"I've missed you," I said. "Enough that your dinner is safe from Shannon's evil clutches." I picked up the bags and carried them to the kitchen.

Anders followed me, before he slowed his step and stopped altogether. "You didn't get a tree," he said.

I set the bags on the counter and returned to him to survey my living room. The little tree on the end table wasn't much. "It's no fun to do those traditions by myself. I figured I'd wait for you to have time." We'd always picked out potted trees to decorate for the season and then donate to be planted. It was our way of helping to make peace on earth and good will to man.

He tensed so slightly that someone who was not schooled in the every-movement-of-Anders would have never noticed it.

I noticed.

"What?" I asked.

He licked his lips. "Let's maybe sit on the couch for a minute."

"Okay." I wanted to throw out a sarcastic comment, something silly to lighten the mood, but my brain could only think of the way he'd licked his lips and averted his gaze for that briefest of moments.

I sat on the couch.

He sat next to me and took my hand in both of his, his thumb tracing a circular pattern on my wrist.

He didn't speak.

I didn't either.

But it seemed we were both waiting for the other to do something, so I tightened my fingers around his.

"I'm moving to Sweden." The words expelled from his lungs in the same way they had when he'd told me he might be engaged. Fast, mystified, terrified.

It was like he'd injected ice into my veins. I shivered involuntarily from the sudden cold. "What? Why?"

But I knew. As soon as I asked. I knew. His grandfather. Hadn't Magdalena come to town to discuss how to handle the care of their grandfather? It all fit. Even before he offered a word of explanation, I knew. Why else would he decide to work such insane hours to save up money?

He then explained everything I had already understood without him speaking at all. How his parents had gone for a few months but really were too old themselves to be making such a move permanent and needed to get home to take care of their own affairs. How Mags had so much on her shoulders with the clinic and the new baby coming. How that left only him.

When he was done, I said, "You're leaving me." Not a question.

He didn't respond right away. I slipped my hand from his and edged away from him on the couch.

"I don't want to leave, Lettie, but I have to. He's all alone. He's sick. He needs a twenty-four-hour caregiver." He scrubbed his hand over his blond hair, those Asgard golden locks that I had always loved. "I'm not going forever. But no one is better qualified to take care of him. I have medical training. I have a job that isn't as set in stone as my sister's. But I'm not leaving you, not like you make it sound."

"How else is it supposed to sound?"

"I'd like you to come with me." As soon as he saw my immediate shock at those words, he amended them. "Not to live — not unless you want to live there. But no.

Just to stay for a while. For the holidays. Come with me from Christmas through the New Year."

"You're leaving so soon?"

"I have to. He needs help now. Mags is there at the moment, but she can't stay. I fly out in a week and a half."

"And when were you going to tell me?"

"Today. Right now. I'm telling you right now." He reached for me, but I shifted out of his reach.

"But you knew before now," I countered.

"Not really. Mags was going first to assess the situation and see if he was well enough to travel to Canada to live with her, because I didn't want to leave you and my life here. But when she got there, she found he was so much worse than we believed. He can't move much most days. So we've been discussing things to see what to do."

"But you started working overtime forever ago."

"Because I figured I would be needed somewhere at some time. But I didn't know when. Not really."

"Anders, how am I supposed to function without you?"

He smiled at that. "We'll work that out. Let's take this a step at a time. Kind of a first-things-first thing. Will you come to

Sweden for the holidays?"

The holidays.

The award ceremony.

My bedroom door was open wide enough to let me see the edge of the dress bag on my bed.

My book was receiving this once-in-a-lifetime award. Once in a lifetime was exactly that. The rejection letters Jen had finally decided to send me were evidence that this might be my one and only chance at a night where my work would be recognized and praised and awarded.

Going with Anders to Sweden meant missing that chance.

There was only one choice to make.

"Of course. You know I'll always be there for you."

Because that's who we were. We were best friends who dropped everything for each other — even the important things. Because nothing else was more important.

CHAPTER EIGHTEEN

"Glass slippers and dreams have a lot in common. They are both beautiful and breakable and endangered by midnight deadlines."
— Charlotte Kingsley,
The Cinderella Fiction
(The "Make Your Own Magic" Chapter)

Anders's relief at my agreeing to go with him for the holidays showed in his every movement: the way his shoulders rolled back instead of slumping forward; the way the creases between his eyebrows had relaxed to smooth skin; the way his fingers stopped raking through his hair, leaving blond spikes sticking out from every angle.

Here he was again. I had the Anders I knew and loved back. I'd been so worried that he'd decided he was done with me. It hadn't occurred to me that his altered personality might have come from the many stresses of job and family responsibility and not because of me. Kat's texted responses to the news that I would be out of town for Christmas weren't exactly supportive, but my family all seemed to understand my need to go to Sweden with him.

He was scheduled to move out of his apartment the day after his photography exhibit. Months ago, he'd jokingly promised me a shoulder massage before the event. Instead, I got to help him pack up his apartment.

Every item we put in a box cracked open the tear in my heart wider. What would I do with my best friend on the other side of the world? I tried not to think about it. Anders said we'd work it out. So we would. Somehow.

The day of his exhibit, I stayed back and finished packing a few last odds and ends for the movers to pick up in the morning while he went to make sure everything was ready at the exhibit hall. He would be sharing this exhibit with three other photographers. They had done the right thing and changed the exhibit name from "Many Faces," or whatever creepy thing they were calling it before, to "Masks."

After everything I'd managed to overcome and become through my writing, the thought of his work out on display for everyone to see made me happy. *Look at us, Anders,* I thought, *chasing our dreams and goals with ferocious grit and guts.*

I checked my watch after the last box had been taped up and added to the stack for the movers. There was just enough time to get ready and get to the gallery. I showered and slipped into the dress I'd purchased for the awards ceremony. Letting a dress of that quality go unworn would be criminal. With my feet in the silver shoes, my hair pinned up in a half twist, and the skirt of the dress swirling around my legs like quicksilver, I was ready.

Everything was perfect until it wasn't. Traffic on the Mass Pike was less than ideal. "I should've taken the T," I muttered to my windshield. But to drag my dress through the subway? Unconscionable.

I was on track to be only fifteen-ish minutes late when the sudden flash of red brake lights streaked through my vision. I hit my own brakes but not soon enough. My car connected to the car in front of me with a dull thud.

We both pulled over to the shoulder to keep from furthering the traffic jam and got out to inspect the vehicles. The woman I'd run into was in activewear and had her hair

389

up in a ponytail. She scowled at her bumper. "There doesn't seem to be any damage," I said, looking at my own bumper as well as hers. Nothing indicated any kind of altercation had taken place.

"We need to call the police," she said with a stoic arch of her eyebrow at my desire to dismiss the whole thing by daring to say there didn't seem to be any damage.

But there really wasn't any damage.

Not so much as an exchange of paint on the cars.

The woman in activewear refused to be calmed. She wanted to call the police. So we did. The police showed up thirty-seven minutes later. Fifty-four minutes and a ticket for me after that, I was on the road again. I'd texted Anders to let him know what had happened, not wanting him to worry about me the way I'd worried about him when he'd missed my book launch. Since his exhibit was only a two-hour event to begin with, I would be catching the last few minutes.

And even then, just barely.

I parked my car in the hotel parking area, gathered my skirt so I didn't get highway sludge on me, and exited the car. The exhibit was being held in one of the primary ballrooms. And if the crowd was any indicator, the evening had been well-attended. I stood still and took several deep breaths before entering the ballroom. Anders was talking to some people I didn't know. Not wanting to intrude, I decided to give myself a tour of the work on display before going to him. The room was divided into four wide aisles, one aisle for each photographer. On one side of each aisle was the masked version of the photographers' subjects. On the other side was the unmasked version.

The other three photographers showed obvious talent. I walked through their exhibits and enjoyed what I saw for the most part. One photographer's work leaned toward the abstract in a clever way. One of his masked subjects was an apple. The unmasked version was apple seeds. His entire aisle was comprised of photos that were unexpected.

Anders had ownership of the last hall, and I wanted to make sure to walk through his last so I could savor his work properly.

His aisle started out in a way that could only be described as literal. There were several images of his paramedic friends wearing face masks. There were a few of kids in Halloween masks. He had a few abstract concepts as well, and then it got personal. Approximately halfway down, I

391

stopped short and stared at the picture on the wall.

The picture staring back at me was me.

It was of me after I'd received the rejection letter that had led me to write *The Cinderella Fiction.* I was sitting on my old couch with the tub of ice cream in my lap and the scoop full of ice cream in my hand. Shiny tears lined my red eyes. Everything about the picture was vulnerable, broken.

So sad.

Without wanting to, I turned to see its masked version. It was of me dressed in Toni's designer clothes with the auburn tinting in my hair and eyelash extensions. I was laughing in the picture, but, somehow, that laughter didn't reach my eyes. In the unmasked version, the tears and the sad were all in my eyes; here, there was nothing.

Horrified, I stepped down to the next set. Masked: my manicured fingers on my book. Unmasked: my chipped and uneven nails at my laptop keyboard.

The next set. Masked: my feet in strappy, green-clothed heels crossed on my new coffee table. Unmasked: my feet in my favorite green Yonder Castle socks on my old coffee table.

The next.

Masked: a bowl of organic mangoes on

my counter. Unmasked: mango sticky rice.

The next.

Masked: me wearing the Cora original Toni had given me. Unmasked: me in my old six-impossible-things T-shirt.

Masked: straight, tamed auburn strands. Unmasked: my red curls, messy and tangled in the wind.

Masked: me looking soulfully out the window. When I had shown Toni the image, she'd told me to post it to Instagram immediately and caption it "Dreaming." Unmasked: me amidst a background of fireflies, with my hands uplifted so it looked like a celebration of light and dark and me.

It continued on to the final pairing.

I started on the unmasked side, fearing what could sum up Anders's feelings regarding my masked self. The unmasked was a shot of the title page of my fairy-tale book *Daughters of the Sea.* I slowly turned to see the masked, and found myself facing the cover of *The Cinderella Fiction.*

Everything. My whole life.

Anders had laid bare my entire life in a hallway of photos he'd taken of me.

My cheeks burned as I glanced around to see others in the area, others who were looking at pictures of me, prying into my soul with each image.

I ducked my head in case they looked my direction and recognized me as the girl from the series. I found a shadowy corner behind some potted trees and waited for people to leave, for the exhibition to start closing up. A text came in on my phone. Anders had written. "Where are you? I know you're here by now, but I can't find you."

"I'm here. When people are gone, we'll talk."

He texted several more times, but people weren't gone. It wasn't time to talk.

Finally, when the many voices had quieted into a few, and my phone felt like it was exploding with texts from Anders, I texted him my location and waited. He found me instantly, his face shining. He wore a suit. I knew Anders wore suits every now and again, but it was rare enough for me to wonder if he'd considered doing a masked-unmasked photo exhibit of himself with the suit and his favorite Red Sox T-shirt. Who was wearing the mask now?

"Lettie! Wow. You look amazing. You won't believe the amount of press the exhibit received. They're going to be running a feature article in the entertainment section of the *Boston Herald.* The whole exhibit got great reviews! And I received some commissioned work from it."

"How nice for you," I said, not able to keep how not-nice I felt out of my tone.

"Lettie? What are you doing hiding here in the trees?" He tried to take my hand. I tucked myself deeper into the shadows.

"It seems to be the only place I'm hidden."

"What? What are you talking about?"

"You've got a whole aisle dedicated to pretty much everything about me. And now you tell me they're going to do a feature article? My whole life available for everyone to analyze. Yep. That's nice for somebody who isn't me."

"You're mad." He seemed baffled by the realization.

"You think?" I snapped.

"Lettie, I thought you'd like it. I thought you'd —"

"That I'd what, Anders? That I'd jump up and down and clap my hands with the sheer joy of being humiliated publicly? Of having this available to an online source where it will go everywhere? Toni's going to be furious!"

"Who cares what Toni thinks?"

"I care!" I'd stepped forward enough to know I was no longer covered by the safety of the trees or the shadows. "Toni has done a lot for me. You think I want it thrown back in her face? You think I want to ruin every-thing she and I have worked so hard to build? Did you for even a moment stop to think about how this will affect me?"

He seemed taken aback. "How can this affect you? It's not like you're putting it on your social media."

"But other people will, Anders. Others will put it on their social media, and it will all come back to me. That's the whole point of social media! It's social!"

He stared at me, clearly mystified.

"You're overreacting," he said slowly — slowly but not carefully. "This isn't going to be anything. This was a small exhibit. No one is going to connect this to you."

"No one? Are you kidding? You used pictures you took as a favor to me for my social media? People know those pictures are me. They're already on my social media pages. The *Dreaming* one has thousands of likes!"

"Yes, but your fan group isn't going to know about my exhibit. It's not like you've ever allowed your social media and mine to cross paths. Seriously, Lettie. This isn't that big of a deal."

I didn't remind him that because he wouldn't keep his social media private, our paths crossed all the time. "It is a big deal.

It's a big deal to me, Anders. You used me."

Anders reached for my hands, but I swatted him away. "Used you, Lettie? How do you figure? You asked me to take those pictures."

"But you used them to market yourself!"

He blinked and then put his hands on his hips as if to scold me. "You're being crazy. You told me I could use them for my portfolio."

"But not like this! This isn't a portfolio!" The accusation hung in the air like a hiss.

"Really? Okay. What is this then?" His voice had grown cold.

"This —" I swept my hand toward the halls. "This is an exposé of my life. It's you using those pictures to position yourself as a leader in the photography world, not caring who it hurts in the process."

"You mean like you used those pictures to position yourself as a leader in the self-help world with a *book* that's supposed to make other people feel better because they can't get their crap together on their own? Like you giving life advice to people whose lives you don't know and have no business butting into?"

I caught the way he'd twisted his lips at the word *book*. "Why did you do that?"

"What?"

"Make fun of my writing."

He groaned. "Lettie! I did not make fun of your writing."

"What do you think this *book* is besides my writing?"

He scrubbed his hand over his head and pressed his lips together. His groan turned into a growl. "It's not a book. It's a rant you wrote because you were mad at the publishing industry."

I fell back as if struck.

His eyes went wide as if he couldn't believe what had exited his mouth. "I didn't mean that."

But he did mean it. Anders didn't say what he didn't mean.

I blinked back the sting of tears searing my eyelids. "You sold me out."

He shook his head. "No. You. You sold you out. You let a hashtag replace your humanity. You let these people tell you that you aren't good enough without some smoke-and-mirrors nonsense of the right clothes and the right furniture and the right food and the right entertainment, and you actually believed them. You actually bought into the lie that you're not good enough. They did this terrible thing to you, and you don't have the backbone to stand up to them and tell them they're wrong. Even now, after seeing my exhibit, you refuse to see. But maybe I'm blind too because I don't think I've ever seen you as clearly as I do now, Charlotte, and I've never been so disappointed."

I flinched at him calling me Charlotte and not Lettie. "Disappointed." The word released from my lips as an exhale. It burrowed into my skin, between my ribs, and into my heart. "Did you hear that?" I whispered.

"Hear what?"

"The snap of climbing too high. Too high. The branches. And they're too small to hold my weight. Every crack, snap, and splinter is running its way from my feet and through my body and into my heart. I've climbed too high. I'm about to fall."

"Lettie." He shook his head. "I don't know what you're talking about."

"I know." I sucked in a hard breath. "Look, I have an awards ceremony on the 27th. I actually bought this dress to wear to it, but then you asked me to go to Sweden so I decided not to go. But now that I'm thinking about things, I think it'd probably be a good idea if I went to that."

"But —"

"Yeah. I think maybe it'd be best if you go to Sweden and I go to my awards ceremony and we both chalk up this whole thing between us to experience."

Complete understanding registered on his face. "You don't mean that."

I lifted my chin, determined not to let it betray the scream of my insides. "I do mean that. The thing is, I don't just do things because Toni tells me to. I enjoy a lot of the interaction I get through the people I communicate with online. I like who I am right now."

Splotches of red crawled up his neck from the collar of his white shirt and onto his face. "Oh yeah? Did you enjoy telling people that you and I weren't together? That we were just acquaintances, as if I was the janitor in the apartment building? Do you like being the girl who denies having me in her life?"

I should've seen that bite coming, but I was unprepared for the way it tore a piece out of my center. Not a single response came to mind as I stared into his eyes watching his emotions flicker through a range I'd never seen in him before. I don't know how long we would have stayed like that if it hadn't been for a security guard coming to tell Anders that they were closing up.

"You know what, *Char.* You go to your awards ceremony." He turned to the security guard. "I'm leaving, Mike. You can lock up when the lady decides she's ready to go. Merry Christmas, Lettie." He walked away. I didn't move until the soft thud of his shoes on the carpeted ballroom floors ended at the doors, which opened and slammed shut with a crack.

"Ma'am?" Mike the security guard said.

"Please give me a second," I told him.

I walked back up the aisle filled with pieces of me and looked at each picture. The masked. The unmasked. As I walked down the middle between the two sides, I realized that I belonged right where I stood. I wasn't the peasant serving girl of the unmasked. I wasn't the woman in the glass slippers of the masked.

I was me. The woman who was sometimes one and sometimes the other and sometimes both at the same time.

I was Charlotte Kingsley, and apparently the man who took those pictures didn't know that woman.

"Thanks, Mike," I said to the security guard. "I'm leaving now."

I drove home and moved toward the elevator.

"Are you okay?"

I whirled to see Shannon standing just down from where the elevators were dinging open. Seeing her shouldn't have bothered me, but it did.

"I'm fine. Merry Christmas, Shannon."

She frowned without responding. I entered the elevator and made my way back to my apartment. I locked the door behind me.

And only then did I allow myself to fall to pieces.

Chapter Nineteen

"You are the writer of your own story. If you want the fairy tale, be prepared to fight for it."
— Charlotte Kingsley,
The Cinderella Fiction
(The "Make Your Own Magic" Chapter)

Anders left for Sweden the next day. He knocked on my door that morning. I recognized his footfalls, the way he shifted from side to side while waiting for me to answer. With the practice I'd had at avoiding the creaky floorboards during hours and hours of pacing, I made my way to the door in silence and put my hand on the wood. I could have opened it and opened up the whole mess again, the pain and humiliation. But the emails I'd received from Toni, along with screenshots of what had run in the *Boston Herald* and demands to know what was going on, saved me from the temptation of opening the door and falling into his arms to beg for forgiveness.

He'd stayed on the other side for a long time, the two of us as divided as the photos in his exhibit. This side and that side and no middle ground.

It hurt that he was there. It hurt worse when he walked away.

I watched from my window as the moving truck pulled into a space it didn't really fit into at the front of our building. I watched the boxes we'd packed and the familiar furniture leave the building and my life for forever. I watched the familiar person, who owned that familiar furniture, standing at the edge of the sidewalk, his camera bag over his shoulder and his keys in his hands, point to the driver, giving instructions I couldn't hear.

The driver nodded and closed the gate on the back of the truck before locking it into place, getting in the truck, and pulling away. Anders's car was also parked out front. He'd loaded luggage into it, but no boxes, no furniture, no moving things. He was not going to wherever the truck was headed. That luggage was making a trip to the airport. A trip out of the country. A trip out of my life. I waited for him to turn and look up to my window. He had to know I'd be watching, that I would see.

He didn't turn, ripping open the wound all over again so my emotions could bleed out.

Snow started to fall sometime that afternoon — too late to stop an airplane from taking off.

I stayed in my apartment and lived off the remnants of food in my pantry because even ordering from The Thai Guy or Bob's Grocery felt like too much effort. Aside from doing the "cleanup" Toni had ordered me to do, I binge-watched a full TV series and had started a second when Anders wrote me a text saying he was sorry.

But then he sent another text saying that he was sorry the exhibit had hurt me, but that he wasn't sorry that the exhibit had happened or that I saw it because being my best friend meant being completely honest with me. He called the exhibit the most honest work he'd ever done.

I didn't write back.

I also did not throw my phone against the wall, which, to me, showed a great deal of progress. Instead, I went to my mother's house. It was the Christmas season. She would need help decorating and cooking and serving in soup kitchens and volunteering.

I needed to volunteer, to work hard, to lose myself in something and someone else before I went completely mad.

My mother opened the door. She looked at me, peered hard into my face, and opened the door wider to let me inside without asking why my eyes were red.

Kat flew into me from where she'd been on the stairs, trying to see who'd come. "You're here!" She nearly knocked me over in a hug before pulling away and saying, "Wait. Why are you here? Shouldn't you be in Sweden?"

My mom's eyes met mine over Kat's shoulder. "Not anymore."

No one asked more, sensing the raw ache in me. Instead, we got to work finishing off all the details Mom viewed as being essential to a successful Christmas.

While Edward and Kat were out delivering neighbor gifts, my mom watched me while I made bows for her gift baskets.

"I've been thinking," she said.

My broken heart had made me careless enough to ask, "About what?"

"About you and the situation you've landed yourself in."

Don't engage, I thought even as the words "And what situation is that?" fell out of my mouth.

"You could have been anything."

"You're right," I said, imagining the fight that would follow the fact that I couldn't stop myself from engaging. "I could have been. And I am what I want to be. We've been through this."

"You could have cured cancer or been on the Supreme Court. But you did what you wanted in spite of my aspirations for you."

"Right."

She put down the bow she'd been working on. "Yes, you were."

"What?"

"You were right. I wanted you to change the world for good, to make a difference — and you did, but you did it your way, not mine. I hated the pretend worlds you and your father lived in. I hated how he never understood that the real world was stability and honesty. But you grew up like him. You always dive into the make-believe thinking that everything will work if you just believe hard enough. But running away from a good relationship isn't one of those things that works out no matter how hard you make believe."

My hands froze. My eyes slowly raised to meet hers.

She shrugged. "Well, it won't, Charlotte. You can't throw pennies into fountains and wish on stars and think that life is going to just be what you want. You have to work for it. I didn't work for it with your father. I got angry and walked away. I learned my lesson and vowed to not make that mistake with Edward. You sighing every ten minutes while helping me isn't actually helping me. Why don't you get on a plane and get to work?"

"Mom, you don't understand what he did. You don't understand why I can't."

"No, I don't." She refused to understand right up until the time I left to go home for the night.

I went home but didn't go to sleep. The worst part of being home was knowing the apartment underneath mine sat empty. No one underneath me would care if I paced over every single creaky floorboard in my apartment.

Lillian's phone call found me on the couch while I ate mango sticky rice and watched *Sleeping Beauty*.

I wished she'd been there in person and not just on the phone. I could have used one of her incredible hugs. How much I needed the contact of another human being. Anders had once told me that an embrace was a powerful tool for healing. He called it that exchange of energy where the giver loses nothing, but the recipient and the giver both gain everything.

I blinked away those thoughts. Who cared what Anders the Asgardian thought about anything?

"This is going to sound like I am busy-bodyin' my way into your life, but I've seen some of the things online regarding that neighbor of yours and you and that exhibit he did and I wanted to check and see how you're doing."

I told her the truth. All of it. She had asked, and, unlike when my mother had asked, I couldn't keep myself from giving a full confession.

She stayed silent long enough it seemed we'd been disconnected, until she said, "Lettie, I'm going to be hurtfully truthful, and I'm not even going to say sorry because I'm not sorry. If a thing needs saying, it's a smart person who says it. Your biggest problem, girl, is that you wrote one of the most beautiful books ever written."

"That's my biggest problem?" I wrapped myself deeper into the lap blanket I'd bought to give cushion to my couch.

"Well, no, not that. Your biggest problem is that you've never read that beautiful book you wrote. And so you don't believe it's true for you. You believe it's true for the rest of the world but not for you. There's a world of wisdom in those pages. A prescription from doctor me would be for you to draw yourself a hot bubble bath, crack the spine on one of your author copies, and get to reading. Call me if you need anything. Good night, Lettie."

But it wasn't a good night. The night was filled with restless tossing and turning until I finally reached for my phone, opened my reading app, and bought my book . . . so I didn't have to get out of bed and get out one of my author copies. By the time morning came, I understood what Lillian meant.

I understood what Anders and his exhibit meant.

I understood what I meant when I wrote my book.

And I knew what needed to be done. Mid-morning, I sent Lillian a text with a link.

She texted back, "What's this?"

"Two minutes inside my head. I'm owning my own fiction."

By the time my suitcase was packed, Lillian was calling, which meant she'd watched the video I'd made.

"Hey, Lillian. What do you think?"

"Is this really what you want?" she asked. "Telling the world and taking whatever the world will dish out to you? I'm assuming you know what it will cost you?"

"I do know. I've already written to Jen and Melissa so they won't be blindsided."

"Don't worry about them. Actually, don't worry about anything because what's done is done, and you can't put the jelly back in the broken jar."

She wasn't wrong about that.

"Lettie?" she said.

"Yeah?"

"Turn your phone off. Take the holidays off to meditate and have peace. The internet and its monsters with opinions will be there when you get back to it. But shutting it out for a while might help you realize how little you need or care about it."

"Too late," I sighed.

"What do you mean 'too late'?" she asked.

"I have my computer open in front of me right now. Comments are already happening. They aren't good. They're comparing me to that diva fitness enthusiast who always does those snapchats of her finishing her daily mile run when someone else filmed her from start to finish and found that she only ever ran ten steps. They're calling me a fraud. Maybe I made a mistake. Do you think I made a mistake?"

"Shut your computer right now, Charlotte Kingsley. Because this is nothing but a tempest in a teacup."

I tried to process that for a minute, but my brain was short-circuiting. Or maybe it was broken entirely from the kinds of comments that had immediately started filling my inbox. "What exactly is that supposed to mean?"

"A teacup is a little thing. The tempest is all the ways that little things get blown out of proportion, but those storms stay in the teacup. It all seems like a big deal because the storm is in *your* teacup. But I promise you, there's a big world out there that doesn't give a fig what's in your cup. Consider the choices you have right now as a breath blowing the storm away. Whatever you decide, the storm *will* blow away, Lettie. A little tea tempest can't last forever."

"I don't know what I did to deserve your friendship but thank you, Lillian. Living honestly is the right thing no matter what kind of storm follows, right?"

"Does that include living honestly with yourself about the fact that you and that boy are good for each other?

"Yes. It does. Which is why I have to go. I have a plane to catch."

CHAPTER TWENTY

"The fairy tale is the reality happening in your life while you're not looking. Pay attention to the person who has been there through all your once-upon-a-times. Notice the one who helps you slay your demons. Who can heal with a single kiss? Who do you want by your side for Happily Ever After?"

— Charlotte Kingsley,
The Cinderella Fiction
(The "Reality Check" Chapter)

When the ticketing agent on the phone gave me the total for my just-days-before-Christmas flight to Luleå, Sweden, from Boston, a piece of my soul died. "You're not poor anymore," I reminded myself before taking a big breath and rattling off the numbers on my credit card. I splurged and went with the first-class ticket so I could sleep on the flight. Granted, book

413

sales might come to a halt after what I'd posted online, but I'd been thrifty enough to live for a long time on the sales that had already happened. Maybe if I was lucky, my international sales wouldn't be affected.

But that didn't mean the cost of the airplane ticket hadn't made my stomach churn.

Anders had been willing to pay this sort of cost in order to have me come with him. The amount would have been nearly an entire month's salary, and yet he'd wanted me there enough to make the cost worth it. He'd very likely been working all that overtime just so he could afford it.

And what had I done?

Cast it back in his face like the monster I was.

The flight from Boston to Luleå took forever. Even though I had the nice seat that would've allowed me to sleep, I didn't sleep for a long time. Instead, I thought about all the things I could say to Anders to keep him from slamming a door in my face.

I also surfed the web to find out more about the tempest in my teacup. Sure, Lillian had told me not to, but habit had become my enemy. Toni had trained me to keep my finger on my internet-value pulse at all times. She had also called while I'd still been waiting for my flight at the airport, but I hadn't been brave enough to answer the phone. Lillian's texts assured me I'd made the right choice no matter what Toni might have to say about the topic.

Shortly after Toni called, she texted, asking me to call her back. She texted that same request seven more times. Finally, I followed Lillian's advice and shut off the phone for the last few hours of the trip. Toni wanted to run crisis management for me. She wanted me to get online and defend myself. But I'd already given my defense, and nothing gave me the right to go back with the jury while they deliberated over how they felt about me.

Between the time in flight and the time in layovers, more than a full day passed. Somewhere in that, I'd caught little snatches of fretful sleep. By the time the hired driver dropped me off in front of the address I'd managed to talk Mags into giving me, I was exhausted in body, mind, and heart. I'd arrived on Christmas Eve.

Luleå was a forest much like the ones I wrote about in my fairy tales. It had been a surprise when a break in the trees had opened up into an actual town center. The break had closed up again around us as the road led us to a home on the outskirts of town.

The house was something out of a post-card created specifically for the Christmas season. The light spilling from the windows illuminated the snow, making it look warm and cozy instead of the freezing cold it actually was.

From the tree in the yard hung a motionless tire swing with half a foot of snow covering it. The scene might have been tranquil — even charming against the backdrop of the house — if I hadn't known what waited inside the house. Anders had come to this place to help his grandfather die. The tire swing, so perfectly still it was like it had been frozen in place, felt more like the exhausted life of the man who owned it. Motion was too hard to manage against the heavy winter, and so it had stopped struggling against the cold and had iced over, allowing the winter snows to bury it.

The walk had been freshly shoveled and sanded to prevent falls — signs that Anders was taking care of things.

How did I approach any of this? How did I feel it was my right to intrude on this situation after having already cast it aside? I took a step toward the tire swing, going off the freshly shoveled path and into the snow. The powder squeaked under my step, and the noise I made echoed into the cold air in a way that made it feel like it was tattling on me for daring to enter the yard. I took another step and then another until I reached the swing. I reached forward to the frayed rope and grabbed hold, unprepared for the shock of cold. The ice on the worn and unraveling rope almost felt like it sliced into my palm. I checked my hand to see if it bled or not.

It didn't.

I gripped the rope harder, setting aside the feeling of cold, and pulled myself up onto the swing, displacing the snow and freeing the swing from the frozen spell it had been under. I rocked, forcing the swing to move back and forth. The creaking echoed in the still air. The rocking motion soothed me in a way that putting off things that are incredibly hard usually did.

"Mari?" The gravelly man's voice from behind me made me twist on the swing to try to see who had approached so quietly in this place where the air itself seemed to carry an echo. The twist from my precarious perch on the swing made me fall off, dumping me unceremoniously to the ground and shooting the swing out from me in a violent arc that came back, aiming for my head. Seeing I was about to get clocked by a heavy, oversized tire, I flattened myself to the ground and let it pass over me.

A hand mottled with blue veins and liver spots shot out and grabbed the rope, stopping the swing from causing any more trouble. He peered down through the hole of the tire at me. I tried to smile.

"Du är inte, Mari. Vem är du?"

I had no idea what the man had said, but his bushy, gray eyebrows that crowded together above his bridge, and his mouth turned down into a decided frown, said enough. "Hi . . . hello. You must be Anders's grandfather . . . *farfar* . . . ."

He narrowed his ice blue eyes. *"Ah, ja. Du är min sonson's Amerikan."* He grumbled this but seemed to have properly identified my nationality.

I scrambled to my feet, keeping a hold as best I could on the swing to use as both a help up and to make sure it didn't try to take another swing at my head. Anders's grandfather also helped to hold it steady.

Who knew an icy tire could be so slick? Well, probably everyone who drove in icy conditions knew that. And, since I had often driven in such conditions, it should have

418

followed that experience had taught me such a thing as well, but I didn't know what I knew anymore.

Once my feet were under me and no longer in danger of slipping *out* from under me, I smiled again at the old man.

He sighed heavily and whispered, *"Inte Mari."* Whatever those words meant, they made him sad. He shook his head, tried at returning my smile, and greeted me with a *"Hej, Lettie. Det är trevligt att träffas."* He almost turned, as if having nothing else to say, but then he frowned. "Good meet you." He nodded as if that bit of broken English was as much as he felt like dealing with at the moment. He turned away then and motioned for me to follow him up the sanded walk.

I did as told and fell into step behind the man whose pinstriped pajama bottoms had been half tucked into winter boots.

When we were inside, I expected to see Anders, but, from all appearances, only his grandfather and I were in the house. Which made sense. If Anders had been home, he likely would have dealt with me himself. He would never have sent his ailing grandfather out to deal with me.

His grandfather kicked off his boots at the front door and shed his coat, revealing that

419

he hadn't been wearing a shirt underneath. He sat heavily in a chair that was likely once a light beige color but was now gray and worn with age so that the man and the chair matched. He filled it in the same way liquid filled a glass, molding himself to all the curves and lines until they were one thing.

"The boy return soon." The dusty voice made me want to cough.

I nodded, not sure what to say, and not trusting myself to say anything.

His home held the smell of a fire burning in a wood stove, freshly cut wood, pine needles, and heavy cheeses. His open windows allowed the frozen forest smells to live in the fabrics of the furniture and rugs and even the walls. Why he had a window cracked open when the world outside looked and felt like it had been sculpted from ice and snow confused me. There was also the faint scent of fermenting yeast and baked bread — faint enough to make me think I'd imagined it rather than actually smelled it. There were other scents, too. There was an undertone of cinnamon and nutmeg, like a hint of Christmas lived perpetually in this place.

The tree in the corner had a garland made of straw. It also had straw hearts, straw horses, and what looked like straw angels.

There were other ornaments as well, but the straw garland and ornaments took up the bulk of the tree's space. White lights were woven into the branches. A few presents were under the tree.

An elaborately carved grandfather clock ticked a steady rhythm, and the hum of a heater provided a base level of noise. The open window and humming heater cancelled each other out so that the room was actually refreshing to be in.

My mother, thin and angular, had a tendency to be perpetually cold. She overheated our house in the winter while I grew up so that it felt like the heat had made a goal to smother me in my sleep at night. During all those years, it had never occurred to me to open a window to balance out the heat into something comfortable. Fresh air and warmth mingled together into something cozy.

"*Pepparkakor?*" the old man asked from his chair.

At my confused look, he nodded to a small shelf where a box of thin, heart-shaped cookies sat. I took one and nibbled on it. It tasted like a gingersnap. The old man smiled and looked like he might say something, but must have decided the trouble of making himself understood wasn't worth it.

I finished the cookie and then ate another one without being invited to. That made the old man laugh.

I think we were both relieved to hear noise on the porch that had to be Anders. I stood and held my breath.

When the door opened, Anders stood before me, but his eyes weren't on me; they were on his *farfar*. *"Jag hittade några glögg. Det var svårt, men —"* That was when he noticed his grandfather trying to get his attention. *"Har du ont?"* His grandfather shook his head, nodded in my direction, and said, *"Din flickvän är här."* Anders actually looked like he might be sick as he slowly turned in my direction.

"Lettie," he breathed.

"Stäng dörren," his grandfather said.

Anders shut the door, so I could only assume his grandfather had given him that direction. "What are you doing here?"

"It's Christmas." I shrugged, suddenly wondering if this crazy seize-the-day thing was a bad idea. "You did ask me to come for Christmas."

"But then you said you weren't."

Not a good beginning. "But I'm here, so . . . Merry Christmas?"

"Give me a moment." He murmured some things to his grandfather, turned on the television, and found a station that was playing a Donald Duck cartoon, of all things.

Anders then turned to me, took my hand, and led me toward the back of the house to the kitchen. He had a bottle in hand. He held it up to me and said, "*Glögg.* It's our tradition."

He released my hand so he could set the bottle down on the counter. Never had I felt so disappointed by any single act than that of him letting go of my hand. When he turned back to me, I dove into my confessions.

"I came clean," I told him, to make sure he understood in what way I had come to him. "I told pretty much the whole world all at once. I put it up on YouTube and then sent the link to a few news stations who I assumed would run with the story. I explained all the ways that the social media me wasn't always compatible with the real me." I had come to him honestly, which meant I had to be entirely honest. "So I'm coming clean with you, too. Even though the social media me and the real me aren't always compatible, they're more compatible than I ever would have thought in the beginning."

"I'm not sure I know what that means."

He had a white-knuckled grip on the chipped, tiled countertop behind him.

"It means I love my Cora designer shirts. I love having the online dialogue between me and the people who love my book and think they love my lifestyle. I love being a friend online to so many people. I love my coffee table. Sometimes I just sit and smile at it because it's the most beautiful piece of furniture I've ever owned. Sometimes I like wearing my Sleeping Beauty pajamas all day. Sometimes I like dressing like I'm on my way to an important event even though I'm just taking a walk in the Common. Sometimes I like the healthy choices. Sometimes I need the ice cream."

"Lettie —" he started.

I cut him off. "I need you to know this about me because all of this is all of me, and if it's too much, then that's okay. At least you're making an informed decision. I don't regret writing that book — that book that is *not* a rant, but is a real book and is really out in the world doing real good in that world. I don't regret hiring Toni because she taught me to connect digitally with people. She taught me to be brave. Don't you remember how afraid I was to go to your work Halloween party a couple of years ago because people would be staring at me in my costume? I'm not afraid to stand out in a crowd anymore. I'm not afraid of having a voice and making it heard. The only regrettable thing is that I didn't shout from the rooftops how I felt about you. I should've done that. I should have been honest. I'm sorry I hurt you."

He took a step forward and reached out for me — in a way I'd feared he would never reach for me again.

His hand slowly moved my direction, a slight tremor in his fingers as he trailed the back of them down my jawline.

"I'm sorry, too," he said. "I didn't mean what I said about it being a rant. I was angry. I'm not always awesome when I'm angry. You know . . . I didn't actually read your book until I was on the plane here." He took another step forward, allowing his stretched-out arm to relax even as his fingers slid up my neck, through my hair, behind my ear. "Don't be mad I didn't read it. It wasn't personal. I really did think of it as a rant you wrote to the publishing world — like an essay or something. And I just never pegged myself for a guy who needed to read a self-help book of any kind. But reading that book . . . It was like reading the story of our friendship. All our inside jokes and the advice we've given each other over the years. It was our story. So. Now that you've told me a story, let me tell you a story, Lettie."

"Anders, I —"

"Shh. It's story time." He cleared his throat. "Once upon a time," he said, "in the middle of a stone forest lived a fair princess named Charlotte Kingsley. Her stone forest looked like beanstalks climbing into the clouds, just waiting for the day when they might become interesting to giants. She had a friend, a peasant named Anders."

I furrowed my brow. "What are you doing?"

"Shh. I already said. I'm telling you a story." He cleared his throat again and moved closer, twining a curl of my hair loosely around his finger. "Anders was the sort of friend that, if giants ever did crawl down her stone forest to make trouble for her world, would do whatever it took to slay them. But, of course, there weren't really stone beanstalks or even trees for that matter. Her forest was made of buildings. And her tiara wasn't a crown on her head but a pen in her hand."

"Anders —"

He shot me a stern look that told me interrupting was not allowed. "Her friend Anders was, sadly, in reality a peasant, but

426

that's not the point of this story."

I smiled, light and happiness edging into my soul in that place where darkness and confusion had existed only moments ago.

Anders smiled as well. "The point of the story is that Anders would, without hesitation, slay the giants in her life. But first he had to do something very difficult. Something that broke his heart."

"And what was that?" I whispered.

"He felt he had to show her what the giants looked like. She didn't believe him, or maybe she didn't understand him, or maybe he didn't understand her when she'd told him to be on the lookout for such monsters. Maybe they were both wrong about what were — and were not — giants. Maybe they were both right. Either way, their friendship had been attacked. The peasant boy became angry with her for not seeing what he saw. And the fair princess grew angry with him for not seeing what she saw. They parted ways, each one shattered by the loss of the other."

"But —"

He scowled. "Have I said the words 'and they lived happily ever after' yet?"

"No, but —"

He rested his finger — the one not twined in my hair — over my mouth. "Then I'm

427

not done with the story."

I shushed so he could finish his story.

"The peasant spent his days in misery, worried he was wrong, angry because he thought he might be right, hurt that maybe she did not care for him like he cared for her. He picked up his magical communication device — that's a phone — where he wrote her long letters of apology and pleadings for forgiveness and reconciliation, but he did not believe his contact would be welcomed, so he deleted them."

"Oh Anders . . . I —" I remembered to shush before he had to tell me.

He continued. "His agony was unprecedented. His loss and need had no parallel. He was no longer poor in means but poor in soul." He blinked the shimmer in his eyes away and cleared his throat again. "But then, at a time when the peasant faced his greatest trial and when he felt so very alone in that trial, this pen-wielding princess showed up at his doorstep. She had given up much to be with him, and his gratitude was so great he forgot his anger and felt shame in his own behavior."

He stopped there, his eyes never leaving my face. When the pause went on for several moments, I asked, "Is this where you say 'and they lived happily ever after'?"

"I don't know, Lettie."

My heart sank down into my toes, every nerve in my body tracing its fall with a searing fire. "Oh," I whispered and finally broke the spell of his gaze on mine by looking away. I moved to pull away, but he took my hand in his and gave me a light tug to keep me with him.

"I don't know," he said, "because it's not really up to me. You know how I feel about you, about long-term, about commitment. After my time here with *Farfar,* I believe more strongly than ever in things that last. But I also know how you feel. I think maybe our ideas of happily ever after might not match up. I'm not really up to waiting around on something that isn't certain."

Relief flooded through me and somehow found my missing heart and buoyed it back up into my chest where it belonged. He wasn't rejecting me. And he also wasn't pushing me. He wanted me to choose, to choose him, to choose us. But he wanted it to be my choice.

I smiled at him. "Then let me finish your story. The princess also wrote long messages that were pleas for forgiveness. She paced her floor and felt sad that her peasant wasn't downstairs, hearing the physical evidence of her lamentations. She wanted to make things right with him because she knew she could not live without him. She had not been understanding. She had not been entirely honest. And the only way to make it right was to confess the truth. So she told the truth to the world about her identity, and she boarded a plane and flew to the frozen land where her peasant had selflessly banished himself to care for his aging grandfather. When she saw him, she knew something had shifted in her. She now believed in long-term. She now believed in commitment. She told him she loved him — I love you, Anders — and she knew he returned that emotion because he had shown her in so many, many ways throughout their time together. They embraced, they kissed with the passion of fiery hot coals, and they made plans for their future because they were going to live happily ever after."

At those words, he reached for me and held my face in his hands while he searched for any sign that I might not mean what I'd said. "Really? Are you sure?"

"I've never been more sure about anything. And because we will be together, you need to know that you're no longer a peasant. I'm financially secure enough to at least bring you up to middle class. Maybe first class if the internet doesn't execute my reputation based off of my video."

"I'm sorry if this hurts your sales and messes up your chances for new books, Lettie."

I shook my head. "Don't be sorry. It was the right thing to do. It was becoming too much for me to keep everything that I should be doing and saying and shouldn't be doing and saying straight. So . . ." I pulled on his tie, forcing his face close to mine. *"Jag älskar dig,"* I whispered.

"You learned to say 'I love you' in Swedish." He looked like he might cry full tears. This time, he closed the distance between us. There was no need to wait to gauge my feelings for him. I'd laid it all on the line. We both knew where we stood.

We were standing on the same side.

CHAPTER TWENTY-ONE

"Dance, live, and love like there is no
such thing as midnight."
— Charlotte Kingsley,
The Cinderella Fiction
(The "Make Your Own Magic" Chapter)

I called Kat later that night to explain to
her what had happened and why I had to
leave her alone for Christmas. She forgave
me. It didn't hurt that Edward agreed to allow me to buy her a ticket to join me in
Sweden for the rest of the holidays. My
mom wished me a merry Christmas and
told me she was proud of me.

Christmas dinner was what Anders and
his grandfather called *julbord*. It was pretty
much a bunch of deli meats, cheeses, various pickled things, and breads. They exchanged presents that night instead of in
the morning. As if Anders knew I'd be coming, he had a present under the tree for me.

"But you didn't *know* I was coming," I said.

"I *hoped* though."

His present to me was a wooden Swedish troll that was used as a stand for a fountain pen. It was perfect. I had a present for him as well. It was a new camera bag, one that had all the pockets and zippers. Anders had been wanting this bag for a long time and was excited to open it.

Anders gave his *farfar* a black-and-white photo that had been stretched on canvas and framed. The woman had hair that was red, though a darker, more elegant shade of red than mine. His grandfather got teary-eyed as he traced the outline of her face and said, "Mari . . ." over and over. Anders told me the picture had been one of their wedding photos that had been badly damaged in a flood. He'd taken months to try to recreate the picture through his digital tools and then to add color.

Later, I told Anders how his grandfather had come out and met me in the yard and called me by that name. Anders was shocked to hear his grandfather had made it out that far when he could barely leave his chair. His grandfather even slept in the chair because getting to the upstairs bedroom was impossible.

Christmas wasn't like my mom's extravagant celebration with all of the people she invited. The humble evening in a small home that was filled with warmth and love reminded me of those days when I believed in Santa Claus. This was what magic was all about.

Over the course of the next few days and weeks, I learned that social media wasn't the dragon I thought it would be. Okay, some people were burning my book in the streets, but most people thought it was courageous for me to own my own identity and to find comfort in my own skin. It wasn't the PR circus Toni thought it would turn into. Sales remained steady.

Jen believed that the new press and the fact that my name was now associated with a bestseller would help when she went on a submission run again.

In Sweden, while sitting between the fire and the open window and listening to the quiet conversation of Anders and his grandfather in a language I couldn't understand, I found myself again.

I wrote something new — something for myself — for the first time since I'd come up with the crazy idea to write a nonfiction title. It was a story about a peasant boy named Anders, and a girl named Lettie who had to get lost in the woods to find herself.

Maybe my mother was right. Maybe reality was a place I wanted to live after all. Sure, I'd keep writing the fairy tales, but I would live in my real life with this man and his love wrapping around me.

We'd settled into a routine during our time together. And while his grandfather slept in his chair, Anders and I went to the kitchen to get things ready for the midday meal. We stood close together while we worked. And when I turned to set the peeled potatoes in the pan, Anders took my hand and tugged me close to him.

His mouth met mine with warm tenderness, then traced over my lips, my cheeks, and my jawline before going back to my lips. I didn't mind because, as a wise woman named Lillian once told me, "What's the point of being together if you're not caught kissing in the kitchen?" or something like that anyway.

We took our time with this kiss that sealed the beginning of this new chapter in our story. We took our time because that was the gift of happily ever after.

Time.

ACKNOWLEDGMENTS

This book is *not* autobiographical, even if it is written about a writer. But there were times where it felt like it might be a smidge more true than any other book I've written — only a smidge, though. It takes a village to raise a child, and it takes a team to create a book. All my gratitude is completely earned by Heidi Taylor Gordon and Lisa Mangum. So much of what is on these pages is there because these two women had the faith that I was capable. I loved our brainstorming session and loved even more the product that came out of that afternoon. Thank you so much! A big thanks to Sara Crowe, for everything. To the Shadow Mountain team, I can never be grateful enough. You are all such a huge part of every page. Thank you!

I'll be honest: 2018 was a hard year with lots of changes. Writing became extra difficult as I navigated new challenges. There were several people who helped me through those challenges: James Dashner, Jeff and Jen Savage, Crystal Liechty, Heather Moore, Josi Kilpack, and Annette Lyon. Thank you all for being my friends. It matters. So much.

In fairy tales, the heroine is often mistreated by family, but that was never the case in my personal fairy tale. Thanks for being supportive and amazing, Mom and Dad! And while all my siblings are awesome, for this book, a shout-out goes to my dear sister Kat, who promised not to complain when I used her name for my character in this story. And though you don't need mascara or eyeliner, and though I look pale and sickly next to you, I will love you forever for buying me hot chocolate at 7-Eleven so we could drive all over town and rock out to eighties music.

I am grateful for my children, McKenna, Dwight, Merrik, and Chandler, for putting up with all the ways their lives were altered by having a mom (and mom-in-law) who decided to be a writer rather than a professional dishwasher.

And to my own happily ever after, my own Prince Charming, my own Mr. Wright. Thank you, *min kärlek,* for always believing in me, for always supporting me, and for

being my personal GPS. *Du är min lyckliga*
någonsin efter. Du är min alltid.

DISCUSSION QUESTIONS

1. We all have versions of ourselves that we display to different people at different times. Are the masks we wear important? How do the masks you wear make you feel?
2. It's easy to look at someone's social media posts and believe they don't have any problems. How does social media misrepresent others to us, and us to others? Where is the line between posting only the positive, happy things and sharing too much baggage online?
3. Cinderella was either the peasant or the princess in the ball gown. In what ways do we tend to see people as either/or? How can we see past the stereotypes we place on people?
3. There are a lot of Cinderella story characters throughout this book. Who do you believe plays the fairy godmother?
4. The publicist is called "HNT Media

Group." HNT stands for "Hot New Thing." How can we stop searching for the "hot new thing" and start searching for authenticity?

5. Lettie's mom could be seen as the evil stepmother in this book. Do you think she truly embodies that role? Do you think she is redeemed in the end?

6. Fairy tales are often considered moralistic. What moral fits this book?

ABOUT THE AUTHOR

Julie Wright is the author of more than twenty novels, including the Proper Romance novels *Lies Jane Austen Told Me* and *Lies, Love, and Breakfast at Tiffany's.* She is a Whitney Award winner and a Crown Heart recipient. She is represented by agent Sara Crowe. She loves reading and writing, playing on the beach or hiking with her husband and kids, and watching her husband make dinner.